C

"Katherine, you stay here," said Matt Pilgrim. "I'm going down for a closer look at the Bonner hideout."

They had come by buggy from Central City up the steep, rocky wagon path gouged, over the years, by miners hauling down their gold into town. Now the tall, young Pinkerton man and the lovely young heiress he'd brought along, much against his will, could look down on the shanty that housed the outlaw Bonner gang.

"I'm coming with you," said Katherine, seizing his arm.

"Stop where you are," said a high-pitched voice from behind them. They wheeled around to see a ragged young man with vacant eyes standing next to their buggy, a Springfield rifle pressed tight against his shoulder.

"Nobody's supposed to be here," he said in a small, child-like voice. "My brother Seth don't like it."

Matt advanced a step toward him. This was the Bonner with the mind of a child. Perhaps he could be talked out of holding them.

Just then, loud voices from the direction of the shanty caused Matt Pilgrim to turn around. The Bonners had seen them and were riding hell-for-leather up the hill. It was too late.

THE
FRONTIER
DETECTIVES

Lee Davis Willoughby

A DELL/JAMES A. BRYANS BOOK

Published by
Dell Publishing Co., Inc.
1 Dag Hammarskjold Plaza
New York, New York 10017

Dell TM 681510, Dell Publishing Co., Inc.

ISBN: 0-440-02695-4

Printed in the United States of America

First printing—July 1984

THE
FRONTIER
DETECTIVES

1

While sixteen nervous passengers on the Denver and Rio Grande Western coach gritted their teeth and gripped the edges of their seats as the tiny railway car creaked shakily across a wooden trestle over a deep Colorado gorge, the seventeenth, Matthew Pilgrim, sat as still as stone. Try as he might, he could not pry his eyes away from the pretty young woman seated diagonally across the aisle from him. After managing to keep from staring at her all the way from Chicago, he knew now that the trip was nearing its end, he would no longer be able to hold it back. He had to speak to her.

"Are you going all the way to Central City?" he mumbled.

She peered curiously over the top of the orange-colored book in her hands and smiled coolly. "Yes, I am," she answered politely, and continued to read.

Matt shifted his weight on the hard pine bench. There was something about this woman that disturbed and excited him. About twenty-two or so, she was obviously educated and wealthy. She wore an expensive, gray, French-tailored wool suit trimmed in black velvet, with a black hat topped by a pink ostrich feather that matched her blouse. She was probably the most beautiful woman he had ever seen. Tall and graceful, she sat straight and proud in her seat, with a firm back and a high, full bosom. Her oval face, framed in long brown ringlets, was as soft and delicate as any he'd seen in portrait miniatures. And yet she was traveling alone to a rough mining town—and reading an inane little dime novel entitled *Deadwood Dick; or, the Rivals of the Road*.

"Is that any good?" he blurted out over the chugging steam of the locomotive.

"What?" She lowered the book and returned his stare.

"I was wondering if you were enjoying that," he said, gesturing at the book with his head.

"Why would you wonder that?"

"I don't know. You look like you should be reading Henry James, not Edward L. Wheeler."

She set the book down in her lap. "I'm not sure if that's a compliment or an insult."

"What I meant was, it's a surprise to see you reading a Deadwood Dick."

"Is it?" she asked, not bothering to conceal her annoyance.

"It's all romantic fiction," he fumbled. "Real lawmen and outlaws are not like the ones in those stories."

"Tell me, what does a man who boarded the train at Union Station in Chicago know about real Western outlaws?"

He flinched as he watched her bright green eyes disappear behind the book again. If she had waited for an answer, he might have told her how he knew about outlaws. He was paid to know about them. He was a Pinkerton detective.

At least, in theory, he was. Actually, Matt Pilgrim, twenty-four years old, dressed in the black sack coat and matching trousers of a midwestern businessman, but with no hat to cover his thick, lion-colored hair, was on his first case. It had been Robert Pinkerton himself who had issued him his orders, the day he completed his training at the Chicago branch of the agency. Pinkerton instructed him to proceed to his home state of Colorado to investigate possible sabotage in a certain gold mine in Central City. After six weeks of minor incidents, the Harrison Get Lucky Mine had been hit with an explosion and a cave-in. Two Pinkerton detectives, working undercover, and the young owner of the *Banner* newspaper had been killed in the blast.

His job was to contact the mine's supervisor, Barton C. Canfield, investigate the situation, and send his reports directly to Robert's brother William at the Denver branch. The assignment was his because, of all Pinkerton employees, he was the one most familiar with the mining camps of Colorado.

The son of a prospector who died poor, Matt did know the territory well. He knew the legend of John Gregory's strike twenty-two years before, in 1859, knew of the great Gulch of Gold in Central City and of the adjoining Blackhawk, of the strange mixture of saloons and opera houses, schools and gaming halls, and churches and brothels in this isolated little mountain town of ten thousand that currently was producing over two million dollars a year in high-quality gold ore.

Before moving to Denver to live, he had grown up in a dozen towns like Central City. Owners and managers and supervisors usually controlled the mines and the town with Eastern money. Merchants and doctors and lawyers always struggled to keep some of it flowing in the community. And parasitic gamblers and prostitutes snatched as much of the loose change as they could before grabbing a train or a stagecoach out. At the core of this raucous little world were the deep miners themselves—hard, rough-chiseled immigrants who worked for pennies a day to bring out the precious gold. The best of them were Cornish, "Cousin Jacks," who had worked the copper and tin mines of their native Cornwall. But others labored shoulder-to-shoulder with them: Irish, Welsh, Italian, and German.

Robert Pinkerton had said to him that day, in the Rogues' Gallery of the Agency on Washington Street: "Some day, towns like Central City will have to change, Matt. America is growing up fast. Times are changing. Before long, telephones and electric lights and phonographs are going to bring people together. Industry will civilize the country. And when this happens, the West will have to change, too. Wild Bill Hickock and Billy the Kid are dead. Jesse and Frank James are on the run. Like it or not, an era of business is upon us. And the day of the outlaw is over."

He didn't have to add that it was one of the aims of the Pinkerton Detective Agency to prove that statement correct.

"Looks like we got trouble out there, folks," a thick man in a blue shirt and faded jeans announced as he pressed his round nose against the glass of his window. "Right at the top of the pass."

"What is it? What's at the top of the pass!" a gray-haired woman asked worriedly. She instinctively gathered her two little boys under her arms like a mother hen.

"Bunch of men on horses," he answered, looking back at her. "Appears to me they're just sitting there waiting for the train. Looks like a holdup!"

"Oh, gracious, no—"

"Anybody got a gun?" The man pulled on a Western hat and gazed around the crowded car. "What about you, son?" he said to Pilgrim.

Before Matt could reply, the conductor, a thin black man in a dark brown uniform, burst into the car.

"Get down!" he shouted. "Everybody get down!"

"What's wrong!" the gray-haired woman cried.

"The Bonner clan's on the track ahead! If you folks don't want extra holes in your heads, get 'em down!"

Stunned by his words, no one budged until a few moments later, when a shot rang out. Then, as the people in the car sprang into motion, Matt reached out, snatched hold of the arm of the young woman across the aisle, and yanked her down to the floor.

"What are you doing!" she shrieked as they both struck the rough pine boards.

"Stay down!" he ordered.

"I will not—"

"Stay *down*!" he demanded as a bullet crashed into the pane of his window and sent slivers of glass flying across the car. Pilgrim shielded her with his body the five minutes it took for the train to puff up the grade past the men on horseback.

"Do you mind?" she finally said, exasperated. "You're crushing me!"

"Sorry." He unwrapped himself from her and helped her to her feet.

"Thank you."

"What happened?" the older woman inquired from the floor. "Why didn't they attack?"

Matt smiled at her. "There isn't enough room on this pass for anybody to attack the train. They were just playing with us."

"Some playing." she grumbled, rising to her feet.

"Yes, ma'am."

In the noisy confusion of the various passengers rising from the floor to find their seats, Matt took the opportunity to slip next to the girl. After looking out the window at a half-dozen men on horses lingering on the tracks, he casually picked up the Beadle novel and opened it. "Looks like I've managed to lose your place," he said.

She made a point of glancing over at the vacant seat across the aisle. "Looks like you've managed to lose yours, too," she said.

"I meant your place in the book," he said, handing her the novel.

"I know what you meant."

After she took it from him, he took a deep breath. "You're Katherine Haynes, aren't you?" he asked her.

She didn't look at him. "You just know everything, don't you?" she commented as she thumbed through the novel for her place. "Outlaws, women, everything."

"I saw your picture in the paper in Chicago," he explained.

"Oh."

"I believe the article said you were the daughter of Gardner Haynes, Jr., the steel magnate."

"Yes, it probably did. Now, would you mind letting me read my book, please?"

He nodded politely and surveyed the people in the car. The Irish and Cornish immigrants, the Westerners, the Yankee tenderfoot, the woman with the two boys—all were buzzing excitedly about the "attack" on the train. "Didn't that gunshot scare you?" he said.

"I was too busy trying to breathe to be scared."

He paused a minute, gazing out the window at the sheer

mountain cliffs in the distance. He recognized Silver Hill. They would be nearing Blackhawk soon. "Would you mind if I asked you why you're going to Central City?" he said.

She sighed and shook her head. "You know, I guess I've read the same line at least twenty times."

"Then why don't you put it down?"

"I don't want to put it down," she retorted, then changed her expression. "I'm trying to . . . keep my mind off something," she added in a serious tone.

"Off me?" he said hopefully.

"No." She stared through the glass. "Off my brother. He was killed in a mine accident a few weeks ago."

"I'm sorry," Matt said sympathetically. But he couldn't help but chide himself secretly for neglecting the basic Allan Pinkerton technique of pulling together every single similarity in a given maze of circumstances. He had failed to connect the Alexander Haynes who had perished in the Harrison mine with either Gardner or Katherine.

"I never knew him very well," she lamented. "At least, not as a grown man. I was only eight years old when he left home." Her chin trembled slightly as she touched it with her fingers. "Alex was always so independent," she recalled. "He could never stand the idea of following in Poppa's footsteps. He just had to come West and do things his own way."

"So he started a newspaper in Central City."

She arched her dark eyebrows. "How did you know that?" she asked.

"I've heard about the cave-in at the Harrison mine. Does anyone know what he was doing down there when it happened?"

"No, but it's something I'm going to find out. Alex was

the last person in the world to go slithering down a hole in the ground. Even when he was little, he couldn't abide getting his hands dirty.''

"Did he ever write to you about the Harrison mine?"

"Alex never wrote to us about anything. Why do you ask?"

"I ask because the two other men who were killed in that cave-in were Pinkerton detectives."

"Meaning . . . ?"

"Meaning that's why I'm here."

"Are you saying you are a Pinkerton detective!"

"That's right. My name is Matthew Pilgrim. I'm from the Denver agency."

"Well, why didn't you tell me that before you wrestled me to the floor and flung yourself on top of me!"

"I didn't have a chance to tell you anything—"

"Well, if you had, we certainly wouldn't have stayed there long. Excuse me." She raised the novel again and began to read.

Irritated at the abrupt rebuff, Matt stared at her for a moment, then boldly grabbed the book and forced it down. "What is it, Kate?" he asked her. "What did I say?"

"My name is not Kate, Mr. Pilgrim. And what you said was that you were a Pinkerton detective. It just so happens that I loathe and despise Pinkerton detectives."

"Why?"

"Because you're nothing but a tool used by greedy and ruthless capitalists who will go to any length to crush any display of individualism that could threaten the almighty system."

"That's quite a mouthful."

"Well, believe me, to a lot of people in this country, it's also a stomach full."

"Now wait a minute, ma'am. I don't know where you get your information, but the fact is, the Pinkerton Agency is not the tool of anyone. We are an independent organization that has worked with the Secret Service, with Scotland Yard, with the Sûreté, and even with the Belgian police."

"Whoever you work with, you work *for* capitalists, Mr. Pilgrim. Men like Benjamin Franklin Gowen."

Matt winced at the sound of that name. The case she was referring to was already an infamous one throughout the country. A Pinkerton detective named McParland had worked undercover for years to expose a violent ring of coal miners in Pennsylvania who called themselves the Molly Maguires. Unfortunately, the controversial case was still making news; only a year before, in 1880, nineteen of the men were tried and convicted and hanged on the gallows.

"The Pinkerton Agency was hired by Gowen to end a reign of violence in the coal mines, Miss Haynes," he defended. "A great many of the Molly Maguires were cold-blooded killers."

"But most of them were poor, destitute Irish miners who were living and working in holes that a rat wouldn't crawl into."

"That doesn't justify murder, Miss Haynes."

"And what justifies the Pinkertons' murders, Mr. Pilgrim? Or are you forgetting your great agency once blew up a house and killed an eight-year-old boy?"

"That's not fair, Miss Haynes. The Pinkerton Agency has handled hundreds of cases without any such accident—"

"Well, I don't want to hear about them."

"You'd rather read romantic nonsense about Deadwood Dick," he charged.

"As a matter of fact, I would," she declared stubbornly.

"At least, in novels, there is some respect for the individual— even if he happens to be an outlaw."

"No outlaw deserves respect, Miss Haynes," he stated flatly.

"That's what my father says about strikers at his mill. That's why he hired you Pinkertons to come in with clubs and ax-handles to beat them into the ground. The outlaws are the same as the strikers. They're both victims of powerful capitalists like my father."

"An outlaw is not a victim, Miss Haynes," he argued. "He's a criminal who must be put away for the safety of the rest of society."

"I don't happen to think so."

"Well, you happen to be wrong."

Without another word, Katherine Haynes turned away and resumed her novel. A while later, Matt excused himself, rose from her bench, and returned to his own. Sweeping off the broken glass with his handkerchief, he plopped down, heaved a deep sigh, and leaned back. The bracing mountain air gusting in through the jagged hole in the window made him shiver, but it felt like a warm summer breeze compared to the occasional icy glances he was now getting from Katherine Haynes.

When the train switched at Blackhawk, he sat behind her and watched the succession of bare hills and dry gulches out the window. On narrow gauge rails of the Colorado Central Railroad, they puffed noisily across the iron bridge over Gregory and Selak Streets, above a dark cluster of sombre-looking mills, depots, saddle shops, warehouses, and blacksmith shops. Then the locomotive strained and choked over the high trestles at Running Gulch and Packard Gulch, on its way to Central City, a mile away.

After negotiating the long switchback down Clear Creek,

then up Running Creek, in order to gain the momentum for the upgrade into Central City, the train finally pulled into the depot.

"Well, it's about time," the thick-set man in the Western hat grumbled as the passengers began to rise. "Took me three days to get here."

"At least, we're safe now," the mother of two offered.

"I wouldn't be so sure about that, ma'am," the conductor offered as he passed by. "You might be seeing those outlaws again before you know it. Central City's where the Bonners live."

"Oh, my—"

"Central City!" he boomed out to the rest of the passengers, who were already trying to file out of the car. "Home of the mother lode! Richest square mile on earth!"

"Conductor?" The woman gently touched his arm.

"Yes, ma'am."

"Do those Bonner men really live here?"

He nodded. "Sure do. Live up on Casto Hill. I'd stay clear of that place, if I were you."

"Don't worry; I will."

As the passengers scrambled to get off, Matt held up the line to allow Katherine to take down her carpetbag and slip into the aisle. She thanked him grudgingly and walked briskly ahead of him to the door.

He had to smile when she stepped down and practically gasped at her first look at a gold-mining town. As he surveyed the place himself, he could well understand what a startling sight it must be to a well-bred woman from Chicago. Nestled uncomfortably among hard rock hills and bald mountains and deep, rain-washed gulleys, Central City was a dismal-looking little settlement that was covered with the clutter of the implements of mining. There

17

were veins of tracks and roads all over town. Stacks of the lumber used for cribbing, Comstock-style, in the mines filled every vacant lot. Every place you looked were abandoned ore cars, broken rails, discarded Cornish water pumps, pulleys, ropes, and bars.

Standing behind Katherine, he watched her eyes follow a wagon loaded with a dozen barrels of sloshing water, bouncing down toward Main Street. Three feet above the driver's head was a whitewashed sign with blue-painted letters that read: "Water—35¢".

"No water system," he explained from behind. "You'll probably have to pay a quarter for every bath you take, too."

She stood tall and erect and said nothing.

"They tell me the best hotel up here is the Teller House," he offered. "It won't be as elegant as the Palmer House in Chicago, but it's supposed to be comfortable."

"I won't be staying in a hotel, thank you," she returned.

"Oh."

"Are you waiting for someone, Mr. Pilgrim?" she asked after a time.

"Nope. I just find it hard to leave you."

"Well, try; please."

"Do you really mean it?"

"Yes, Mr. Piligrim, I mean it!"

"Then I'm on my way," he said. But as he picked up his grip, he noticed a bright red surrey pulling up the grade from Main Street. He waited next to her until the black driver reined the two white horses to a stop. Instantly, a tall, thin man about thirty-five, dressed in a brown business suit and a matching derby hat, slid out of the carriage.

"Katherine!" he called out to her. "Is that you?"

18

Matt leaned over and whispered into her ear. "Better forget this one—looks like he can barely see."

"He's an old friend. He hasn't seen me since I was six years old."

"Then he's been neglecting you."

"Mr. Pilgrim—"

"All right, I'm going. But watch this fellow, Kate. He's not wearing boots. My father used to say, never trust a man who wears shoes in a mining town."

"I'll try to remember that."

He nodded and began walking, making sure to brush past the man rushing up to greet Katherine. Pausing by the surrey long enough to see an embrace, he turned back to them and glanced up at the driver.

"That's a lucky man," he observed.

"Sir?"

"Never mind. I wonder if you could tell me where Mr. Barton C. Canfield lives?"

"Well, yes, sir. That's his big white house down the hill there, on Pine Street. See it? Right back of the Teller House."

"The one with the red roof."

"That's the one, all right."

"Thank you," he said, tucking his grip under his arm. Then, leaving the sound of Katherine's excited voice drowning in the shrill whistle of a steam locomotive, Matt Pilgrim strode down the slope into Central City.

2

By the time Matt reached Pine Street, he had begun to feel an annoying chill crawling up and down his back. The closer he got to Eureka Street, the more aware he became of a certain tension in the air. Even the buildings in town seemed to be shuddering in the cold wind. Soon he could see the evidence of an imbedded fear in the anxious faces of the people he passed on the street. A dirty, stooped miner trudging home from the hills pushed by without even looking up. A couple of red-faced boys in rags flinched and scampered away when he drew near. A Chinese woman in a white coat, lugging a basket of laundry toward Teller House, smiled nervously at him, but then hurried away as fast as she could.

He decided that this cloud of dread hanging over the town was due to the nearby presence of the Bonner clan. Now he began to believe their mock attack on the train could be leading up to an eruption of violence in Central City. It could be that he was walking down a fast-burning fuse into a town that was set to explode like a keg of California powder.

At the door of the two-story frame house near the hotel,

Matt was greeted cordially by a pretty blonde girl in a ruffled, blue-checkered dress. She was small and plump, with an abundance of curls bouncing on her shoulders and bosom, and an innocent, charming smile.

"Yes, sir?" she said brightly. "May I help you?"

"Is this the Canfield residence?" he asked. "I'm Matthew Pilgrim."

"Oh, of course you are!" she blurted, smiled, then covered her mouth with her hand. "I'm sorry, I should've known. Please, don't mind me. Come in."

"Thank you." Stepping across the threshold, he stole a look inside the house from the foyer. It was dim and lavish, in a Victorian decor, with massive brocade drapes hanging in front of the tall windows and ornate, blood-red carpets and upholstered Louis XVI furniture.

"My name is Alice." She offered her hand. "I'm Mr. Canfield's daughter, the one nobody probably told you about."

He smiled as he squeezed her soft fingers. "Somebody certainly should have," he said admiringly.

She blushed as she pulled her hand away. "Well, for some reason, they never do. If you'll come this way, Daddy's back in the library, smoking his cigars, as usual."

As he followed her down the wide, dark hall, he noticed that she dragged her right leg slightly as she walked, but she seemed quite unaware of her infirmity. She opened the door and announced him to her father.

"I'll give you fair warning, Mr. Pilgrim—" she took time to whisper to him before she turned away—"Watch out for Reuben. He's set to pounce!"

"Who's Reuben?"

"You'll see." She laughed and called out to the man lingering at the fireplace. "He's all yours, Daddy."

Matt was comforted by the stalwart appearance of Barton C. Canfield. He was a stout but firm man of about fifty, with reddish, balding hair and a thick moustache. Dressed in a dark blue linen suit, he had the look of no-nonsense solidity about him. Clenching a smoldering cigar between his teeth, he moved out from the fireplace, shook hands with Pilgrim, and asked him to sit down.

"How was your trip?" he asked abruptly, in a deep, sonorous voice.

Settling down in an armchair, Matt pushed the attractive image of Katherine Haynes sitting in the railroad car out of his mind and concentrated on business. "It was uneventful," he answered. "Until we were shot at, on the other side of Blackhawk."

"Shot at by whom?" he asked, puffing bellows of smoke. "Outlaws?"

Matt nodded. "Someone called the Bonners."

"Damn it!" he growled, and flung his cigar into the burning fireplace. "Central City was a peaceful, law-abiding place before that bunch dragged themselves in. We've never been like those California mining camps, Mr. Pilgrim. Oh, we might have a brawl or two over at the Shoo-fly, maybe even a shootout with the Irish miners from Nevadaville once in a while, but never anything like this. This is something we don't know how to handle. Burning houses, detached rails, explosions, cave-ins, mysterious deaths—it's just too much!"

"Then you think the Bonners are responsible for the deaths in the Harrison mine?"

"I think they are, but then I honestly don't know, son," he confessed. "That's why Mr. Harrison contacted your people in Denver. He knew Allan Pinkerton back in the

23

Lincoln days. He believes a Pinkerton detective can solve any mystery the human mind can devise.''

"We do have a good record," he admitted proudly.

"I know you do." Canfield fondled the gold watch chain dangling from the pocket of his vest. Then he crossed his arms. "Do you own a gun, Mr. Pilgrim?" he asked.

"No, sir. I know how to use one, but I'm an investigator, not a lawman."

"Good. You may be just the kind of man we need—a man who'd rather use his brain than his pistol. You and Reuben ought to get along fine."

Reuben again. "Me and who, sir?" he said.

"Forget it. I want you to give me an expert opinion on this." He flipped a sheet of folded paper out of his coat pocket and handed it to Matt. "I found that in my mailbox two days ago. I don't have to tell you, it put the fear of the Lord in me."

Matt slowly unfolded the paper and read the note. It was penned in large, bold, awkward letters spaced unevenly across the page:

Mr. Canfield. . . . If you do not clos the Getlucky Min immedetly, your dawter will never reach New Yorke.

Seth Bonner.

Matt puzzled a minute over the message. "Why would an outlaw want you to close the mine?" he wondered.

"I've been racking my brain for weeks for an answer to that one, son. But so far, I've come up with nothing. I can't figure these Bonners out. They seem to be terrorizing the town for the pure fun of it. Is that possible?"

"I doubt it," Matt said, getting up. He ambled slowly over to the window and let his eyes follow a wagon outside that was budging up a hill toward the loading tram on the other side of town. "It would help to know who these Bonners are, Mr. Canfield," he said. "How long have they been in Central City?"

"That's what's so strange about it: only a few months. All I really know about them is that there are six of them—all brothers. People say the mother was a prostitute and every one of those boys has a different father."

Matt searched his brain for a Pinkerton lesson on motive that would apply to the profile of this case, but he could find none. He read the message again. "According to this, your daughter is planning a trip to New York," he led him.

"That's right. Alice is supposed to be going back East in three days. She's a very clever girl, Mr. Pilgrim. My late wife used to say Alice's good sense was the good Lord's compensation for giving her that gimp leg. I don't know about that, but I do know I'd do anything on this earth for that girl. So if she wants an Eastern education, I'm going to see to it she gets it."

"I wonder how Seth Bonner would know about her plans?"

"I have no idea."

"I do!" interjected a lively, exuberant voice that came bursting through the door, into the library. It belonged to a young man in a neatly pressed brown suit and a stiff bow tie approximately the color of the bristling red hair slicked back from his forehead. Leaving the door wide open, he marched briskly into the room and heaved a black box the size of a suitcase on top of Canfield's rosewood desk.

"The fact is, that note is not even from Seth Bonner!" he announced in a loud, excited voice.

Matt glanced over at Canfield. "This must be Reuben," he guessed.

The other man nodded as he took a seat on the sofa.

"Here, I'll show you," Reuben proceeded, snapping the note out of Pilgrim's fingers. After half-reading, half-mumbling the message out loud, he popped the page emphatically with the back of his hand. "This isn't the language of an outlaw like Seth Bonner," he declared. "Since we don't know much about the Bonners, it's possible the man may have actually written this. But the point is, he couldn't have *composed* it."

"Why don't you tell me how you know that, Reuben?" Canfield offered resignedly.

"Please," Matt invited. "Go ahead."

Reuben beamed a smile that flashed white teeth. "Well, for one thing," he began, "it's written in correct grammatical syntax, which is hardly likely for a man who spells the way he does. For another, the threat is *indirect*. An outlaw like Seth Bonner wouldn't care about where Alice was going next week. He'd say, 'Close up that mine, or else I'll kill that girl of yours.' "

"Reuben—"

"Well, face it, Dad; that's what the message is. It's just that it's so indirect, I know there is the mind of a more sophisticated person behind it."

Fascinated, Matt cleared his throat. "So you assume someone must have dictated this message to Seth Bonner?" he inferred.

"Ha! I knew we'd think alike, Mr. Pilgrim!"

"You might as well give him all of it, son," Canfield

muttered, pinching another cigar out of his vest pocket. "I'm sure he can hardly wait."

Pilgrim scratched his chin. "What else do you have?" he asked.

"Only the clincher!" Reuben exclaimed. "Take a look at this!" he said, whipping back the lid of the mysterious black box on the desk. "What we have here is absolutely the latest thing in scientific investigation. I put this together myself."

Matt peeked over into the box at a collection of dark little jars of grease and ink, a magnifying glass, a can of Marvin's Talc, a stack of glass panes, and a bone-handled penknife, all arranged neatly on a stack of charts and graphs. He recognized the equipment from an experiment Robert Pinkerton had performed once at the Agency.

"Fingerprints," he said.

"There, you see, Dad, I told you Mr. Pilgrim would be up-to-date. I told you the Pinkertons were the most modern police force in the world today!"

"I think I should tell you, the Agency doesn't use fingerprints in its investigations," Matt informed him.

Reuben's eyes widened in a state of profound shock. "I don't understand," he said. "Why doesn't it?"

"It's still experimental, Reuben."

"But didn't you read what Henry Faulds wrote in *Nature* last year? He said the best use for fingerprints is to identify criminals. And isn't that exactly what the Pinkertons want to do?"

"Yes, but the process is so new that no one has started acquiring the prints."

"But it's so simple! Using a little wax and printer's ink, I managed to get two perfect specimens." He slid a card out of his inside coat pocket. "These prints were taken

27

from this letter allegedly written and composed by Seth Bonner. If you examine the lines closely, you'll notice there is absolutely no resemblance between the two. The arches are not the same, and neither are the loops.''

Matt scrutinized the prints carefully under Reuben's magnifying glass. ''These are impressive, Reuben,'' he complimented.

''But the important thing is what they tell you! One of them belongs to Seth Bonner, the other to someone else—the mastermind who is behind all these mysterious goings-on in Central City.''

''You could be right,'' he acknowledged.

''What I can't figure is why the Pinkertons are lagging behind on this. They should be scouring the country for fingerprints right now!''

''The Pinkertons are very conservative, Reuben.''

''But fingerprinting fits perfectly into their system. They can be a crucial part of the Rogues' Gallery. They're every bit as important as the Agency's letters and photographs and telegrams and agents' reports and eye-witness accounts. After all, William Pinkerton himself said it himself: 'Solving cases is merely a matter of weaving together bits and pieces of crime.'''

Barton Canfield had to chuckle at that. ''The boy's damned thorough, isn't he?'' he said.

''Oh, yes.''

''Then you agree that Reuben will make you an excellent partner.''

''Sir?''

''I guess I didn't tell you. I want you and Reuben to work together on this, Mr. Pilgrim.''

''Ah, no, I don't think so.''

''But, Mr. Pilgrim!'' Reuben moaned, deflated.

"I'm sorry, Reuben. You're a brilliant fellow, but you're just not trained for this kind of work."

"But I am trained! I'm incredibly trained! I've read everything ever written about a Pinkerton case. I know every one of them, from the Washington spy ring to the Renos of Indiana to the James and Younger gangs. I've read Allan Pinkerton's book on the Molly Maguires six times. And I've evaluated it carefully. I can't help but agree with *The American Law Review* that the exposure and prosecution of the Molly Maguires was 'one of the greatest works for public good that has ever been achieved in this country.' "

"But all that isn't training," Matt insisted. "If this case gets dangerous, we could end up getting in each other's way."

"No, we won't. I promise I will stay completely out of sight, pursuing clues."

"No, Reuben," he stated firmly.

"Mr. Pilgrim." Canfield got up from the sofa. Sucking in a breath of cigar smoke, he paused, cocked his head back, and spewed out a white stream. "Even though I agree with what you're saying," he began, gesturing with the cigar, "I still want you to reconsider your decision. Look at it from my point of view. My daughter's life is in danger, damn it. However much I trust you to do your job here, I'd feel a lot better if I knew my own flesh and blood was right there with you, every step of the way."

"Mr. Canfield—"

"It's obvious he's qualified; why are you so hell-bent on doing it all yourself? Is that the Pinkerton way?"

"No, sir—"

"What is it, then? Do you always work alone on a case?"

Matt quickly decided it would be better not to admit this was his first case. "I've never had a partner before," he equivocated.

"Well, let's not call him a partner, then. Let's say Reuben will tag along as an aide."

"I don't want to 'tag along as an aide,' " Reuben objected.

"Be quiet, Reuben."

"I can help the Pinkertons solve this case, Dad," he declared, slamming the lid of the box down. "I know I can!"

During the long pause of silence that followed the loud clack of the box lid, Matt exchanged looks with the two men. Canfield appeared worried and disgruntled, Reuben discouraged, but still eager. Relaxing a bit, Pilgrim eased down in the armchair again. "Do you have any idea who this mastermind might be, Reuben?" he inquired.

"I certainly do!"

"For some reason, I'm not surprised."

"I have several strong candidates, as a matter of fact. One of them is Mr. Ben Watkins. He could very well be our man."

Canfield wrinkled his nose and shook his head. "Uh-uh, son," he disagreed. "I can't believe Ben would ever do such a thing."

"Who is this Mr. Watkins?" Matt asked.

"He's the manager of the Get Lucky," Canfield answered. "He's been there ever since it opened, six years ago."

"That's exactly the point," Reuben stepped in. "When Dad got the job of supervisor, Ben Watkins was passed over. He might resent Mr. Harrison enough to destroy his mine and everything in it."

"Enough to make him kill three innocent men?" Matt wondered.

Reuben shrugged. "It could be. He's done it before. He killed a man down in Leadville ten years ago. Walked straight into his bedroom, pushed the barrel of a .45 into his throat, and pulled the trigger."

"That man molested his daughter, Reuben," Canfield reminded. "Besides, he was drunk. And he was never convicted of the crime!"

"But the fact remains, he has killed someone, Dad. And he does have a motive. He could be wanting revenge again."

"Ben may still be a hothead sometimes, but he is not the same man he was in Leadville. I haven't seen him take a drink in six years!"

"But it was that killing in Leadville that made Mr. Harrison pass him over, wasn't it? It could have made him angry enough to start drinking again, couldn't it?"

Canfield chewed thoughtfully on his cigar. "Maybe," he acknowledged. "But I still don't believe he's the one we're looking for."

Matt looked at Reuben. "Anyone else?" he asked.

"There's Alvin Potts, the sheriff."

"Now, Potts is more likely," Canfield concurred. "He's a strange old cuss. He never does anything but fish and drink. I don't know why we keep putting him back into that office every election."

"The sheriff is mean and angry, Mr. Pilgrim," Reuben told him. "I've heard him say he despises all miners and wishes he could drown every one of them in their holes."

Canfield shifted his cigar to the left side of his mouth. "He's bitter because it was a miner who ran off with his wife and son, eleven years ago," he explained. "At least, we *think* they ran off. Some people say he murdered all three of them.''

''What's his relationship with Mr. Harrison?'' Pilgrim asked.

''Simple: He hates him. They used to be co-owners of a mine called the Big Break, right after the war. After digging out a couple of years of gold, the ore finally started coming up sulphuret. In the days before the railroad, you couldn't ship off your ore to be smelted, and nobody knew anything about the reduction process up here. For years, we had pedlars hustling around selling ways to separate the gold from the sulphur—everything from Keith Desulphurizers to Crosby and Thompson Roasting Cylinders. But nothing worked. Many of the mines had to close down.''

''Including the Big Break.''

''Right. Mr. Harrison bought out Potts for six hundred dollars, shut down the mine, and moved to Denver. That was in 1871.''

Matt leaped ahead of the story. ''But he came back to Central City four years later and re-opened it—this time under the name of Get Lucky. Am I right?''

''That he did. And it became the richest gold mine in Colorado. Now Harrison is a wealthy man in Denver City, and Alvin Potts sits on his rump in his office, drawing barely enough money to keep up his supply of E.G. Booze.''

''There's one more prime suspect, Mr. Pilgrim,'' Reuben said. ''Andrea Sherbourne.''

''That's quite a name.''

''Everybody says she's quite a woman.''

''It's not her real name, of course,'' Canfield told Matt. ''She used to be Hilda Jane Barnes, back in the sixties. She was a saloon girl for a while, then a dancer at the

32

Shoo-Fly. A few years ago, she took over the old Mercer Hotel and fixed it up and started hauling in pretty young girls from the South to entertain the guests. In other words, she turned the place into a whorehouse.''

"My mother always said Hilda Jane Barnes and Sheriff Potts were lovers," Reuben added. "Just before Mrs. Potts left Central City."

"I don't see any motive."

"She may have been trying to put an end to all those articles in the *Banner* lately, about the Mercer Hotel. Those papers had the women in town grabbing sticks and screaming for the mayor to close her down."

"The man who was writing those articles was Alexander Haynes," Canfield elaborated. "One of the men who died in the cave-in."

Matt nodded. "I met his sister on the train," he noted.

"I didn't know Haynes had a sister," Canfield said.

"Well, he did. Apparently, she's staying with a friend of the family—a tall man in very expensive clothes picked her up in a red surrey."

"That would be William Henry Aldrich," Canfield deduced. "He knew Haynes' father back in Chicago. Henry's an influential man in town, Mr. Pilgrim. He's a vice-president on the Denver and Rio Grande Western Railroad."

At this point, Reuben's store of patience finally ran out. "Mr. Pilgrim!" he erupted. "Are we or aren't we going to be partners?"

"Reuben, I appreciate the work you've done here, but I don't want you to get hurt."

"But I won't get hurt! I swear I won't. Even if I do, I'm not going to blame anyone for it!"

Before Matt could respond, the door to the library creaked

open, and the fresh, pretty face of Alice Canfield peeped in. "Daddy, there's a miner out here," she said apologetically. As soon as she had made the announcement, a young Cornishman in a faded gray tweed coat and loose black trousers slid past her into the room. Whipping his rumpled hat off his matted hair, he sheepishly lowered his eyes to the floor.

"Sorry, sir," he muttered.

"What is it, Mills?" Canfield anticipated. "More trouble?"

"Yes, sir," he replied. "Bad trouble. I think ye'd better come quick."

Canfield yanked his cigar out of his mouth. "What happened, son?" he asked.

"I don't know, sir. All I know is, Ben Watkins sent me down here to fetch the supervisor. He's spitting nails."

"All right, I'm coming." He looked over at Matt. "Mr. Pilgrim, you might as well come along and get your feet wet."

Matt buttoned his coat. "I'm ready," he said.

"So am I," Reuben declared.

Canfield flipped the cigar into the coals. "Damn it!" he growled. "There's always something happening in that mine! If this keeps up, I won't be able to find a single man in Colorado who'll be willing to work a Harrison mine."

34

3

Despite the close, courteous attention paid her by the tall, nattily dressed man sitting across from her in the surrey, Katherine Haynes felt very much alone. As the carriage rolled to a halt in front of the *Banner* office at the end of Main Street, she drew in a deep breath to ease the ache of the cold, hollow feeling in her chest. All the way from the depot, the image of her brother kept flashing through her mind. In the upstairs hall, twelve years ago last April, he had bent down, pinched her cheek, and ruffled her hair. "See you later, Sis," he said casually— and then walked out of her life forever.

"You should not be doing this, Katherine," William Henry Aldrich stated flatly as he stepped down into the dirty street. "It's altogether unnecessary."

"I don't care if it's necessary or not," she replied.

He straightened his red silk cravat before he offered her a hand down. "Let me take care of all these business details for you, Katherine," he said. "I see no reason why a lady should have to bother with such things. Especially at a time like this."

Reaching the ground, she had to wait—too long—for

35

him to release her hand. "It's not a bother, Mr. Aldrich," she assured him.

"Henry," he reminded.

"I'm sorry—Henry."

"That's better. After all, we are old friends."

"The reason I'm here is to take care of Alex's things," she explained. "Since no one in the family came to the funeral, it's the least I can do."

"I understand. I merely want to spare you a little grief, that's all," he said in a smooth, low voice.

"I didn't come all the way to Colorado to avoid grief. I want to know about my brother. I want to know who he was, what he did, and why he died."

"Why open up old wounds, dear? Your brother was not a popular man. Sometimes that pen of his was dipped in acid."

"Could we go in now, please?"

He heistated, then nodded politely. "The landlord is a mining agent down the street. I'll get him to open the door for us."

"Thank you."

While Aldrich headed down Main Street, Katherine paced slowly back and forth in front of the *Banner* office. Nervously, she slid her fingers into her breast pocket and touched the small metal key inside. She felt compelled to bring it out and look at it, for the thousandth time. No wonder it made her feel better: It was practically all she had to remind her that Alexander Haynes had ever existed.

Mr. Edward Carroll, an undertaker in Central City, had sent the family a neatly wrapped cigar box containing what he had coldly described as "the personal effects of the deceased, removed from same, upon arrival at this office." Inside was a leather wallet with twenty-six dollars tucked in the fold, a blank note pad, a mechanical lead pencil, a pair of Franklin reading spectacles, and the little key. A man's whole lifetime packed away inside a cigar box!

She cringed as she recalled her parents' reaction to the death of their son. Her mother, a weak, silly woman who considered it a cardinal virtue to shop daily at Palmer's and Marshall Field's, who gave more time to United Charities than she did to her family, and who worked for interminable stretches at a settlement house on Wells Street, exploded into tears when she heard about Alex. After she fainted, she had to be escorted upstairs by the maid. Later, she returned downstairs to announce sadly that she had forgiven Alex for leaving them. She was convinced that in spite of his rebellion, her wayward son was very likely on his way to the other world, where he would surely meet his reward. After that brief statement, she said no more about it.

Gardner Haynes, Jr., a massive, domineering, intolerant man, was the one who first opened the cigar box, in the foyer of the lake house. He unwrapped Mr. Carroll's note, scanned it quickly, peeked down into the box for a second, then promptly shut the lid. Extending the container to the butler, he gave the simple command: "Do something with this." When Whatley inquired stocially exactly what he was supposed to do with it, Gardner Haynes snapped back crisply, but indifferently, "Bury it, I guess."

Bury it. Although Katherine Haynes would love her father always, she would never forgive him for saying that. Not if she lived a thousand years.

For some reason, they expected her to want to go out to Central City to settle Alex's estate. Mother gave her a brief lecture on the dangers of traveling in the wilds, as she put it, and presented her with a copy of the latest

Crofutt's *Railroad Guide* for reference. Poppa, on the other hand, made all the preparations for her. "I've written to an an old acquaintance of mine out there, Katherine," he informed her at the station. "You may remember him— William Henry Aldrich. He'll take care of you. Mind what he says and I'm sure you'll be fine."

A while later, as she leaned out of the window of the train leaving Union Station, she could see her mother through the billows of smoke, waving weakly while she sobbed into a handkerchief. Her father had already turned his back and was walking away.

"Katherine, this is Tom O'Reilly," Aldrich introduced the pudgy Irishman trailing him.

"Afternoon, ma'am," he said, tipping his Irish cap. "Fine day today, isn't it?"

"Yes, it is."

"I'll wager anyone you're Alexander's sister—no?"

"Yes."

"Sure I was, I thought when I saw you, that's who you'd be. You resemble the lad a bit, you know." After a pause, he moved toward the door. "I guess I'd best be opening her up, hadn't I?"

"Please." Katherine noticed that Aldrich's eyes were fixed on the key she was rubbing between her fingers. He seemed to be interested in every move she made!

O'Reilly fumbled with the lock. "Sorry you have to see the place in such a shambles, ma'am," he apologized. Finally, he clicked open the door, stepped in, and snapped up the green blind with a loud bang.

As the light filled the room, Katherine stopped dead-still, unable to speak. The word "shambles" was almost a compliment to the room. In truth, it had been wrecked, turned completely inside-out. The press lay on its side; all the printing trays were open, with broken letters scattered on the floor; rolls of paper were strewn about the place. Alex's roll-top desk stood with empty drawers hanging out over piles of printed and handwritten notes.

"I've been keeping her locked, ever since it happened," O'Reilly told her.

"I don't understand—who did this?"

"No telling, ma'am. In a gold mining town, anything can happen."

She took a few steps into the room. Seeing the office this way made her feel sick at the stomach. It was as though someone had torn into Alex's grave and mutilated his body!

"Would you be cleaning up soon, ma'am?" O'Reilly asked.

"What?"

"It's just that I'll be needing to put the place up for rent soon," he explained. "Can't very well do that with all this refuse in here."

Aldrich started herding the landlord out. "I'll take care of it," he told him.

"Yes, sir, I was just thinking of the lady, you know."

"Let me take care of the lady."

"Ah, yes, sir, I see what you mean. I do, indeed."

Katherine felt her shoulders shake uncontrollably as she shuffled a few feet through the debris to Alex's desk. The room seemed so forlornly cold and still!

"I guess we've seen enough," Aldrich asserted. "This is a disgrace, isn't it? I knew someone had broken in here, but I had no idea the place was like this!"

"They were looking for something, Henry."

"Oh, I doubt that. It looks more to me like the work of a few errant outlaws."

She shook her head. "I don't think so."

He moved closer to her. "Katherine," he entreated, "maybe now you'll agree this is no place for you. Why don't you let me take you home? After this shock, you need to rest."

"I don't want to rest, Henry. I want to look through Alex's things."

His voice was firm. "Let me do that, Katherine. That's what friends are for." He smiled as he gently patted her forearm.

The feel of Aldrich's spindly fingers on her sleeve sent a sudden, sharp chill through her body. Moments later, she couldn't help but puzzle over her curious physical reaction to him. As far as she could tell, W.H. Aldrich, a handsome, successful, attentive man, possessed all the qualities women admired in their men. And yet, for some reason, she found herself being repulsed by this single, harmless touch.

Her reaction wasn't the result of her being a flighty, innocent, fumbling girl, either. Since the age of fifteen, Katherine Haynes had been courted and desired by some of the most important single men in Chicago. Generally, she was tolerant of her admirers. Some of them she actually liked. Once she had even come very close to loving one. Harlan McInnis, a chemist in the steel mill, was a bright, eager young man with a burning smile and deep, penetrating blue eyes that simply left her weak. Each time they kissed, he had stirred certain strong currents of desire in her she had never felt before. But soon she had to back away from him. Instinctively, she had known that McInnis was not the man she should give herself to.

What peculiar, irrational things emotions were! A short time ago, on the train, she had felt twice as excited—and frightened—as she had ever felt with Harlan McInnis. And those feelings were produced by a brash, sandy-haired Pinkerton detective she didn't even know. She had far less reason to respond in such a way to Matt Pilgrim than to W.H. Aldrich, and yet she yearned for the touch of one and was repelled by the close contact of the other.

Struggling not to be obvious, Katherine tried to ease her arm away. But the instant she moved, she felt his long, bony fingers slide down her arm, then wrap themselves tightly around her wrist.

"I am your friend, Katherine," he insisted firmly, emphasizing the "am."

"I know—"

"But I want to be more than that. Much more."

"Henry, don't—"

"Listen to me," he ordered, pulling her close. "Don't think I'm trifling with you. I'm not a scoundrel; I'm very serious."

"Henry, would you let go of my hand, please?"

He ground his teeth as he stared at her. "You're making this very difficult, Katherine," he told her. "What I'm trying to say is, I want to consider us engaged."

She could hardly believe her ears. "Engaged!" she exclaimed.

He gripped her wrist harder. "Is the idea so repugnant to you?"

"For God's sake, Henry. I've only been in town thirty minutes!"

"If you'd been in town only thirty seconds, I would still ask you. I knew I would, the moment I saw you get off the train. I'm a man who knows what he wants, Katherine."

"Well, I'm sorry, but I'm a woman who doesn't. Now, would you mind letting me go?"

Gritting his teeth, he relented. "I apologize," he said,

releasing her. "I shouldn't have been so abrupt. I'm used
to going after what I want. I should have merely asked you
to consider the idea."

"Henry, this isn't the time or the place—"

"You're right, it isn't. Forgive me. But promise me,
you'll at least consider the idea."

"How could I possibly promise anything of the sort! I
came here expecting to see my brother's orderly little
newpaper office, and instead I find a room that's completely demolished, and now you're standing there in the
middle of the wreckage, proposing marriage to me!"

He nodded. "I agree, it was atrocious timing," he
allowed. "I should have controlled myself. But I'll make
it up to you. We'll go home and have Su Li prepare one of
his famous Cantonese dishes. He's a splendid cook; I was
lucky to get him."

"It sounds wonderful, Henry, but right now, I want to
look around here. You could go ahead; maybe if I did this
alone, I could start to feel close to him—"

"No," he said in a strained voice. "One thing I will not
do is leave you alone. It's too dangerous. I have a feeling
this is the work of the Bonners. And when that unholy
pack of animals is prowling about, no woman is safe."

She looked at him steadily. "Tell me something," she
challenged. "Why does everyone around here hate the
Bonners? Exactly what have they done?"

"They're outlaws, Katherine."

His blithe response irritated her. "Even if they are,
they're still people, aren't they?" she countered. "If you
were shunned by society, wouldn't you resort to stealing?
All they're trying to do is survive in a world that doesn't
have the human decency to give them a chance to be
anything else. They're not outlaws—they're outcasts."

42

"The Bonners are mad dogs, Katherine. They plunder and pillage and terrorize whenever and however it suits them. And our spineless sheriff lets them do it!"

"They had a chance to attack the train and didn't," she defended.

"So what? Next time they might. They're absolutely unpredictable."

"Well, I don't believe they're so bad," she said, to end the matter. "People don't understand outlaws any more than they understand the strikers at the mills."

Turning around, she walked past three overturned trays of type, past a heap of old metal engravings, and stepped over to the pine wood cabinet standing next to the north wall. She could feel Aldrich's eyes burning into her back as she swung open the first door. Why on earth was this man so persistent?

At the botoom of the cabinet she saw half a dozen full bottles of Fodor Brothers printing ink, an old, warped oak bucket, a pile of cotton rags, and an unopened bar of Gold Dust soap. Inside the second door was a three-foot stack of newspapers, ranging from the *New York Tribune* to the *Kansas City Star* to something called *Grit*.

Aldrich's voice assumed a tone of impatience. "Just what are you looking for, Katherine?" he asked.

"I don't know," she confessed sadly, as she closed the door softly. "I guess I'm trying to find a trace of Alex in all this. But I can't. None of it means anything."

He moved toward her. "This is too upsetting for you. I think you should stop."

She smiled weakly. "I'm not a fragile little doll, Henry," she assured him. "Besides, I still believe there is something here I have to find."

"There's nothing here but Bonner remains," he asserted.

43

"And it looks like it always does—like a mass of picked-over bones."

With her attention now on the walls of the office, Katherine let the reference to the outlaws pass. Over the cabinet, in the center of a straight line of a dozen issues of the *Central City Banner*, was a framed daguerrotype of a slim man about twenty-five years old, with thick, black hair, and thin, arched eyebrows. He was standing with his shiny boot propped on an upholstered chair, wearing a playful, impish expression on his boyish face. She was shocked to see a printed caption beneath the portrait, which read 'Gardner Haynes, Jr., 1849.' "

"I can't believe this is Poppa!" she exclaimed. "He's changed so much."

"I've always thought that was a terrible likeness."

"Did Alex look like this?"

"I don't know; I suppose he did."

"It's so strange to see Poppa's picture in this office," she observed. "He always believed Alex hated him. I wonder if he would soften any, if he saw this."

As she reached up to touch the picture, Aldrich spoke. "We should be going now, Katherine," he announced. "Su Li is expecting us for dinner."

She dropped her hand, gazed around her, and sighed. "Could I be wrong about this?" she wondered. "Could Alex have left nothing important behind?"

"It looks that way."

"But why would he carry around this little key?" she asked, removing it from her breast pocket. "There doesn't seem to be anything here with a lock."

"No," he said, looking at it curiously. "There doesn't."

"He had this with him when he died. It has to mean something!"

"May I see it?" he asked, holding out his hand.

"It's just a key, Henry."

His hand curled into a fist as he withdrew it.

"It has to fit a drawer, or a safe, or a cabinet some-where," Katherine surmised. "If it's not here, then it's somewhere else. Where did Alex live?"

"He rented a couple of rooms here in town," Aldrich answered vaguely.

"Where?"

"Two doors up the street. Above Miller's Mercantile."

"Could we go there now?"

"We could, but I think it would be better if I went alone. I could take the key with me, in case I found anything."

"Thank you, but I want to see his room myself."

He rubbed his sallow cheeks as he watched her slip the key back into her pocket. Then he stepped aside and gestured gallantly with his open palm. "This way, please," he said.

After closing the door to the *Banner* office behind him, Aldrich grasped her arm firmly and guided her up the dirt street to a set of wooden stairs appended to the brick sides of the dry goods store. After glancing up the high steps, he looked at her. "I would guess your key fits that door," he suggested. "Why don't you let me go up and try it?"

"No, I'll do it." She hitched up her skirts a few inches, grabbed the railing, and started up the stairs. With Aldrich hanging close behind, Katherine quickly reached the landing and came to an abrupt stop in front of the door. Slipping the key into the lock, she turned and rattled it loudly a few times, then shook her head. "It doesn't fit," she announced.

"Let me try it," Aldrich volunteered.

But Katherine was already discovering the door wasn't even locked. The instant she twisted the knob and pushed the pine door open, a wave of disgust swept over her. Like his newspaper office, Alex's room had been completely torn apart. The mattress had been ripped open and flung over in the corner; the dresser drawers were gutted; even his trousers and shirts and undergarments were scattered about the room.

"Dear God," she murmured in a low, quivering voice. "What do they want, Henry? What are they after?"

He pursed his thin lips and nodded his head knowingly. "This ought to be enough to convince you to leave it alone, Katherine. Whatever your brother's feud with the Bonners was, I would advise you to let it end with his death."

"But it's so sickening!" Feeling cold, she crossed her arms in front of her chest. "They put their hands on everything he owned! They have no respect for anything!"

"I told you they were animals."

"It's as if he were *nothing*, Henry."

"Sometimes people are like that, Katherine," he claimed, placing his fingers on the nape of her neck. "That's why you need a protector."

She drifted away from his touch, into the room. "All I want to do is find out who did this," she declared, looking around. "Right now, I can't think of anything else."

He advanced slowly, deliberately. "I think what you need more than anything else is rest, Katherine," he determined. "Let me take you home."

"No, Henry. Not now."

"Katherine, dear—"

Just as Aldrich reached out to her again, the startling, deafening sound of a steam whistle suddenly whined into

46

the room through the open doorway. The unrelenting, piercing noise sent a ringing through her ears.

"What on earth is that?" She stepped out to the landing and witnessed a crowd of men thrashing against each other as they banged through the swinging doors of a saloon into the street, then three women in bright new hats from Miller's store hurrying outside. Within seconds, the whole town was teeming with miners, merchants, men, women, and children, all scurrying off in the same direction.

Joining her, Aldrich observed that they were headed toward Nevada Hill. Above the sound of the whistle, he shouted down to the round little man huffing past. "O'Reilly! What's all this about? What's happened!"

The stout Irishman came to a halt. "Looks like it's the Get Lucky again, Mr. Aldrich," he answered. "Those lads have the worst luck up there."

"What is it this time?"

"I'm just about to find out, sir. Just as soon as I can get myself up that hill."

"So am I," Katherine broke in.

"Katherine, wait—"

"The Get Lucky is the mine my brother died in, Henry."

"That's hardly reason to go running up there—"

"It's reason enough for me."

"I advise you not to do this, Katherine."

"Well, I'm sorry, but I'm going to."

"All right," he conceded. "I'll go with you. I'm not going to let you anywhere near that mine without me along."

Not taking the time to respond to him, Katherine yanked the door to Alex's room shut, hastened down the steps, and joined the great exodus to Nevada Hill.

4

By the time Katherine Haynes and W.H. Aldrich reached the crown point of Harrison's Get Lucky Mine, over three hundred nervous, anxious people were already crowding together on the rocky slopes of the mountain.

One of them, Ben Watkins, the stocky, dirty, gat-toothed manager of the mine, was stretched out on his wide belly, straining to see into the main shaft, cupping his ear to hear the faint voices of the men below. Peering over his shoulder were Barton Canfield, Matt Pilgrim, and Reuben.

"Can you hear what they're saying down there, Ben?" Canfield asked.

"Can't hear a thing. The poor bastard ain't got a Chinaman's chance in hell," Watkins answered in a husky, irreverent voice. "He's as good as dead."

"Who is it? Lewis? Hawley?"

Watkins got to his feet. "Apparently, it ain't one of our men," he reported. "Apparently, it's some dub in a slick suit. Now you tell me what a man like that is doing in my mine in the first place!"

"Aren't you going to try to bring him up?" Matt asked.

Watkins turned fully around and glared at him. "Now, just who the Sam Hill might you be, boy?"

Canfield quickly interceded. "Mr. Pilgrim's a Pinkerton detective, Ben," he explained. "Mr. Harrison hired him to investigate the mine."

"Did he now?" he muttered sarcastically. "Ain't that nice? Apparently, we can't do it on our own."

"Can you bring him up?" Matt persisted.

Watkins looked him up and down. "Are you trying to tell me that dude down in the hole is another Pinkerton detective?" he sneered.

"I don't know if he is or not. Maybe if you'd bring him up, we could see."

"Now, you listen to me, boy—"

"Watkins!" Canfield warned.

Catching himself, he emptied a wad of tobacco out of his mouth into his fist and let it drop on the ground, close to Matthew's feet. "Well, as it happens, Mr. Pinkerton detective," he grumbled, "we couldn't bring him up if we wanted to, because our lift cable's broke." Buoyed by the excited response rumbling through the crowd, he added: "Live or die, they're all stuck down there til we get a cable up here and get that lift fixed."

"What about a rope?" Matt asked.

"A rope! Ha!"

"Mr. Pilgrim," Reuben offered, "if the man is dying, he might not survive being hauled up on a rope."

"Apparently, he don't know that." Watkins grinned.

Canfield glanced up at the elevator pulley. "How long will it be before we can get the cable back on, Ben?"

"Soon as they bring that new one over from the Good Times, Mr. Canfield. Half hour, maybe?"

50

"I can't wait that long," Pilgrim said. "I have to talk to that man."

The mine manager slid a fresh plug of tobacco out of his overalls, stuffed it into his mouth, and champed off a hunk of it. "Why don't you go ahead and talk to him yourself?" he invited. After gnashing a bit, he shot a splash of brown tobacco juice over the lip of the shaft. "There's your hole, Mr. Pinkerton. Crawl in it."

Pilgrim started unbuttoning his coat. "Get me a rope, Mr. Watkins," he said.

Barton Canfield quickly grabbed his arm. "Now, wait a minute here, son," he cautioned. "You can't go down there on a rope."

"Do you know any other way to go down there?"

"No."

"Then we're wasting time. Get me a rope!" Matt whipped off the coat, threw it on the ground, and pulled his necktie loose. "Hurry!"

Canfield hesitated a moment, then nodded at Watkins. "Get it, Ben," he ordered.

The manager spewed out a stream of juice that splattered on the ground. "Sure, why not," he mumbled. "If he wants to get himself killed, who am I to stop him?" He shoved his way through the crowd in the direction of the tool shed, muttering as he went on the subject of the "damned Pinkertons."

Peeling off his tie, Matt stepped up to the edge of the mine shaft. Above his head was a wooden rack, containing a tackle hook and a huge iron pulley. Free of its cable, the wheel was revolving slowly in the wind. Below him was a steady draft of cool air blowing up out of utter darkness.

"I don't like this, Matt," Canfield confided to him as they waited for the rope.

"I don't care much for it either, Mr. Canfield. But I have no choice."

The supervisor cleared his throat. "Have you ever been down in a mine before?" he asked.

"No, sir. The only kind of mining my dad knew anything about was placer."

"Then maybe you'd better reconsider, son. It's damned hard going down there."

"Mr. Canfield, I'm sure that man knows something about what's been going on around here. I have to get to him before he dies!"

"I wish I could be sure of that. So much has been happening lately."

Minutes later, Watkins arrived with the rope, which he insisted on personally fastening around Pilgrim's body. "I'm making you a bowline," he explained as he tied the knots. "And I'll tie you up here to the hook with a double Blackwell. That ought to hold you."

"You men handle the tow," Canfield ordered two husky miners. "And be easy with the line—he's never been down before."

When the rope was tied to the hook, Matt jerked on it a couple of times, then announced he was ready. "Reuben?" he said.

"Yes, sir?"

"I want you to stay close to the edge. Talk to me."

"Yes, sir."

"All right," he said to the tow men, "let's go."

With one end of the rope tied securely around his waist and the other wrapped around the hook, Matt dropped the slack in the line down into the silent darkness and began to lower himself slowly into the mire. Canfield had been right; it was hard going. But even though he found the

52

black walls of the shaft damp and slippery under his boots, he somehow managed to keep his balance as he climbed down the sides of the hole. For a time, he could look up and see Reuben's bright face poised over the edge of the shaft. But then that comforting sight became nothing but a speck of darkness in the rapidly shrinking circle of light above him.

Soon his neck and shoulders began to throb with pain; before long he had to stop and wrap the tight rope around his waist, brace his feet against the wall, and lean back, all to ease the pressure. He longed to be able to shake his arms vigorously for a moment so as to loosen his muscles, but all he could do was hang on to the rope and hope the pain would finally pass.

"Mr. Pilgrim!" Reuben's voice, descending from the circle of light overhead, seemed almost to fall down the shaft upon him. "Are you all right down there?"

"I'm fine, Reuben," he called back.

"Have you found a drift, yet?"

Matt had no idea what a drift was, but he was dead certain he hadn't found one yet. "No!" he answered.

"Well, that's no problem. Just keep going, Mr. Pilgrim."

"Thanks, Reuben," he muttered and started down again.

But the agonizing pain in his shoulders was now seeping down into his forearms and wrists. With every change of hands on the rope, his grip was becoming weaker. His arms felt like strips of rubber. His fingers, thick and clumsy now, were starting to slip; he could feel the rope scraping and burning his palms. He had to stop and rest again.

"Mr. Pilgrim!" Reuben called down.

"What!"

"Have you stopped?"

"Yes, I've stopped!"

"According to my count of the rope length, I estimate you are about six feet above a station. Can you see it?"

"I can't see anything, Reuben!"

"Then go down six more feet, Mr. Pilgrim."

Tightening his whole body under the spasms of pain, he lowered himself farther down the shaft, until finally he saw the flicker of a torch on the wall, then the opening of the timber-lined niche itself, measuring almost seven feet high and four feet wide. Thrusting away from the side of the shaft, he swung over into the station and let go of the rope. Even as he landed with a hard, solid thud on the ground, he decided he had never felt anything quite as good as the earth beneath him now.

After lying on his back for a whole, to catch his breath and ease the discomfort in his arms, Matt rose up and looked around. The carved-out niche, dimly lit by a single oil torch on the scorched wall, was the end of the line for a particular ore shaft which led down and back into the mine. Pausing at the tramway, he listened to a low, rumbling noise somewhere in the rock beneath him. He held his breath and tried to determine where it was coming from, but now he could hear nothing but silence.

All of a sudden, a dull, bumping sound drifted down the main shaft. When he leaned out and looked up the hole, he saw something change from a dark, vague form blocking the light to a man in a white shirt dangling at the end of the rope. As he watched him drop down into the mine, Matt didn't even bother to wonder who it might be. He knew it could only be one man.

When Reuben finally reached the level of the station, Pilgrim reached out, snatched hold of his waist, and swung him in. Huffing excitedly, the newcomer straightened two oil lanterns connected by a strip of rope around his neck, and grinned mischievously.

"Hello, Mr. Pilgrim," he said. "Aren't you going to ask me what I'm doing here?"

"I figured you'd tell me."

"I know you told me to stay in the shaft house, but I had to come down." He unbuttoned his shirt and popped something out from behind his belt. "I had to bring you this map of the mine."

"I don't need a map of the mine to go down the shaft, Reuben."

"I know, but I've determined a better way to go, Mr. Pilgrim." He untied the two lanterns, lit them with the flame from the torch on the wall, placed them carefully on the ground, and stretched the map out between them. "Dad says the men are supposed to be digging right here." He pecked a certain horizontal line on the map with his fingernail several times. "They're in a drift on the west side of the shaft, two hundred feet above the water level."

Matt surveyed the soiled, hand-drawn map. "What's your better way to go?"

"I thought we could proceed this way." He traced a jagged, vertical line with his fingernail. "Down through these winzes. Of course, they're mighty steep, but I'm sure we can handle it all right."

"We?"

"The supervisor always tells his men never to go into a mine alone, Mr. Pilgrim. You should always take your partner with you."

"Reuben—"

"I'm not a novice, sir," he said quickly. "I'm bringing you some firsthand mining experience. Not to mention some pretty good lanterns. But if you want to go back down the shaft alone . . .''

Matt couldn't help but smile. "I guess I've had enough of that shaft for a while. We'll try the winzes," he agreed. "But we'll do it on one condition."

"Sir?"

"If you'll stop calling me Mr. Pilgrim," he stipulated.

"Yes, sir." Handing Matt one of the lanterns, Reuben pointed straight at the ore shaft. "We'll have to slide down the tramway to get to the first tunnel," he said. "But after that, it'll be a relatively simple procedure."

As Matt suspected, climbing down into the mine was anything but a relatively simple procedure. The winzes, extremely steep and rugged little tunnels, connected the various horizontal working levels called drifts, which were cut out of the rock to follow the vein of the gold ore. He found the descent almost impossible to manage, until Reuben showed him the proper technique of bracing both hands and feet against the walls and monkey-walking down the narrow channels into the darkness below.

Deeper and deeper they descended, into a maze of crosscut tunnels and passageways, past the ore shafts and chimneys and stopes and stulls, until at last, in a roomy drift, they came to a halt, as Reuben asked Matt to stop and listen.

"I don't hear anything," Matt said after a minute.

"That's what's so strange," Reuben replied. "According to where we are on the map, we should be hearing the water pumps!"

Matt listened. He thought he heard the strange, distant rumble again, but then it faded gradually into the dead silence. "If the pumps aren't working, then the water level must be rising," he concluded.

"Yes, and I wonder how much!"

"And how fast! If that rumbling I keep hearing is water pouring in from the Good Times Mine next door, we're in trouble, Reuben. How much farther are the miners?"

"I figure they're about fifty feet away, through this last tunnel."

"Then let's go!"

The last passageway was the sharpest incline of all, only slightly less vertical than the main shaft. With Reuben close behind, Pilgrim descended slowly through the close chasm of rough, chiseled rock for a few minutes, then drew up.

"I hear it again, Reuben," he said.

Reuben nodded. "So do I. And that's a flood, Mr. Pilgrim. No doubt about it."

"And it's getting closer all the time."

"Mr. Pilgrim, if that is water flooding from the Good Times, we're going to be caught right in the middle of it!"

"Then we'd better keep moving."

Ten feet farther down, Matt was relieved to detect the mumbling sound of voices in the mine. Thirty feet later, the winze opened out into the spacious drift where the miners had been working.

Matt discovered four of them in a huddle, near the main shaft: a trio of tall, young Cornishmen with blondish hair under rumpled caps and baggy gray trousers and sweaters of wool. They were standing near a prostrate man in a black business suit.

"Well, looks at this, lads!" The largest of the Cornishmen cocked back his cap and grinned widely. "Welcome to the Hole of Cornwall, mates!" he greeted Matt and Reuben. "We've been hearing that stirring in the winze for hours, seems like."

Matt didn't stop for introductions. He crouched down beside the man on the ground. "How is he?" he asked.

The Cornishman with big black eyes and a horsey face pinched his long nose. "He's been sleeping like a babe through it all," he replied. "Though I would say the poor devil ain't long for the world, the way he is."

"Has he said anything?"

"Not a peep."

Matt stood up. "What's wrong with the water pumps?" he asked.

"There's nothing wrong with the pumps, mate. They just ain't built to withstand a hundred tons of Mother Nature's urine, that's all."

"Then it's true; the water level is rising."

"Oh, yes, it's a-rising all right. And before too long, it's going to be bursting like a bad bladder down here."

"How high is it?"

"How about it, mates?" he addressed the others. "Fifty feet below us?"

They nodded and mumbled their agreement.

"And it'll probably rise about that much above us, too."

"Then why have you been standing around here doing nothing?" Reuben asked. "Why haven't you tried to get out?"

"Because this poor devil's in such sad mortal shape, that's why. There's a blade in his belly, and Morris here says one of his ribs is broke and sticking against his lungs. We figure it would kill the lad sure as death if we lugged his carcass up five hundred feet of tunnel."

"You don't have to worry about that now," Matt told him. "I'll stay down here with him. You men get out of here while you can!"

58

The Cornishman crossed his arms and shook his head. "We couldn't do that, mate," he declared.

"For God's sake, man."

"We'll wait for the lift wagon, if it's all right. I know they'll be sending one for us before long."

"They'll be sending one, but who knows how long that will be?"

"I guess we'll wait, won't we, boys?"

"Damn, you're a stubborn lot."

"The thing is, Mr. Pilgrim, this lad was on our turf," he explained. "And that means we're responsible for him."

"But you don't even know who the man is."

"Don't know who ye are, either. But I sure wouldn't leave ye hurt and wounded on the floor."

"Reuben—"

"Don't ask me to go anywhere either, Mr. Pilgrim." He pulled out his watch and held it up to the light of his lantern. "I'm assuming my calculations are correct and the lift car will be coming down that shaft in exactly five minutes."

Letting out a sigh or resignation, Matt gave up and dropped to his knees again, beside the unconscious man. Only now did he see the bloody blade of the bone-handle knife piercing through the black coat and white shirt into his stomach, a few inches below the navel.

"Is this where you found him?" Matt asked the Cornishman.

"Has to be. Morris wouldn't let us move a muscle."

With his handkerchief Pilgrim wiped the dirt off the man's face. Despite a bit of grime and a few days' growth of beard, he looked exceptionally neat. What was such a man doing five hundred feet below the surface with a knife in his belly?

By now Reuben had drifted over to the main shaft. "I can hear the water rising up the shaft, Mr. Pilgrim," he reported.

"Any sign of the lift car yet?"

He craned his neck to look up. "No, sir."

"Damn!"

"It'll be here, though, Mr. Pilgrim. Give it another three or four minutes."

"I hope we have that much time left." He blinked at the close, shadowed ceiling above him as a dull noise deep in the bowels of the earth rumbled and vibrated the rock around him. The location of the sound was so indistinct that he had no idea where in the mine the water was rushing or which tunnel would be the next to flood. He simply had to accept the situation: They were trapped, and all they could do was wait.

The man on the ground reached up, snatched Pilgrim's shirt sleeve, and let out a groaning cry of pain as he pulled it down. "Help me!" he whispered painfully. "Please—"

Matt slid his hand carefully behind the man's head and raised it gently. "Just take it easy, sir," he advised. "We're going to get you out soon."

He grimaced and shook his head.

"Try to be still," Pilgrim insisted. "I'll take care of you."

The big Cornishman wrenched his long face into an expression of concern. "If ye don't mind, that's our responsibility," he said. "We'll be taking the lad to the lift wagon ourselves."

What lift wagon? Matt wondered. Where the hell was the thing? The image of the stout, tobacco-spitting Ben Watkins crossed his mind. Could the mine manager somehow be responsible for all this? Could he be delaying the car now, hoping they would drown?

As the injured man choked and gasped for breath, drops of sweat popped out on his wrinkled forehead. Matt wiped his face again and loosened his shirt enough to expose the skin, but nothing helped. He still was heaving up and down to get his air.

"Mr. Pilgrim!" Reuben called out. He was standing at the shaft, holding on to a stull, extending a lantern out into the hole. "I can see the water now. It's rising fast!"

But Matt was responding to a pitiful, silent plea for him to draw close. He bent over the man, near enough to feel his wheezing breath puff against his face.

"What is it, sir?" he asked. "What are you trying to say?"

"Bonanza," he whispered.

"I don't understand."

"Tell them . . . bonanza."

"Tell who?"

"Looks like he's passed out, mate," the Cornishman informed him.

"Sir!" Matt felt like shaking him awake.

"He can't hear ye, Mr. Pilgrim. The lad's out."

Matt looked up in frustration. "But what was he talking about? What kind of bonanza?"

"Now that I wouldn't know, mate."

"Mr. Pilgrim!" Reuben cried from the shaft. "Here it comes!"

For one splendid, excited second, Matt turned toward Reuben, expecting to see a sturdy elevator car dutifully arriving at its appointed stop at the level of the drift. But what he witnessed was a giant pool of clear water seeping out of the main shaft and spreading rapidly across the floor in his direction. Still supporting the man's head with his hand, he watched with horror as the water washed quickly across the chiseled stone, gathered around the soles of his boots, and rose instantly to the height of his ankles.

Then Reuben called out again. "Ah! I was right!"

Matt gritted his teeth. "Reuben, damn it—"

"No, I mean the lift car, Mr. Pilgrim. It's coming down!"

The Cornishman chuckled with satisfaction. "I knew it would," he muttered. "I knew up top they wouldn't let us down."

Matt looked up at him. "Take your men and jump into that car as fast as you can," he said.

The man didn't budge. "I told ye before—we ain't going aloft without this lad here."

Matt raised the head of the injured man higher, to avoid the water. "Go on! There may not be room for all of us!"

"We'll wait and see how much there is," he said simply.

At that instant, every inch of rock around them shook and creaked as a thunderous, rattling sound boomed through the floor, the walls, and ceiling.

"I've got it, Mr. Pilgrim!" Reuben was struggling with the iron car, which was rocking back and forth on the water rushing into the tunnel. "It'll hold us!"

"Then let's go!" Matt said, rising.

"We'll take him, if ye don't mind," the Cornishman said and made a come-here motion with his finger to the other miners. Immediately, two of them formed a cradle of four strong arms, while the others raised the unconscious man up and placed him softly on the support.

Matt and the Cornishmen sloshed their way through the tunnel in knee-deep water to the main shaft where Reuben was still trying to control the car. The heavy metal box was being slammed back and forth against the walls of the shaft by the rising flood.

"Get in, Reuben!" Matt ordered. "Hurry!"

"Yes, sir."

After he rolled over the edge of the car, he helped the miners with their burden. Just as the Cornishmen piled in, the cable above tightened and jerked the car up—without Matt.

"Mr. Pilgrim!" Reuben yelled and reached out his hand.

As the detective lunged toward the shaft, a torrent of water gushed into the drift, nearly sweeping his legs out from under him. He had one chance—to leap out into the shaft, high enough to reach up and grab Reuben's extended hand. Without a moment's hesitation, he sprang forward, groping for the hand stretching out over the side of the car.

His chest struck iron at the same time he felt the firm, sure grasp of Reuben's fingers clamp around his wrist. Groggy for a moment, he soon felt himself behind whisked up through the air into the car by an octopus of powerful Cornish miners' arms.

As the lift car started to move like a snail up the shaft, Reuben eyed the cable curiously, then shook it vigorously with both hands. "Mr. Pilgrim," he said, "this is a very old cable."

Matt steadied himself as he rose up. "Are you trying to tell me it's going to break before we reach the top?"

Reuben shrugged. "I don't know if it will or not. I was just accounting for the slow movement. But you're right about that; a cable this old could snap like a dry twig at any moment."

"That's a very comforting thing to hear right now, Reuben."

"Yes, sir."

The Cornishman leaned over the car, responding to the loud, sucking noise beneath them. "Looks like the Hole of Cornwall is flooded, lads," he announced. "And at the rate we're moving up this shaft, we're all about to join it."

Matt cleared his throat. "What does that mean?" he asked.

The other man was ready with the answer. "It means," he replied, "as soon as that drift fills up, there will suddenly be more pressure in the shaft. When that happens, the water will rise so fast, this old wagon of ours will spill over and go under like a rock in a lake."

"Then it doesn't matter if the cable breaks or not," Matt said, shaking his head.

"I don't know," Reuben said, scratching his chin. "That may not be correct."

Matt looked at him. "If you know something, Reuben, let's hear it."

Reuben turned to address the Cornishman. "You're assuming the water will level off at five-fifty, is that right?"

He nodded. "And that's a good forty feet above us, mate."

Reuben handed his lantern to one of the miners to hold, unfolded his map, and studied it. "If what Mr. Pilgrim assumes about the Good Times Mine is true," he reasoned, "that figure could be wrong. You see, if we're being flooded by a breakout next door. . . ."

The others watched in interested silence as Reuben whipped a stubby yellow pencil out of his trousers pocket and began scratching numbers on the map.

"The Good Times is working at nine hundred feet.

We're at seven hundred. Now if they stopped the pumps and let the level rise—let's see. . . ." He ran a string of numbers across the page. "It could be that. . . ."

Matt could bear it no longer. "It could be what, Reuben? Tell us, man!"

"It could be, if my numbers are right, the water will reach its level in our mine at five hundred feet—in other words, ten feet below us."

Matt heaved a sigh. "What do you know—good news, for a change. I hope you're right."

"I am right, Mr. Pilgrim. That is, if you were. Of course, there is a second possibility. The water could be coming from a break underneath us instead. But when that happens, there is usually a release of suffocating gas—"

He left the sentence hanging in the air as a great silence all of a sudden surrounded them. Above their own breathing, the only sound they could hear now was the rhythmic creaking of the cable over their heads.

"It's over!" Matt announced. "The water's calm!"

"Then you must have been right, Mr. Pilgrim," Reuben said happily. "Congratulations!"

"*We* were right, Reuben," he corrected. Then he added pointedly, "Maybe I should say, 'We were right, partner.' "

"Why, thank you, Mr. Pilgrim," he said, ingenuously.

Matt turned to the man in the arms of the Cornishmen. "Now, if we can bring him back to health," he said, "and get some answers to a few questions—

"Ah, I'm afraid ye'll have to be getting your answers elsewhere, Mr. Pilgrim," the big Cornishman said, wearily. "This poor devil here just didn't make it. The lad was dead the minute we lifted him into the wagon."

5

The last person on earth Matt expected to see at the top of the shaft was Katherine Haynes. But the moment the car reached ground level, he caught a glimpse of her bright, beautiful, and very worried face shining in the crowd, as if it were bathed in light. In the one exciting moment their eyes met, they exchanged a simple confidence. She revealed to him her joy at seeing him safe; he confided to her how much her concern meant to him. Although he was eager to communicate more, she broke the connection, turned away, and spoke to the man next to her, Mr. W.H. Aldrich.

As the lift car creaked to a stop, the whistle screamed loudly, and a noisy, jubilant round of cheers erupted from the mass of people gathered on the hill. While the wives of the Cornishmen, mixing tears with smiles of delight, raced to the arms of their husbands, other women huddled around, offering warm woolen blankets and cups of hot, steaming coffee to the survivors.

In the confusion, Barton Canfield sought out his son and greeted him with a passionate hug. Then he draped Matt's shoulders with a blanket and pumped his hand emphatically.

"Good job, Matt," he congratulated. "But very close," he added with a smile.

"Very," he agreed.

"For a while, we really thought we'd lost you."

"Aw, we knew what we were doing, Dad," Reuben offered.

"Did you, now," he replied skeptically.

"Of course we did. Don't forget, Mr. Pilgrim is a Pinkerton detective!"

"I know he is. But you, my son, are not. And since you first learned to read and write—which may have been a mistake, by the way—I can never, ever tell what you're going to do next."

"Well, I can tell you that exactly, Dad. Next I'm going to be Mr. Pilgrim's partner. Isn't that right, sir?"

"Not if you keep calling me Mr. Pilgrim."

"Coffee, sir?" A pretty Chinese girl in a coolie hat smiled warmly as she handed Matthew an empty cup.

"Thank you." He shrugged his blanket off his shoulders, caught it in the crook of his left arm, and received the cup from her hand. As she poured the coffee out of the gray metal pot, he looked over at Katherine Haynes again. Once more their eyes met. She seemed to be on the verge of moving toward him when Aldrich took her attention again. But even while the railroad man was talking to her, she managed to steal a few quick glances at Matthew Pilgrim.

The clamor of the crowd trailed off sharply into silence the moment the miners hauled the dead man out of the elevator car and stretched him out on the ground. Matt immediately handed his coffee to someone and covered the corpse with his blanket.

"Who is he, Matt?" Canfield knelt down beside the

man and peeled the cover off his face. "I've never seen him before."

Ben Watkins interjected with a spray of tobacco juice on the ground, near the body. "Whoever the hell he was," he offered, "apparently, he was up to no good. Look at that Arkansas toothpick in his guts."

"He never got a chance to tell us who he was," Pilgrim answered Canfield's question. "He died right after we reached him."

Watkins spit again. "In other words, he never said anything, right?"

Matt hesitated, remembering the dead man's strange words. "Nothing that made any sense," he replied.

"Then nobody knows why he was down in my mine," he concluded.

"Not at the moment."

Canfield rose to his feet. "I can find nothing on him," he said. "I guess we will never know."

"Oh, we'll know, Mr. Canfield," Matt promised. "The Agency will tell us that."

"I don't see how."

"From photographs, Dad," Reuben offered. "It's a standard Pinkerton technique."

Matt looked at his new partner. "Reuben, we need a room where we can thoroughly examine the body," he told him. "A place that's private and unused—" When he caught the eye of Katherine Haynes again, a thought occurred to him. Without a moment's hesitation, he marched straight to her. "Miss Haynes," he said in a calm, easy voice, "would you mind if we used your brother's newspaper office?"

"Would I mind what?"

"We need it to examine the body. Your brother did own a camera, didn't he?"

"Why on earth would you need a camera?"

"To photograph the body, Miss Haynes."

"Good Lord!"

"Now hold on there, Mr. Pilgrim," interrupted W.H. Aldrich as he raised a protesting hand. "Miss Haynes has had a long trip. She's in no condition to stand by while a couple of young ruffians go plundering through her brother's private belongings."

"I assure you, we're not going to plunder, Mr. Aldrich."

"Anyway, Alexander Haynes's office is simply in no condition to be used by anyone. It has been wrecked."

"We'll straighten it up."

"I believe the idea is preposterous, sir."

"It probably is. What about it, Miss Haynes?"

Katherine swallowed drily. "I guess Alex's office would be convenient for that—"

"Katherine!" Aldrich exclaimed.

"Yes," she decided, nodding. "You may use it. But you must allow me to be there—"

"Oh, I wouldn't have it any other way," he said. "Reuben?" he called to his partner.

"We're loading the body now, Mr. Pilgrim," he anticipated.

When the procession reached the *Banner* office, Reuben Canfield guided the miners carrying the corpse into the building, while Matt stayed outside to disperse the crowd. After a few minutes, he had managed to clear the street, except for Katherine Haynes and the tall, stiff man clasping her elbow.

"I insist on going in, too, Mr. Pilgrim," Aldrich was saying. "After all, Miss Haynes is my responsibility."

"But she's not your property."

"Now, just a minute, sir—"

"I'm sorry, I don't have a minute."

"You young—"

"Henry," Katherine cut in. "Please—it's all right." She pulled her arm gently out of his grip. "Why don't you go ahead without me? I'll be there later."

"Katherine, you haven't stopped since you got off the train. You need your rest."

"I'll get my rest later," she said, a little annoyed.

He glared at Matt from under his thin eyebrows, then looked at her solicitously. "I don't approve of this," he stated.

"Well, I'm not sure I do either," she confessed. "But I'll be fine."

Grinding his teeth disapprovingly, Aldrich lingered a while, then excused himself politely, wheeled around, and headed up the street.

Matt watched him. "You know, Kate," he observed bluntly, "I don't think you're going to marry that man, after all."

"I beg your pardon."

"My mother used to say, a man who hangs on a woman's arm like a snake on a tree is just about as trustworthy as the snake. And from what I've seen, you're every bit as wise as my mother."

"Mr. Pilgrim," she retorted, "for you information, he was not hanging on to my arm."

"Well, no, he wasn't. Not for long anyway. You had the natural wisdom to yank it loose."

"I did nothing of the kind—" she protested.

But Matt was already striding into the *Banner* office, where Reuben and the two miners were stirring about, diligently trying to put the place back into order. "Somebody did a thorough job of this," he commented, gazing around at the jumble.

As soon as Katherine saw the still, human shape laid out on top of her brother's work table she turned her back. "First someone tries to wreck Alex's office, and now you bring a dead man in here."

"They weren't trying to wreck the office, Kate," he disagreed. "Whoever did this was looking for something."

She looked at him eagerly. "That's what I thought!" she told him. "But Henry said it wasn't very likely—"

"Henry was wrong," he stated. "And from the looks of things, they didn't find what they were looking for."

She shrugged her shoulders. "But what could it have been?" she asked. "And why would this happen now, right after his death?"

"I would say the two events are related, Kate," he answered. "The Pinkertons believe that coincidences are part of a logical, predictable pattern of behavior. If we knew why this office was turned inside out, we would probably know why your brother was killed in the Harrison mine."

She was doubtful. "Somehow, I can't see the great Pinkerton Detective Agency bothering to find out why a maverick like my brother died mysteriously in a mine explosion," she said. "They only work for wealthy industrialists, after all."

"The Pinkertons work for money, Miss Haynes," he corrected. "Not people. Anyone can hire them."

"You make it sound like a business, Mr. Pilgrim—when I know it isn't. I've seen that awful sign in the shape of a human eye over Allan Pinkerton's office on Washington Street. Everyone knows a Pinkerton detective is the eye—he works for powerful men like my father. He spies on strikers and outlaws, and sends in his reports—''

"He has to. The Agency uncovers every truth that's necessary in any case."

"Every truth?"

"Yes."

"Then you really could find out what Alex was doing in that mine?"

"Yes, we could," he answered confidently.

Katherine slid a thumb and finger into her breast pocket. "I mean *you*, Mr. Pilgrim," she said. "Would you find that out for me, if I hired you?"

"You have to hire the whole Agency, Kate," he pointed out. "Not merely one of its 'eyes.' "

"But if you do this for money—"

"I said the Pinkertons do it for money, Kate—not me."

She extracted her fingers from her pocket. "Then, why—"

Her question was severed by a sharp exclamation from Reuben Canfield, who was crashing out of the closet loaded down with bulky, cumbersome photographic equipment.

"Look at this, Mr. Pilgrim!" he announced. "I found a Talbot camera, some dry plates, a tripod, even a magnesium flash. Everything we need." He gave Matt the plates and flash and started rigging up the camera.

"Is it damaged?" Pilgrim asked.

With his head shrouded by the cloak, Reuben peered through the camera lens. "It seems to be all right," he reported through the black velvet cloth.

"Good." He addressed the two miners: "Now, if you men will help us slide the table back against the wall. . . ."

Katherine turned away while they scraped the table

across the floor and raised the corpse into a sitting position against the wall. While the two miners, out of camera range, held the body erect, Reuben ducked under the cloth and raised the flash up high.

"That's perfect!" he hollered. "Hold it there!" Suddenly, the flash exploded in a burst of white light and a cloud of smoke. "Let's do two more," he said, snapping out the plate.

While Reuben was busily photographing the subject, Matt watched Katherine Haynes linger near the window, silently staring out over the reverse lettering on the *Central City Banner* sign on the glass. As he studied her, he couldn't help but wonder what she was thinking. Beautiful and poised, she always seemed to be in complete control of herself. She carried her body gracefully, spoke clearly and directly, and stated her opinions succinctly and confidently. And yet, for all that, there was an air of uneasy anticipation about her. It was as if she were searching for something.

As he stared admiringly at her lovely form in the golden light of the setting sun pouring through the window, he felt a need for her begin to stir in his body. He tightened under an almost overpowering desire to rush over to her, spin her around, take her into his arms, and kiss her. But he sucked in a deep breath and held himself in check. He knew Katherine was not ready for that. There was still a barrier between them. . . .

"Mr. Pilgrim? I'm through," Reuben cut into this thoughts. "We have three pictures."

Matt sighed, looked around, and acknowledged. After thanking the miners for their help and sending them away, he and Reuben again stretched the body out on the table.

"Now, let's see what this fellow can tell us about

himself,'' he said. He tested the arms and legs for broken bones. Three of his ribs were crushed. ''Kate?'' he called to the woman at the window.

She faced him. ''What is it?'' she asked.

''Would you get us some more light, please?''

After hesitating, she discovered an oil lamp in the half-straightened room and brought it over.

''Thank you,'' Matt said as he set it down on the table.

''Mr. Pilgrim,'' she said to him, avoiding a direct glance at the body, ''I want you to know that for once, I agree with you. After thinking about what you said, I believe all of this is related, somehow: Alex's death, this office being broken into, even that poor man there—''

''Do you think you could find us another lamp, Kate?''

She paid no attention to the request. ''As I was saying, Mr. Pilgrim,'' she continued, ''like it or not, I need you. The Pinkertons, I mean.''

Matt looked at her. ''Are you trying to say you want to help us?''

''Yes, that's what I'm trying to say. I will do anything to find out why my brother died in that mine.''

''If it is related to the case, we'll do it. But first we need to examine this body.''

''If that's what you have to do,'' she shuddered.

''But we need more light.''

''When I said help, I didn't mean fetching and carrying.''

''I'll get it, Mr. Pilgrim—''

''No, Reuben.'' She stopped him. ''I'll bring the light.''

While she was getting another lamp, Reuben was examining the long, white fingers of the dead man under his magnifying glass. ''He certainly wasn't a working man, Mr. Pilgrim,'' he concluded. ''There's not a trace of grime under his nails.''

"That's consistent with his Boston suit."

"No mine dust on the bottom of his shoes, either. He never set foot down there."

Matt thought a minute as Katherine brought the extra lamp and hesitantly shoved it next to the corpse. "The broken ribs mean he must have been thrown down into the shaft, but he landed, accidentally, in an elevator car part of the way down."

"And when the elevator car stopped on the Cornwall level," Reuben deduced, "he managed to pull himself out and crawl a few feet into the drift, where the Cornishmen found him."

"Which accounts for the dirt on his face and chest," Matt agreed.

"But why was he stabbed?" Katherine interrupted.

"I don't know," Matt answered. "But we can eliminate robbery as a motive. He has no money or identification, but he was still carrying his watch. No thief would overlook that."

Reuben examined the timepiece under the light. "It's a Waterbury," he said. "Which tells us he wasn't rich."

Katherine raised her eyebrows suspiciously. "And what good does it do to know how much money the man had?" she said.

Matt took the watch. "We're looking for the reason he was murdered, Kate," he replied. "A man who owns a dollar watch like this one probably has to work for a living. He might have been on a job when he was attacked."

"So finding out who he worked for could lead us to a motive for the murder," she surmised.

"Yes, it could," he acknowledged, pleased that she had said "us" instead of "you". He looked at his partner. "Reuben," he invited, "since you brought that box of yours with you, why don't you see what the murder weapon can tell us?''

"Gladly!" Without a pause, Reuben scooped his black box up from the floor and swung it up to the table. As he removed the little jars and set them down in a line next to the body. Reuben explained that he was going to attempt to lift a fingerprint off the handle of the knife.

"The ridges on the finger are recorded on hard surfaces by the oil in the skin," he said. "But since the prints are invisible, you have to show them up, somehow. I use this." He held up a jar of black powder. "It's a mixture of lampblack and resin. I dust the surface to reveal the print, then lift it off with resin on paper—"

"Hold it, Reuben!" Matt held him up. He plucked up the magnifying glass, leaned over the body, and examined the knife handle. "Look at the grooves of the bone handle." He waited while Reuben eagerly peeped over his shoulder into the glass. "Do you see it?"

"Yes, sir, I see it. Looks like black dust."

"You're close: it's black powder."

"Oh!"

"What is black powder?" Katherine asked.

"Another name for explosives," Matt replied.

Scrutinizing the knife handle, Reuben nodded his head and clucked his tongue. "That's what it is," he confirmed. "The murderer definitely had his hands into black powder recently."

"Can you take a sample of it?"

"Nothing could be easier, Mr. Pilgrim. Here, I'll show you."

Matt watched him carefully lift off some of the dust with resin paper. Then he sprinkled his lampblack on the handle and removed the latent fingerprints from the surface of the bone with another sheet of resin paper. After ten minutes of meticulous labor, he raised himself up and proudly displayed the results.

"We now have a specimen of the black powder and one partial thumb print of the murderer's right hand," he announced proudly.

"That's good evidence," Matt allowed. "We'll start tracking it down tomorrow."

"Why don't we start now, Mr. Pilgrim?"

"Because it's late, Reuben."

"Yes, sir, but I would be happy to investigate myself," he offered. "Honored, in fact."

"It's almost dark. The stores are closed."

"They'll open for me," he returned. "They're too anxious to do business with Harrison mines to turn away the supervisor's son."

Matt was too tired to argue. "All right," he agreed finally. "While I'm arranging to send these plates to the Denver office, you find out where that black powder came from."

"I'll have that piece of information for you before the sun rises tomorrow," he promised. After packing the black box again, he closed the lid quietly, tucked the heavy container under his arm, and rushed out the door into the golden sunset.

"He's very eager, isn't he?" Katherine observed.

"He's also very helpful," Matt added. "Only don't tell him that. Not yet anyway."

"Do you think he'll be able to trace the explosives to the cave-in that killed Alex?"

He shrugged his shoulders. "With Reuben Canfield, who knows what will happen?" After drawing the blanket over the dead man's face, Pilgrim took a quick last survey of the office, gathered up the negative plates, and started for the door.

"Good night, Kate," he said abruptly.

"What are you doing!" she asked.

"I'm going to send these pictures to Denver."

"Well, yes, but aren't you forgetting that?" she gestured with her head at the corpse.

"No," he answered simply.

She wrinkled her thin dark eyebrows. "You're not going to leave it here, are you?" she asked.

"Why not? He's not going anywhere."

"And I'm not either, as long as there is a body in my brother's newspaper office!"

"Good. That's what I hoped you'd say." He stepped out of the office to the plank walkway.

"What I meant was," she said, following him out, "aren't you going to do something with it?"

"Like what?"

"I don't know. It's not my body—"

"All right, Kate. If it bothers you, I'll send the undertaker over for him."

"Meanwhile, what am I supposed to do—entertain it?"

"That might be a good idea. Pretend he's Henry Aldrich."

As he turned to go, she called out. "Mr. Pilgrim—wait!"

He stopped, turned around. "The man's dead, Miss Haynes," he pointed out. "There's no way he can hurt you."

"I know that. I'm just concerned about Henry. He's expecting me."

Matt looked at her closely, grinned, and shook his head. "You won't ever learn, will you?" he teased. "I've told you what two wise parents think of such men as Henry Aldrich, and yet you insist on uttering his name in public!"

"We are not discussing Henry Aldrich, Mr. Pilgrim."

"You know, it's odd that everybody in this town keeps calling me that," he said, moving toward her. "What is it—am I that frightening?"

She backed into the doorway. "Certainly not—"

"Then why don't you try Matt for a change?" He reached out with his free hand, circled her waist with his arm, and pulled her next to him.

"Now just a minute, sir—"

"No, no sir," he murmured, close to her lips. "Matt."

He felt her chest and shoulders grow rigid as he kissed her. But as he slid his tongue between her moist lips, he detected a slight quiver in her bosom, which he was holding hard against his chest. Moments later he could feel her whole body start to respond—but then she withdrew.

"That's enough, sir!"

"I've been wanting to do that ever since we left Chicago."

"Well, now you've done it. Good night, Mr. Pilgrim!"

With his heart pounding hard in his chest, he watched her pivot quickly, march into the newspaper office, and slam the door behind her. Then, blowing a gust of air through his closed teeth, he wheeled around and hurried down the street.

6

The instant Katherine Haynes realized that she had just made a dramatic exit only to shut herself up in a room with a dead body, she felt completely ridiculous. She slipped over to the window and followed Matt Pilgrim's tall, lean form as he moved purposefully through the gathering darkness up the street, until finally he disappeared around a corner. How, she wondered, could a man get to be so presumptuous?

And yet, now that he was gone, the air in the room was growing cold, thick, and oppressive around her. It was strange how the atmosphere of Alex's wrecked office had changed in a matter of a few hours. In the room with Henry Aldrich, she had felt weak and nauseous; with Matthew Pilgrim, she had experienced a kind of annoying excitement. Now, standing in it with *that*, she couldn't help but think of the dim little chamber as a shadowy, sombre tomb!

She stayed at the window until the undertaker, Mr. Carroll, arrived for the corpse fifteen minutes later. While this tall, lanky, clammy gray-haired man in a thick, black broadcloth suit ceremoniously and slowly directed two

Lee Davis Willoughby

boys in the proper removal of the body, Henry Aldrich's driver appeared to take her to the house on Pine Street.

But for some reason, seeing the big, two-story, white frame house lighted at every window didn't cheer her up at all. She carried the oppressive feeling of gloom right into the foyer, where a rotund and cheery-faced middle-aged woman wiped her chubby hands briskly on her yellow apron and opened her round face with a warm smile.

"Good evening, Miss Haynes," she greeted her with an awkward bow of the head. "We've been expecting you. Can I take your bag?"

"Thank you."

"I'm Beatrice Hatter, the housekeeper," she identified herself as she took the carpetbag.

"Hello, Beatrice."

"Oh, everybody calls me Bea," she said, leading her to the stairs. "Which I'm certainly busy as," she added. "Let me tell you, it's no small trick, taking care of a bachelor gentleman like Mr. Aldrich in a mining town."

"I suppose not." She regarded the house as she climbed the stairs. The place seemed practically barren—under-furnished, uncarpeted, with bare walls and ceilings. The spare furniture consisted of the essentials and nothing more. The chairs and sofa and cabinets were of a thin, curved beechwood, in the style of Thonet.

'Of course, what a man like Mr. A. needs should be perfectly obvious to anyone with a decent pair of eyes in his head," Bea commented as they reached the landing. "Between you and me, Miss Haynes, it's the same thing every other man needs—a pretty young wife to keep him company, if you follow me."

Katherine resisted the temptation to reply to the house-keeper that she had no intention of being anyone's pretty

82

little wife—least of all, Mr. Aldrich's. Instead, she smiled politely and followed the stout woman to the closed door of the bedroom.

"Our Mr. A. would be quite a catch," Bea continued as she pushed open the door. "If I wasn't as old as I am, let me tell you, I'd be right in there with the rest of you, dropping my little perfumed hankies all over the place. This is your room," she said, crossing the threshold.

Katherine trailed her into a delightful little chamber, glowing in the flickering light of oil lamps and burning coals in the fireplace. She was just about to comment to the housekeeper about how warm and cozy the room was, when her eye snagged on a colorful array of garments on the bed.

To her dismay, she recognized her own clothes! She was stunned to see everything she had brought with her— silk petticoats, lisle stockings, patent shoes, hats, dresses, and coats—spread out on the mattress in neat piles. She could hardly believe what she was seeing. Not even the maid at home presumed to handle every single piece of clothing she owned!

She held her tongue while the housekeeper fidgeted about the room, straightening up lamps and vases and pulling closed the seagreen velvet drapes. When she had composed herself, she asked her, "Who unpacked my things?"

Bea let go of the drapes and looked at her. "Ned brought your trunk in from the depot," she answered. "But I unpacked it. I hope you don't mind."

"Well, no," she said politely. "It's just that I naturally expected to do it myself."

"I'm sorry, Miss Haynes, but, you know, Mr. Aldrich insisted."

"Insisted? I don't understand."

A grin widened her mouth. "He's never done this before, Miss Haynes. To tell you the truth, I think he's very interested in you. In fact, I expect the staff to be informed very soon that you are the girl he intends to marry."

"Bea, I swear to you, I am not here to get married," she corrected her. "I'm staying in this house only because Mr. Aldrich is a friend of my father's. I see no reason why he should *insist* on my personal things being taken out and laid on the bed, like a display in a department store widow!"

"I guess I don't understand it either," she admitted. "But that's what he did. He supervised the unpacking himself."

"Do you mean he saw everything?" she asked in a strained voice.

Bea looked bewildered. "Yes, ma'am," she replied.

At the bed, Katherine gazed over the clothes, reached down and picked up a sheet of wrinkled and folded paper. It was the letter the undertaker had included in the cigar box, informing the Haynes family of Alex's death.

"This, too?"

"I guess so, ma'am."

"Did he read it?" she asked.

"Oh, no, ma'am." Bea shook her head emphatically. "Mr. A. is quite a gentleman. He would never do such a thing!"

She dropped the paper on top of the nightstand next to the bed. "The strange thing is, it wouldn't matter if he had. I don't have any secrets. Why would he bother to do this?"

"I'm sure I don't know, Miss Haynes."

"Well," she sighed, "I shouldn't be upset with you about it, Bea. I'll talk to Henry."

"You know, all I was doing was following orders," she said.

"I know. It's all right."

"I'm so glad." She quickly beamed. "I'd dearly hate to offend a lady like yourself. Dinner will be at eight. I hope you like Chinese cooking, because that's all we ever have around here."

"I love Chinese cooking," she responded agreeably.

"Oh, and Mr. A. said for you to join him in the library before dinner."

"Thank you, Bea."

"You're welcome," she said, moving toward the door. "I hope I didn't hurt any of your clothes. They're such pretty things." Reaching the door, she paused. "And not a bustle among them," she noted.

"No."

"I was wondering: Aren't bustles in style, any more?"

"They're in and out of style, Bea. This year, they happen to be out."

"Oh," she said, her pie-shaped face clouding with a puzzled frown. Then, shrugging her plump shoulders, she walked out of the room and closed the door quietly behind her.

Listening to the housekeeper's steps retreating in the hall, Katherine eased down in one of the Thonet chairs next to the bed and tried to collect herself. She couldn't understand why she had been so rattled by the simple act of unpacking her clothes without her permission. It wasn't a crime, after all. Why did she feel that her privacy had been invaded?

Katherine decided that she was being much too sensitive.

The ordeals of a long day had rubbed her senses raw. She had to get hold of herself. She would wash, dress, and go downstairs for a calm, restful evening with a gentleman.

She rose slowly from the chair, unpinned and removed her hat, and slipped out of her wool waistcoat. She placed Alex's key inside the undertaker's letter on the nightstand and laid the coat neatly on the chair. Next she unhooked the matching gray skirt, stepped out of it, and peeled off the pink silk blouse.

Stripped to her pantalets, Katherine took a moment to warm herself by the coal fire, then walked across the room to the mirror over the dresser. She knew that the radiant flush on her face now was caused partly by the heat of the fire, but mostly by her recollection of Matthew Pilgrim. Why, she wondered, hadn't she slapped him when he boldly grabbed her waist? And why, when he kissed her, had her body begun to vibrate with a warm and powerful sensation that seemed to surge through her veins? No man had ever caused such a reaction in her before!

Remember, he is a Pinkerton! she chastised herself. Don't let yourself fall in love with him! You despise what he represents.

At least, she thought she did.

Actually trembling, she poured a stream of cold water from the white pitcher into the basin, soaked her hands, and patted her cheeks with her dripping fingers. When that had no effect, she splashed her face and rubbed vigorously. But still the hot, tingling sensation in her skin remained.

Scolding herself for allowing a man to invade her thoughts and emotions this way, she quickly swabbed her arms and chest and dried off with one of the towels Bea had left.

Later, after some deliberate thought, she chose the blue dress to wear downstairs. She decided it was proper, without being sedate. It had a draped skirt and a slightly ruffled bodice, with a high neck that gave it the formal look she wanted now. Requiring no corset to shape her figure, she stepped right into the gown and fastened the hooks behind her back.

By the time she reached the library door fifteen minutes later, she was convinced that she had a tight rein on her feelings. But the image of the thin, erect W.H. Aldrich standing with his sharp elbow propped against the mantle of the marble fireplace triggered her anger all over again.

"Katherine," he greeted her coolly, almost formally. "Come in, please." After a minute, he added, "I hope your room is satisfactory."

She paused next to one of the six-foot mahogany bookcases. "Henry," she began, "I don't understand why my trunk was unpacked," Her words sounded odd to her ears. As provoked as she was, her complaint, stated in such a direct way, seemed downright trivial. But since she had made it, she was committed to it. "It was quite a shock," she said.

Gesturing with the glass of whiskey in his hand, he indicated the table of dark bottles nearby. "May I pour you a drink?" he asked.

"No, Henry. You may give me an explanation."

"About the clothes, you mean. Yes, well, I had no idea that would offend you. I was only trying to be accommodating. But then, when one has had to live in a wilderness for fourteen years, one naturally tends to lose his sense of decorum, Katherine. At times, one even forgets his manners."

"Yes, but—"

"Why don't we forget it, Katherine? I apologize to you. What more do I have to say?"

"Henry—"

"I promise to respect your privacy as long as you want me to. Is that what you want to hear? Is that enough for you?"

It seemed pointless to pursue the matter now. She nodded her head silently.

"Good," he said. "Now let's talk about more important things." He sipped some of the whiskey, swallowed, and cleared his throat. "Let's talk about your conduct at the Harrison mine this afternoon. I suppose I'll have to forgive you for that because you're new here, just as you have to forgive me for being too accommodating to a lady."

"Forgive me for what? What have I done?"

"Oh, you've done nothing, Katherine," he assured her. "But you can't deny your deportment at Alex's office looked, shall we say, improper—"

"Let's say nothing of the kind!"

"Now, don't lose your temper, dear. I'm only trying to instruct you."

"Forgive me if I don't think I need instructing!"

"And you don't. I agree. Not on Michigan Avenue in Chicago anyway. But trust my judgment out here, Katherine. In a mining town, a lady of your distinction cannot freely associate with single men like Matthew Pilgrim and Reuben Canfield."

Katherine could feel her face starting to burn. She dug her fingernails into her palms to keep from screaming. "I am not accustomed to being treated this way, Henry," she managed to say in a strong, if slightly fluttering voice.

"No, of course you're not." He set the whiskey down on the table. "That's why I'm trying to help you adjust. But once again, I'm afraid my Western coarseness has gotten in our way, hasn't it? That's going to be one of

88

your little jobs, dear. I'm going to need you to polish some of this roughness I've acquired out here.''

"Henry, I'm not going to be here long enough to polish the silverware!''

He gritted his teeth and glared at her. "Now, don't try to spoil my plans, Katherine," he said. "Someday, I'm going to be a powerful man in this country. I need your help to become that man.''

"I'm just not interested, Henry. I thought I made that clear this afternoon.''

He arched his eyebrows. "Your father is interested," he noted with obvious pleasure.

"I don't care.''

"Would you like to see a letter he sent to me before you arrived?''

"I'm not interested in anything my father wrote to you, Henry.''

"Well, you should be, because he advised me to marry you, Katherine. Now would you stop and think about that for a moment, please? One of the most influential men in America has sent me a letter advising me to marry his only daughter! Do you honestly believe I could simply ignore that advice?''

"I think you should forget he ever said it.''

"Now, why should I do that, Miss Haynes? Because you said so?''

"Because I'm not going to marry you, that's why!''

Gritting his teeth, Aldrich took three long strides over to the liquor table and replenished his drink. Silently, he gulped a fourth of a glass of whiskey, contemplated her for a moment, then, all of a sudden, slung the rest of the liquid into the fire with a loud *spat!*

"Do you think you're wise enough to slight the wishes

of men like Gardner Haynes and William Henry Aldrich?''
he charged.

''I think I'm wise enough to act on my own.''

''I'm afraid you're living in the past, dear. The days of
romantic individualism are over. America's no longer a
free, open country. It's a nation controlled by a few select
men. We all know their names—Rockefeller, Carnegie,
Gould, Vanderbilt, Haynes—''

''Those men control businesses, Henry, not people.''

''Those men, my dear, would control God Himself if
He were a resident of these United States. We're an indus-
trial society now, Katherine. The railroads are connecting
the remotest points of the country. Businesses are developing electrical power for heating and lighting. Telephones
are being produced. At last, we're a nation that is beginning to prosper.''

''But we're still a nation of people!'' she contended.

''Not anymore. Today, a man is nothing unless he
possesses wealth and power. Nothing!'' He slammed the
glass down on the liquor table for emphasis.

At that moment, Katherine concluded that she had nothing to gain by their swapping views of the subject of the
people versus the nation. She allowed herself a few shakes
of the head and some polite, token opposition to Aldrich's
arguments, and let it go at that.

The dinner, an elegantly prepared Cantonese meal offered by a nervous, anxious little Chinese man with a
graying pigtail, was a delicious roast duck in a sweet wine
sauce. Unfortunately, she had little chance to enjoy it.
Elaborating on his favorite theme of the need for personal
power in a growing country, her host threw out an armload
of facts and figures to illustrate how most of the nation's

currency and resources were maniuplated by a handful of wealthy men.

"Rockefeller's Standard Oil Company now controls fourteen thousand miles of underground pipeline and every single oil car on the Pennsylvania Railroad," he revealed to her. "Joseph Wharton controls ninety-nine per cent of America's nickel production. If Gustavus Swift's new refrigerator cars are successful, he'll have a monopoly on our meat products—"

"There are still the people," she occasionally argued.

But he always had a ready response. "The people are paupers, Katherine. They get poorer every day. Did you know we are letting over six hundred thousand dirt-poor immigrants a year into the country?"

"However poor they are, Henry, they're the public. And it's for the benefit of the public that men like my father must work!"

He laughed at that. "Let me quote you what William Vanderbilt said about that, the other day. When a reporter from the *Chicago Daily News* asked him if his railroad was run for public benefit, he answered, very honestly, and to the point: 'The public be damned!' Excuse my language, Katherine, but that happens to be the reality of the situation."

After the meal, Katherine excused herself, complimented Su Li on the dinner, said good night to Bea Hatter, and slowly climbed the stairs to her room. Wearily, she stepped in and closed the door behind her. The pleasant thought of being able to shut out William Henry Aldrich's relentless polemic with the solidity of a heavy oak door lifted her spirits tremendously.

Inside the cozy little room, with the coals glowing brightly in the fireplace, she felt happy and comfortable as she began taking off her clothes and thinking once again of

Matthew Pilgrim. The thought of the handsome young
detective made her feel adventurous, for some reason. For
the first time in her life, she lounged in front of the fire,
completely naked. She found something extremely sensual
in the mere act of exhibiting herself to the heat of the live
coals. The waves of heat reached out and caressed her bare
skin, warmed her blood, and stimulated a gnawing ache in
her loins. It was an exhilarating feeling. Never before had
she felt such an intense longing for . . . what? As real as
the desire was, it was still vague and unfocused.

Dropping her smooth silk nightgown over the curves of
her nude body, Katherine turned back the coverlet on the
bed and slid in. As she sank down in the feather mattress,
she pressed her eyelids together and summoned up an
image of Matt in his business suit, soaked from the thighs
down, rising from the mine. She wondered: did it matter
so much, after all, if such a man was a Pinkerton detective?

As she recalled the last time she saw him, she could
almost feel the firm grip of his hand on her waist and the
touch of his lips upon hers. Luxuriating in this strange,
new feeling of a slowly warming desire, Katherine finally
grew drowsy and drifted quietly off to sleep.

At some time in the night, though, she awoke with a
start. Had she heard something? A chill shot from the back
of her neck to the tips of her toes as she jumped up in the
bed and strained to hear another sound. For a few minutes,
there was only silence in the cool room. Then she heard a
soft, muffled sound outside her door.

Moving toward her, the noise quickly materialized as
slow, deliberate footsteps, moving from a rug to the hard-
wood floor of the hall. Just as quickly, the sounds stopped.
Katherine imagined she could hear the easy, rhythmic
sound of someone breathing outside her room. She swal-

lowed her breath and listened closely. But the only disturbance in the night was the dull, distant clamor of mine work on the hills, and—she imagined—the heavy, rapid thumping of her heart.

Just as she was about to chalk the whole business up to her overactive imagination, the footsteps commenced again, becoming louder and louder as they approached her door. With the tightness of fear in her chest, she waited for a voice to call out to her. Instead, the slow creaking of the brass knob turning in the door broke the icy stillness of the room.

Katherine lay back in the bed, waiting apprehensively as the latch clicked open, and the door began to move. A pencil-thin block of light from the hall expanded to a yard's width before Henry Aldrich appeared at the threshold. He stood bathed in it for a moment, then pressed forward into the room.

Charged with feelings of annoyance and fear, Katherine chose to lie still, pretend to be asleep, and hope he would go away. But what did he want? Why hadn't he announced himself? Even under the shield of a stack of heavy cotton quilts, she couldn't help but feel vulnerable and exposed. Through squinted eyelids, she watched him amble over to the bed and look down at her.

"Katherine?" he whispered. "Katherine—it's Henry."

When she didn't respond, he cracked the door wider to let in more light, and began to search her room! He let nothing elude him, turning over and examining every item of clothing, even her underwear. Quietly and efficiently, he worked his way around the room to the other side of the bed.

"Katherine?" he murmured again.

Still she pretended to be asleep.

"Damn!" he cursed in a whisper.

It was all she could do to keep from flinching as he lowered his thin arm to the bed. She almost cried out when his long, spindly fingers clasped the edge of the quilts and tugged at the covers.

She decided to move before he touched her. But it was too late: Henry was already racing through the doorway. In a heartbeat, the block of light behind him shrank to nothing, as the door clicked shut.

Under the quilts, she curled up and hugged herself. Shivering violently, Katherine suddenly burst into tears. She chided herself for acting so foolishly, for hiding in the bed and crying like a baby. But her tears kept flowing anyway.

It was a day of firsts for Katherine Haynes. Never had she been so aroused and excited by a man—and never had she been so repulsed and afraid of one.

7

"You're the first one down, sport," the sleepy-eyed cook said to Matt Pilgrim the next morning in the Teller House Cafe. He was a chunky fellow with a handlebar moustache under a wide, pink nose and a high forehead. "Waitress won't be in for another half-hour, at least."

Matt took the first table in the room. Covered with a red-and-white checkered cloth, it was already set for four people, with a folded newspaper resting on its side in the center of the table.

"Am I too early for coffee?" he asked.

The cook, knocking around behind a counter, knotted a crisp white apron behind his back. "I got a pot on now," he said. "What's the matter with you this morning—have a bad night?"

"Nope, I had a bad day," he replied, recalling the adventure in the mine.

The cook brought over the coffee and poured it. "You must be that Pinkerton detective everybody's been talking about. Tell me something: What's it like, being a Pinkerton man?"

Matt raised his cup and allowed the steam of the coffee to warm his face. "Right now, it's being hungry."

"Yeah, I know that. I meant when you're out chasing outlaws and everything. I bet that's plenty exciting, huh?"

"Plenty," Matt confirmed, after a drink of the soothing coffee. "I wonder if I could get some breakfast now?"

"Yeah, sure, why not? I may not have an exciting job like yours, but what I do, I do good. You know what I mean?"

"I think so."

"Well, what'll it be then? You just name it."

"I'll have three eggs, a thick beefsteak, and a plate of biscuits, if you have them."

"Whatever you want, we got," he replied confidently. "And if you can say it, I can cook it."

"Glad to hear it."

"You just sit there and wait. You've never seen a beefsteak like the one you're about to get."

Matt let more of the coffee slide down his throat, then casually picked up the copy of the week-old issue of the *Rocky Mountain News* from the table. His attention naturally landed on an article about a bloody shootout in the town of Tombstone in Arizona Territory. At the O.K. Corral, Wyatt, Virgil and Morgan Earp, along with Doc Holliday, had blasted the wild Ike Clanton bunch out of town and into Boot Hill. The news was typical of what was happening these days. Matt wondered if William Pinkerton hadn't been right, after all. Perhaps the day of the maverick outlaw was finally drawing to a close.

Ever since President Garfield was gunned down earlier in the year by a disgruntled victim of the spoils system, the country had begun to take a closer look at the suspicious activities of many wealthy and "respectable" men in business and government. With sophisticated, covert crime on the rise, some day only elaborate, nation-wide agencies like Pinkerton's would be capable of coping with the major crimes in America.

As Matt turned the page to read a piece on Lillian Russell, the attractive young star of the touring opera *The Great Mogul*, a red-headed man came dashing through the lobby of the hotel, then sprinted into the cafe.

"Mr. Pilgrim!" he called out.

Matt laid his newspaper down as the man hurried across the room to his table. "Good morning, Reuben," he said.

He bumped the corner of the table as he sat down, spilling coffee on the tablecloth. "I've been waiting an hour for you to come down," he said. "I'm ready to report. Where do you want to start?"

"Why don't we start with breakfast?" He signaled for the cook to come over. "I have a feeling it's going to be a long day," he observed to his partner as the cook headed their way.

"I don't think I'm very hungry," he said.

"Well, I am."

Reuben shrugged his shoulders. "I guess I should have something," he relented. "I did forget to eat yesterday."

"What'll it be, Mr. Canfield?" The cook appeared at the table, wringing his hands on his apron. "Couple of spicy sausages maybe?"

"I'll have the same thing Mr. Pilgrim is having," he answered.

"Oh, yeah? Does that mean Barton Canfield's son is a Pinkerton man now?"

"I'm just helping them out, Sam," he explained. "That's all."

"Oh. I thought maybe I'd missed something along the

way. You can miss a lot, working behind the scenes the way I do.''

''What did you find out about the black powder, Reuben?'' Matthew asked after the cook had left.

Reuben leaned forward. ''I located the source!'' he said brightly. ''It was simple! After only six stores, there it was, at Miller's Mercantile, on Main Street. Four kegs of powder were missing from the back of his storeroom. He figures they were stolen two or three days ago.''

''Does he have any idea who took them?''

''No, sir. He assumes it was miners, since they've done it before.''

''Did you find out what kind of black powder it was?''

Reuben smiled. ''I knew you'd ask that, Mr. Pilgrim. As a matter of fact, Mr. Miller claims it wasn't his usual stock. Since it came in from Denver two months ago, nobody's even asked for it. He called it a No. 4, Coarse Grain.''

Matt leaned back in his chair. ''That's the favorite powder of train robbers,'' he revealed.

''Really?'' Reuben was obviously impressed. ''How do you know that?''

''It's in the Pinkerton files.''

''But this isn't a train robbery we're investigating, Mr. Pilgrim. It's a mining incident.''

''I know, but criminals tend to stick to their habits. And they have a habit of using No. 4, Coarse Grain for trains, not mines.''

''But what train would they be using it on?''

''You tell me. Is there any special shipment going out on the railroad in the next day or two?''

A light dawned in the other man's face. ''Of course there is!'' he exclaimed. ''The Harrison payroll is coming in from Denver tomorrow night, unless that's only a coincidence—''

"I don't believe in coincidences, Reuben. Somebody is planning to rob that train before it reaches Central City."

Reuben wrinkled his brow as he considered the idea. Finally, he shook his head doubtfully. "It still doesn't make sense to me," he said. "What is the connection between a train robbery tomorrow night and the death of those Pinkerton detectives two weeks ago?"

"I think we should ask the local sheriff that question, Reuben. Maybe he can put it together for us."

"I'm not sure we should, Mr. Pilgrim."

"Why not?"

"I told you about Sheriff Potts. He's a suspect!"

"He's also the law in Central City, Reuben. And Pinkerton detectives are instructed to cooperate with all local authorities."

"But Alvin Potts is a bitter old man that hates everything and everybody, Mr. Pilgrim. We can't trust him!"

"Then we won't. But we still have to work with him."

"Yes, sir."

Matt finished his coffee and pushed the empty cup aside. "Let's look at what we have to show him, Reuben," he suggested. "We have a mysterious cave-in that kills the Pinkerton detectives who were investigating possible sabotage in the Get Lucky Mine."

"As well as killing the owner of the *Banner* newspaper, Alexander Haynes," Reuben added.

"Yes. Then we have another death connected with that mine—a man who was a stranger in Central City."

Reuben followed the thought. "And he was probably working for someone else when he was killed," he said.

"We know from his Filene suit that he wasn't poor and from his Waterbury watch that he wasn't rich."

Matt nodded. "We also know that he was murdered by someone with black powder on his hands—the same kind of powder outlaws use when they blast train rails and express company safes. And since we have a payroll train due here tomorrow night, we can assume our murderer will be trying to rob it."

Reuben sighed. "Everything points to the work of outlaws then—probably the Bonners. Maybe my theory about a mastermind was wrong."

"I don't think it's wrong, Reuben. Too many things don't fit the pattern of an outlaw. First of all, an outlaw would rob a train for money—but why would he bother sabotaging a mine? There's no profit in it. And then we have the wrecking of Alexander Haynes' office."

"There's no profit in that, either."

"No, there isn't. Unless . . . there was something in that office somebody wanted."

"Such as what? We don't have the slightest bit of evidence that will connect any of this together."

"Look for the motive, Reuben! Maybe the detectives, Alex Haynes, and our mystery man were all killed for the same reason—because they knew too much!"

"Yes! And each of them could have been in the process of finding out something when they were murdered!"

"They probably stumbled upon a plot, Reuben—a plan that involves the mine and the railroad. And one so profitable to somebody that he was willing to kill four men to keep it from being discovered."

"A plot by a mastermind," Reuben concluded.

"That's right."

"I knew it! But why take all this to Sheriff Potts, Mr. Pilgrim? He could be our mastermind!"

"We have to follow standard procedure, Reuben."

"I know, but—"

"Besides, he could help us. He may have collected some evidence of his own—"

"Not Sheriff Potts."

"Now, Reuben."

"Wait, Mr. Pilgrim! I forgot about the other evidence!"

Just as Reuben plunged his hand into his inside coat pocket, the cook arrived with the breakfasts.

"Now what do you think of that, men?" He stood back and waited for a response. "Quite a couple of slabs of meat, huh?"

"They look good, Sam," Matt complimented.

"And the biscuits are coming."

"Thank you."

The cook lingered. "Uh, I was wondering, since you Pinkertons move around the country a lot, do you reckon you could tell me how our food here measures up to the Windsor or the Palmer House—places like that?"

"I'll let you know, Sam."

"Now I would appreciate that, Mr. Pilgrim. A man likes to know how good he's doing. I'd say you'd better eat those eggs before they get cold, Mr. Canfield," he advised Reuben before he made his way back to the counter.

"What have you got, Reuben?" Matt asked as his partner shoved the food out of the way, opened up a sheet of paper, and spread it out on the table.

"This is a drawing I made of a bootprint I found in the black powder on the floor in Miller's storeroom."

Matt examined the drawing. It was clear and precise, but partial. "It's mostly a heel," he observed.

"Yes, but it's a very distinctive heel, Mr. Pilgrim. Notice the inside of the leather is worn, instead of the usual outside. And right here, at the bottom, are three small holes in the shape of a triangle, probably caused by walking on jagged rocks. In other words, this print is unique."

"And you think this boot belongs to the murderer."

"I would say it's very likely."

"Why don't we see what Sheriff Potts will say?"

"Mr. Pilgrim—"

"Bring the evidence, Reuben," he said, rising from the table.

"Yes, sir." Resignedly he pushed back his chair. "But I'm not sure we ought to show it to anyone."

As they headed toward the door, the cook hollered at them from behind the counter. "Hey, what's the matter, men? You didn't eat your breakfast!"

"Put it on my bill," Matt told him.

"But where are you going? The biscuits are almost done!"

"Keep them warm, Sam," Matt told him. "We'll be back."

8

Matt couldn't help being a little startled at the sheer magnitude of the figure in high boots towering over the sooty pot-bellied stove in the sheriff's office. Wearing soiled, baggy wool trousers, an old, crumpled, gray shirt, and a limp, black string tie, Alvin Potts stood at least six and a half feet high and weighed well over two hundred pounds. He had an unruly mat of gray hair, bushy eyebrows running together over steel-gray eyes, and an angular face full of deeply etched wrinkles that crisscrossed his skin like the ridges and gulleys in the mountains of Colorado.

"What do you want?" he growled at Matt and Reuben the instant the door opened. Not bothering to look around, Potts poured some steaming coffee into a tin cup.

The detectives paused just inside the office. Then Reuben quickly stepped forward. "Sheriff Potts, this is a detective from Chicago," he said eagerly.

The big lawman shook his head. "I didn't ask who you was, boy," he said. "I only asked what you wanted."

"What we want to do is talk to you, Sheriff Potts," Reuben offered. "This is a Pinkerton detective—"

"I know who he is." Potts brought the coffee over to

his desk. Jerking out the drawer, he snapped up a bottle of rye whiskey. "And what's more," he added, popping off the cork, "I don't care."

Matt waited until he had sloshed three or four ounces of liquor into the coffee before he spoke. "Sheriff, the Pinkerton Agency would appreciate your help—"

"Don't give me any applause, boy," he interrupted. "Alvin Potts don't help anybody. I keep the law, and I help myself when I need it, and I expect everybody else to do the same when he can. Now, is that enough said?"

"No, it's not—"

"Then let me give you some straight advice, son. Get on the next train out and go back to Chicago and leave us alone. There's enough rats crawling around this town now, without a new bunch coming in every time the train whistle blows."

Matt looked at him. "We have some evidence we'd like you to see," he told him.

"I can't see a thing till ten in the morning," he replied. "Why don't you come back then? Better yet, don't come back at all."

"It's about the cave-in at the Get Lucky Mine, Sheriff," Reuben said.

Potts swigged some of his coffee. "You think Alvin Potts gives one holler in Hades what happens at the Get Lucky Mine? No, sir. If the whole thing caved into hell this minute, I'd probably buy myself another rye whiskey to celebrate."

Pilgrim gritted his teeth. "Sheriff, however much you may hate Mr. Harrison for buying you out of that mine, the fact is, people are getting hurt down there. Four men have already died!"

"Now that's on Tom Harrison's conscience, not mine."

After gulping down the rest of the coffee, he filled the cup with straight rye. "Of course, I'm not sure he has a conscience to begin with."

"Sheriff, it was Mr. Harrison who hired the Pinkerton Agency."

"Doesn't surprise me he went outside. He wouldn't trust me to throw his cook into jail. But like it or not, I am still the law here, boy. So why don't you head on out, huh?"

"I can't do that, Sheriff."

Potts winced as he drank more liquor. "You know," he said, "You Pinkertons may not think so, but us local lawmen can still handle ourselves in a pinch. Let me remind you, it wasn't the Pinkerton Detective Agency that got Billy the Kid last July; it was Sheriff Pat Garrett. And it wasn't the Chicago police that cut down the Clanton gang in Tombstone; it was Marshall Earp and his deputy brothers. Seems to me like we're still holding our own out here."

"I'm not questioning that, Sheriff."

"In this town, you don't have the right to question so much as a cowlick on a bull's ear, unless I say so. You dudes may ride into the gulch on your fancy railroad expecting us old-timers to sprawl out on the dirt and wait to be spit on, but this is one of them that ain't laying down, so forget it."

Matt stood still for a moment, wondering whether he should go or stay. Finally, he decided to try another approach. "Would you mind if I had some of that coffee?" he asked politely.

Potts peered up from under his eyebrows. "Go ahead," he mumbled.

"Thank you." Matt stepped over to the stove, filled a

cup, and took a sip. "It's good. Tastes like my father's coffee. He always added grain to his, too. Back when he was prospecting, he used to say only dried-up old bankers and single women had the constitution to stand pure coffee."

"The man was right. The grain takes out all the bitterness," Potts said. He added, after hesitating, "Just where did this pa of yours do his prospecting—Chicago, Illinois?"

"No, in Colorado."

"Is that a fact? Whereabouts in Colorado?"

"All over. Fair Play, Jefferson, Aspen, Canon City, Columbia—"

"I hear they're calling that Telluride these days."

Matt laughed shortly. "I'm surprised they're calling it anything these days. It never was much of a place—even as mining camps go."

"A real spit on the sidewalk, I'd say."

"That's about the way I remember it, Sheriff."

Potts wiped a smile off his lips with his hand. "What's your name, boy?" he asked.

"Pilgrim."

He raised his bushy eyebrows as he tried to name silently on his mouth. "You wouldn't be Jake Pilgrim's boy, would you?" he asked.

"Yes, I am: Matt."

"I'll be damned. I think maybe your pa and I panned a stream together once, for about an hour and a half. Can't remember where it was, even. I just remember him saying he had to always keep moving on, because his name was Pilgrim, like those folks that come over from England to Plymouth Rock."

"That sounds like him," Matt confirmed. "He always said people changed themselves to fit their names."

106

"Yeah, he said with a handle like Potts, I was going to wind up being a tinker or a cook." He laughed at the idea. "I'll be damned. I haven't thought of him in years. Whatever happened to him, anyway?"

"He died, four years ago. Right after my mother. He never struck it."

"Ah, too bad. I know well enough how that is. I've lost a few in my time."

"He had a good life."

"That's a damn sight more than I have," he noted cynically. "Most folks have to stomach things they can't stand or never wanted, you know? Like being a sheriff in an ugly one-horse mining town and sitting around trying to live through all this dry weather we've been having for months. Seems to me it'll never rain again."

"Sheriff?" Matt tried to bring him around to the subject again. "Reuben has found some evidence that links the cave-in with the railroad—"

"I don't want to hear it," he said abruptly. "Just because I run into your daddy once don't mean I'm going to turn myself inside-out to please you." He slid open the drawer to his desk and drew out a shiny fishing hook dangling at the end of a fishing line. "Look at that, Reuben," he said, holding it up. "Looks like a star, don't it? They call that 'stainless steel,' Ever see such a thing?"

"No, sir."

"Sheriff," Matt persisted, "at least hear us out. Let us tell you what we know."

"Don't you understand anything, Pilgrim? I don't want to know!"

"Why don't you? Because then you may have to help Thomas Harrison?"

"Maybe. He did cheat me out of my mine, Pilgrim. I'll

swear to God he did; he cheated me out of the Get Lucky Mine.''

"All right, he cheated you. But what he did to you ten or fifteen years ago is no reason to refuse to help innocent people, is it?"

Potts sighed loudly, lumbered over to the window, and gazed out. "Damn, I hate dry weather," he complained. "It makes my skin itch. I wonder if it's ever going to rain again."

"Sheriff—"

Potts spun around. "You just won't let up, will you?"

"No, I won't."

He eased over to the oak chair by the gun rack and slumped his huge body into it. "Ah, why fight it?" he moaned. "The fact is, since I can't help you anyway, boy, I'd rather not even know anything. How's that for facing the truth, Pilgrim?"

"You could have something we've missed—"

"I tell you, I don't have anything, boy. All I do is round up drunks from the Shoo-fly and go fishing on Saturdays and Sundays. Only reason folks keep electing me sheriff is because they haven't found anybody better."

Matt came closer. "Sheriff Potts, Reuben and I believe that someone is planning to rob the Harrison payroll train tomorrow night."

"Now how in hell could you boys know that?" he said skeptically.

"We have scientific evidence, Sheriff Potts," Reuben said.

"Evidence of what? Even scientific evidence can't predict the future."

"Sometimes it can—"

"Well, I don't happen to believe in magic, Reuben

108

Canfield," he stated. He got to his feet, plucked a ring of keys off a nail on the wall, and rattled one of them in the door to the jailroom. After a minute, he shoved it open. "All right, O'Hara!" he growled at the prisoner inside, "time's up—let's go!"

Matt watched the big lawman swing open the unlocked jail cell and step inside while a thin, little bald-headed man sheepishly slid out.

"How can I be sure he's gone, Sheriff?" he muttered in a low voice.

"He's always gone by this time of day, O'Hara."

"I know; I just wouldn't want a confrontation."

"Go on home, Tim, before that woman comes looking for you."

He nodded his head. "If I didn't have to be gone all the time," he murmured as he pushed a derby hat down on his head, "she wouldn't be doing this, Sheriff."

"Yeah, sure."

"No, really, Sheriff Potts."

"Get out of here, O'Hara."

"Yes, sir." He meekly tipped his derby at Matt and Reuben and walked out of the office.

"The poor bastard's a drummer," Potts explained as the door closed behind him. "Every time he goes off to sell his kitchen tools for a week or two, he comes back and finds his wife in bed with a miner. He's so scared he'll get hurt, he never says anything to her about it. Just me. He comes crying to me and I have to let him sleep here till the coast is clear."

Through the window, Matt followed the halting steps of the little man as he trudged with uncertainty down the street, paused, looked at his watch, threw a nervous glance back at the sheriff's office, and finally pressed on hesitantly toward his house.

"I wonder why he keeps on going back to her?" he said.

Potts seized the cup in his big hand and returned to the coffee pot. "He goes back to her because that's all he knows to do, Pilgrim," he answered, pouring. "He thinks that's where he belongs. He's got no better sense than to think he's going home."

Reuben looked at him quizzically. "But if he loves her—"

"You don't love somebody that treats you like a pack animal, boy," he observed. Wincing, he inhaled half a cup of coffee and broke out the rye whiskey again. "Of course, nobody's shown me a woman yet that don't act like a twenty-five-cent whore and pose like a hand-carved saint at the same time. So what Tim O'Hara's got is nothing different. You take your chances with anything in skirts."

"Sheriff—" Matt began.

"Let me tell you boys something," Potts interrupted. "I'll grant it may be the stupidest thing in the world, to be alone. But when you are, by God, you just are. And no amount of pretty talk and fine clothes and references to old prospector friends is going to change that. Do you follow me there, Matt Pilgrim?"

"Sheriff, I'm not trying to force you to do anything," Matt protested. "I'm simply following procedure. The Pinkerton Agency uses a network of local law enforcement officers around the country."

"Well, you make sure you don't get yourself snagged up in that network of theirs like a fly in a spider web. I know what I'm talking about. I used to be one of the drudges on the hill, a couple of lifetimes ago. I used to work sixteen hours a day, every day, just trying to cut a couple of ounces of third-rate gold out of the ground. I did it all—picking, blowing, loading, carting, pumping, you name it. I worked so long sometimes, I couldn't move my little finger at night. And I didn't get pee in the bucket for my labor, either. When the bust came in '71, I lost it. Every last timber, nail, and shovel of it.''

"To Tom Harrison," Matt said.

"That's the one. And in the meantime, my wife hustles herself out of town with this skinny-necked miner that used to play-act in the Montana Theatre on weekends. This Bantam rooster named Hales, or Holes, I forget which, fluttered around my wife and son with his comb up and red as a damned beet, and then, all of a sudden, flew the coop with the both of them. I should've hauled off after them with a couple of Colt Peacemakers, but I didn't. I may have been stupid not to, but I didn't.'' Turning up his nose, he slurped down coffee and rye and sucked a draught of air through his teeth, and moaned with pleasure.

Matt drew closer. "What happened to him, Sheriff?" he wondered.

"Who knows what happens to people, Pilgrim? And who cares? When I stood on the street and watched the Montana Theatre burn to the ground a couple of years later, I told myself that Ella Mae and that peckerwood Hales was burning up with it. So be it. I don't even think about them anymore. And let me tell you this: If a twenty-one-year-old kid named Bill Hales or even Bill Potts walked in here today and grabbed my hand and called me Pa, I'd take him out and drown his ass in Lake Gulch, like a blind cat. I mean that. And I'd never feel a thing for him, either, not one way or the other.''

"What about Mr. Harrison? Do you still hate him?"

Potts plopped down in the desk chair, set his cup down, and looked at Matt askance. "Sure, I do. But I don't hate him enough to screw up his precious mine, if that's what you're getting at."

"I'm just—"

"Yeah, I know, you're just following procedures. Bless your heart, boy. Be sure you do it all their way. Let some hostler in a three-piece suit in Chicago, Illinois, run that scientific brain of yours. You, too, Reuben. That's what it's all coming to anyway, I reckon."

Annoyed at this gruff and bitter man, Matt decided it was time to force the issue. "Sheriff," he said, "I want you to look at this and give me your expert opinion on it." Taking the fingerprint card and the boot print from Reuben, he laid the evidence in front of Potts.

The lawman wrinkled his brow. "What in the name of spring is this supposed to be?" he asked.

"It's a fingerprint and a drawing of a boot print, Sheriff Potts," Reuben explained proudly. "I did them myself."

He avoided looking at them. "Good job, Reuben. Now do you think you can take them away yourself?"

"Sheriff—"

"Take this hen-scratching away! I don't want to look at any of your scientific mumbo-jumbo, all right? I don't believe in it!"

"These prints belong to a murderer, Sheriff."

"If they belong to him, then give them back to him."

Reuben frowned at that, but said nothing.

"We know he's already killed one man, Sheriff," Matt informed him. "And apparently, he's threatened someone else."

"Apparently, bull. You sound like Ben Watkins. Either he has or he hasn't. Which is it, as if I cared?"

"Sheriff, it was Alice!" Reuben cried.

"What?"

"The person he threatened to kill was my sister, Alice."

Potts wrenched his face, loosened his limp string tie, and unbuttoned his shirt collar. "I figure you must be wrong on that one," he said, rubbing his chin. "Who'd want to hurt that little girl?"

Reuben eyed him closely. "The same person who's planning to rob the payroll train tomorrow night, Sheriff," he answered.

Potts cleared his throat. "I just don't believe you can know that, boy," he said stubbornly. "I don't."

Matt reached over and shoved the papers under his nose. "Will you at least look at them!"

Obstinately hesitating, then clenching his teeth, Potts finally dropped his eyes to the prints and examined them for two or three minutes. Then he shrugged his shoulders. "All right," he announced, "I've looked at them. Now what?"

"Thank you," Matt said, relieved.

"Don't see why you wanted me to look at them. To my mind, they don't mean a thing."

"Maybe they will later," Matt said hopefully.

"I doubt it."

"Well, I'm sorry we took so much of your time."

"Forget it happened, Pilgrim. Now, if you don't mind, I've got coffee to drink. Weather's so damned dry these days, I can't quench my thirst with anything."

Matt handed Reuben the papers and headed for the door. Before he opened it, he turned around. Potts was already looming over the stove, draining the last drop of coffee from the blue metal pot. "We'll stay in touch with you, Sheriff," Matt called out to him.

Potts toasted him with his cup. "You do that."

"Meanwhile, if you hear anything, we'd like to hear it."

"Why don't you hear one last bit of advice instead, boys," he offered. "I don't mean for your sake; I mean for that sister of yours, Reuben. You're both making all this too complicated. You're losing the fleas by sticking your noses in the dog tracks, if you know what I mean."

"We're dealing with a complicated crime, Sheriff Potts," Reuben explained.

"It ain't as complicated as you think, boy," he insisted. "All crimes are simple. If you want the people responsible for all this killing and threatening you've been telling me about, then go find yourself some outlaws."

"There's more to it than that, Sheriff," Matt offered.

"No, there ain't. There's only one bunch these days capable of this: the Bonners."

"We're going to investigate them, too—"

Investigate, bull, Pilgrim. Don't investigate them. That's too civilized. What you need to do is go out there and get rid of them the way you would a pack of varmints."

"Just what would you suggest, Sheriff?"

"With roaches like that, what does it matter how it's done? Burn them out; blow them up with black powder; mow them down with a Gatlin gun—who cares, as long as it happens? Do that, and you'll solve your crime and keep little Alice Canfield alive and do the town of Central City a favor in the bargain. Just don't ask me to help you do it."

"Sheriff—"

"You mind what I'm saying, boy. In fact, I'll make you

an offer. If you'll go up to Casto Hill and rid the earth of that infesting vermin up there, I'll swear to you, you'll never have to spend a single night in jail. And that's compliments of Alvin C. Potts, Sheriff of Central City.''

9

While Clayton Bonner waited impatiently for Deke to bring the newspaper to the mining shack on Casto Hill, he was forced to sit and watch his four other brothers eat supper. And that was making him sick.

He felt his stomach become queasy and start to burn as Mick, Buck, Thomas, and Seth tore at their food like hungry wolves. They scratched and clawed at the platters of half-cooked rabbit, then stuffed bits of legs and thighs between their teeth and ground and crunched and snorted until streams of white saliva dribbled into their black beards. He wished he had courage enough to whip out his Colt .45 pistol and blow their revolting heads off into their plates.

"What the hell's the matter with you, Clay?" Seth snarled over the rib bones of a rabbit.

"The name is Clayton," the blond, good-looking boy corrected. He was eighteen, the youngest of the clan. "How many times do I have to tell you? My mother called me Clayton."

Seth, the oldest of the Bonners, a hulking, hairy man, approximately the size of a young buffalo, chucked the picked ribs on the floor and cocked back his brown wide-brim Western hat. He had always worn that hat, inside the house and out, even to bed.

"All right, Clayton," he mocked. "What's your problem —you think you're too good to eat grub with us?"

"I'm not hungry." He turned up his fine-chiseled nose and shoved his tin plate away.

"That don't matter. Eat anyway."

"I can't, Seth. I can't stand all this slobbering at the table. It's disgusting!"

Seth aimed his dark, probing eyes straight at Clay Bonner. "You better start showing a little more respect for you own flesh and blood, Clay," he cautioned.

"That's right, Clay," one of the twins broke in. He wiped his greasy hands on his leather vest. "We may not all have the same daddy, but we all had Momma—"

"Keep your big nose out of this, Mick," Seth ordered.

Buck quickly defended his twin. "All he was doing was agreeing with you, Seth," he said.

"I don't need no agreeing with. I reckon I know how to handle one prissy little momma's boy, if I have to."

The twins both raised their eyebrows in anticipation. "What're you going to do to him, Seth?" Mick asked.

"Yeah, Seth. Let's see."

"I'll show you what I'm going to do to him," he blustered. "I'm going to make him eat. Give me that rabbit leg you're chomping on, Thomas," he told the thinnest brother, tall, stooped, and dressed in black. Without waiting for a response, Seth reached over the table and snatched the meat out of Thomas' teeth. Then with a grunt, he flung the mangled leg down to Clay. It landed with a loud clank on his tin plate. "Eat it, little sister," he said.

118

"I don't want to."

"Don't back-talk me, Clay."

"I can't eat it, Seth!"

The oldest Bonner glowered at Clay a minute, then scraped back his chair and stood up, eyes blazing with anger. "Hand me that hare leg," he commanded. "It's time this sassy little maverick learned some respect for his elders."

The slender brother in a black suit reacted quickly this time. Snapping up the rabbit leg, he handed it to Seth. " 'And ye shall eat flesh until it come out at your nostrils,' " he quoted, grinning. "That's in Numbers Eleven—"

"Clap your mouth, Thomas."

"Ram it through his nostrils, Seth, like the Bible says."

"You want some of this yourself, Thomas?"

"I'll hush. Give it to Clay."

Clayton braced himself as Seth tramped toward him. "I'm not going to do it," he declared.

"Oh, yes, you are. You're going to eat every piece of it—I mean skin, meat, and bones."

"Seth, don't. I'm sick!"

"Well, you're liable to be sicker when I get through with you."

"Hey, Seth!" Mick called out. "Give him a drink, too." He rolled a bottle of Kentucky whiskey across the table.

"Good idea, Seth," the twin agreed. "Why don't you make a man out of him while you're at it?"

Seth stopped and held the meat two inches from Clayton's lips. "Eat it!" he growled.

"No!"

"Do what I say, damn it!" With one hand he yanked

back Clayton's blond hair and crammed the meat into his mouth with the other.

A wave of nausea swept over him as he felt the hard bone and mushy flesh of the rabbit leg being rammed hard between his teeth. He gasped, unable to catch his breath. As he gulped for air, two of Seth's huge, rough fingers mashed the slug of meat harder and harder, into his throat.

Suddenly, Seth let go of his head and burst out laughing. The others followed, crowing and guffawing, pointing at Clay and calling him "Momma's boy." When Clayton heaved and coughed, then vomited the food upon the floor, they roared hysterically.

"I'll reckon he'll learn some day," Seth muttered. "Even if I have to kill him first."

Clay wiped his wet mouth with his sleeve. His stomach had turned inside-out. "I hope they get every one of you tomorrow night," he charged. "I hope you all die!"

Seth shook his head in disgust. "Here, little sister," he said, pitching the bottle of whiskey at Clay. "Wash your mouth with this."

Clay didn't move a muscle while the bottle banged against his elbow, careened off the edge of the table, and crashed to the floor. A long, tense moment of silence followed. Then, just as Clay touched the heel of his right hand to the butt of his Colt, the sixth brother, Deke, stumbled into the shack, waving a copy of the *Central City Register* excitedly above his head.

"I got it, Seth!" he announced. "Look at this! I got it!"

"Give me that thing!" Seth snatched it out of his hands.

"I did just what you said, Seth." Deke beamed.

The leader of the Bonners spat on the floor, lifted the

paper near the oil lamp, and ran his eyes up and down the front page of the newspaper. "Is this today's?" he asked.

Deke, a simpleton with a trembling chin, brown cow eyes, and thin, wet lips, nodded defensively. "They said it was, Seth," he replied, frowning. "I don't know, but they said it was. I couldn't know—"

"All right, Deke, shut up and let me look at it."

"Did I do the right thing, Seth?" Deke begged. "Did I? Was that the one you wanted?"

"Yeah, you got it, Deke," he answered. "Just the right one." He gazed around the table at the four anxious men leaning forward in their seats. "Of course, it might not even be in here, you know," he told them. "The *Register* never did pay us much attention."

"Not like the *Banner* anyway," Thomas agreed.

While the others chuckled at Thomas' comment, Seth slapped the newspaper into Clayton's belly. "Read!" he commanded.

"Why should I?" he countered.

"Because I'll break your arm if you don't."

"Go ahead and read it, Clayton," Deke urged. "We want to hear!"

"Yeah, Clay," Mick encouraged him. "We've been waiting for two hours!"

Clay hesitated, then took the *Register* and opened it. The item they wanted to hear about occupied a full column on the left side of the front page. It was an account of the mock train robbery staged by the Bonners the day before. This deed, which they had done for the fun of it, was, according to the reporter, "a harassing act of pointless violence."

"What does that mean, Clayton?" Deke asked.

"It means we're still famous!" the twins croaked.

"Let Clay do it," Seth told them. "Go ahead, Clay—read it and tell us in your own words."

Tracing the words with his finger, Clay silently made his way through the essay. Even though he didn't recognize a third of the words, he managed to wring the sense out of it.

"They're saying they're going to hang us some day," he summarized the reporter's sentiment. "The day of the Bonners is gone."

Seth laughed. "They sure don't know the Bonners, do they?"

"What else does it say, Clayton?" Deke asked, wide-eyed.

"It says there was a Pinkerton detective on that train. And a rich woman from Chicago—the daughter of a steel man named Haynes."

Seth licked his lips. "We don't care about that. What did it say about us!"

Clay wiped his mouth again, but the rank taste of vomit remained on his tongue. "We're supposed to do what we do because of 'pure ma—liciousness,' I think it is. And we had no call to fire a shot into the railroad car with that Miss Haynes in it."

"Come on, now—tell us what we want to hear!"

"Now don't you order me around, Seth—"

"Clayton," Deke begged, "please tell us what they said. Did they mention me at all?"

"Yeah, they mentioned you, Deke. They said you were 'moronic'—whatever that means."

"Is that bad?"

"Hell, I don't know, Deke. Don't be so stupid."

He nodded sadly. "I think it is bad."

Clay swiped his lips with his sleeve again. "They said

122

the leader of the Bonners wears a sheep's-hide coat and a crumpled old brown hat the size of a Mexican sombrero.''

"What about us, Clay?" Mick asked.

"They call you and Buck the silent twins and Thomas the preacher. They say you're always trying to convert the people you rob, Thomas.''

He pursed his lips and nodded knowingly. " 'To those to whom much is given, much is required.' ''

"Don't tell me they didn't say a word about young Clayton Bonner?" Seth pressed him.

"There's a little, here.''

"Did they call you moronic, too, Clayton?" Deke asked.

"No, the bastards called me a 'fair boy.' Sons of bitches. I ought to murder every newspaperman in Colorado.''

"Why?" Seth laughed. "Looks to me like they got you just right, Clay.''

He rolled the paper and twisted it in his hands. "All right, Seth," he warned, "I don't want to hear that anymore. I do my part around here.''

"You cook and wash, you mean. And he don't even do that as good as a woman, does he, boys?''

"But I do it, damn it! And I can shoot a gun as well as any of you. I think I deserve some respect!''

"Go play with your dolls, *Clayton*.''

Clay felt his hands start to tremble around the rolled newspaper. How easy it would be, he thought, to reach down, snap up his Colt, and blast Seth's ugly bearded face all over the wall. Then he'd take care of Thomas, the twins, then the idiot. How he'd love to see them all wallowing in a pool of their own blood on the cabin floor.

"You'd better stop telling me things like that, Seth!" he challenged.

123

"Listen to him, boys. Don't you think he sounds like Ma when he talks like that?"

"Hey, he does!" Mick agreed. "Just like her!"

"Same high little voice," Buck observed. "Same poor little whine, too. Remember, we used to hear her whine like that when she had somebody behind the doors?"

"Watch what you're saying, Buck!" Clay fumed.

Seth leaned his hip against the corner of the table. "I used to wonder what Clayton and Ma did in her room all those hours, didn't you, boys?" Seth said. "What was it, Clay? What'd she do to you in there?"

"I read to her."

"Yeah? I say she put a little dress on you and made you act and talk like a little girl."

"That's a dirty lie."

"Admit it, little sister. That's why you were always Momma's boy."

"Momma loved me because I was like her. Look—" he fumbled in his pocket—"you can see that in her picture."

"What picture is that, Clay?" Seth taunted.

Springing to his feet, Clay rifled quickly through his trousers pocket. A look of sheer panic seized his face as he flicked the white linings out. "Where is it?" he whined fearfully. "Where's my picture!" He scowled at his brothers around the table. "Who stole it?" he demanded. "Somebody tell me!"

"You don't mean us, do you, Clay?" Seth smirked. "Your own brothers? Come on now, we don't even know what you're talking about."

"Maybe Clay means that picture he keeps under his pillow at night, Mick," Buck snickered. "Reckon that's it?"

"Nah," his twin replied. "He wouldn't lose that. He must mean something else."

Clay squeezed his fists together. "You know what picture I'm talking about, Mick," he said. "And if you took it, I want it back!"

"Listen to that, Seth." Buck fluttered his hands in pretended fear. "Clayton's threatening us!"

"I want my picture, damn it!" he yelled.

Abruptly Seth whipped a paper object out of his coat pocket and waved it in the air. "I have here a portrait of Miss Sal Bonner, of Memphis, Tennessee," he said. "Any offers?" He held a dim, four-by-five daguerreo-type by the corner, as if it were filthy or poisonous. The image was that of an attractive, voluptuous woman in a feathery dance-hall costume, with her skirt hiked up, exposing a well-turned calf. She was poised in front of a oilcloth stage drop, beckoning to the camera with a grin and a come-hither index finger.

"Give that to me, Seth," Clay demanded through clinched teeth.

"What do you think, men?" he asked the others. "Should I give this boy this valuable property or not?"

"No, no!" they answered and broke out laughing. "Auction it off!"

"Who is that, Seth?" Deke asked seriously. "Do I know who that is?"

"You don't know a damned thing, Deke. Go play with something."

"Is it Momma?" he asked, cocking his head at it. "Is that what you're all laughing at?"

"Yeah, it's Momma. Now let us handle this, stupid."

"What do you want me to do, Seth?" Clay asked

desperately. "I'll eat, if that's what you want. But don't hurt that picture, please. It's all I have of her!"

Unmoved, Seth raised the portrait high for inspection. "This woman's name was Sal," he informed the others. "Lived in a hundred towns from Tennessee to Missouri to California. What'll you bid for our Ma, rest her soul?"

"Seth—"

"Hush, boy. I'm selling a picture here."

"Give it to me! Now!"

"Who'll give me a penny, men? A penny for a whore!"

"Yaay!" the twins cheered. "Ma Bonner, the penny whore!"

"That's the one. Give me a cent for the finest little chippie in Tennessee."

Trembling with anger and frustration, Clay could contain himself no longer. He slapped his shaking fist against the cool metal of his revolver, gripped the bone handle, and jerked it out of the leather holster with a snap. "I'm warning you, Seth." He directed the barrel of the heavy black pistol at his brother. "I'll shoot you to death, I swear I will!"

Seth chuckled contemptuously and pinched the edge of the picture with the thumb and index fingers of both hands, ready to tear it at any second. "You ain't going to buy our momma with a gun, Clay," he said. "Didn't they teach you that in school?"

While the twins cracked into laughter, Thomas nodded his head up and down. "Hosea took a wife named Gomer from the whoredoms of the Bible. God told him to."

Deke frowned. "Who's Gomer, Seth?" he asked. "Is that Momma's name?"

"Shut up, Deke!" Clay erupted. "Get out of the house! This is between Seth and me." He leveled the pistol at his brother's eyes. "If you don't give that back to me right now, Seth," he threatened, "I'm going to blow you to a hundred pieces!"

"I'll tell you what, little sister. Instead of a penny, make it a spit."

"I mean what I said, Seth!"

The older brother sauntered back around to his place at the end of the table. "So do I, Clay," he said. "Spit on this picture and call this woman a whore, and I'll hand it over to you. Fair enough?"

Clay eased back the hammer of the Colt .45 with a click. "I'm giving you five seconds," he warned. "One, two—"

"Tear it up, Seth!" Mick cheered.

"Yeah, tear up Momma!" Buck joined in.

"Three—"

"Do it, Seth!" Thomas burst out.

"Four—"

"Rip it to shreds! Punish her! Stone her!"

"Five, Seth!"

"All right, Clayton." Seth held up a palm to stop him. "Here it is." He extended the daguerreotype across the table. But just as the tips of Clay's fingers touched paper, he yanked it back, lifted it above his head with both his hands, and calmly ripped it into two pieces.

The long barrel of the Colt hitched in Clayton's hand the instant he awkwardly hooked the trigger. Out of a deafening explosion of white smoke, a bullet whizzed at a rising angle across the table, punctured the crown of Seth's wide-brim hat, and crashed into the wall behind him. Before Clay could squeeze off another shot, he was staggering in the powerful grip of the twins as they locked his wrists and twisted his arms behind his back.

"Drop it!" Mick breathed in his face.

Without a word, he let the heavy revolver slip out of his grasp and clunk loudly to the floor. As he watched Seth striding angrily toward him, he winced under a hot, churning sensation scorching the walls of his stomach. Then a sharp and agonizing pain sawed like a knife through his intestines.

The older brother, dripping saliva, stalked across the room. Then, with every ounce of strength he could muster, he rammed the meat of his big right fist straight into Clayton's groin. When the boy coughed and spit and sagged in Mick and Buck's arms, Seth growled furiously at them, "Hold him up, damn you—I'm not through!"

"Don't, Seth," Clay pleaded. "Don't hurt me again."

But the other man was already pounding his massive fists into his stomach and ribs. Methodically, he hammered six swift blows into Clayton's resisting flesh, then three more to the jaw and throat, until, finally, the boy's knees buckled and he crumbled bleeding to the floor.

"You hurt, Clayton?" Deke's concerned face peered down at him.

"Get away from him, Deke," Seth ordered.

"But Clayton's hurt, Seth. There's blood on his face."

Seth hoisted him by the collar. "Go to bed, Deke," he told him. "All of you—go to bed!"

"Come on, Seth," Mick whined. "We want to see more!"

"Yeah, Clay ain't done a thing yet, Seth," Buck complained.

"I said, go to bed!"

Grumbling, the four brothers finally obeyed the command and filed one after the other into the single bedroom in the old mining shack. As soon as the door banged shut behind them, Clay was heaved up on Seth's great shoulders and lugged outside. A minute later, he felt himself plunging backwards through the air, down into the violently cold water of a horse trough.

Scrambling to keep from going under, he forgot about his pains. All he could feel was the biting cold air piercing his wet trousers and shirt to the frozen skin of his shivering body.

"You're stupid, Clay," he was told as he got to his feet in the trough. "Real stupid."

"You pig!" he mumbled, shuddering in the frigid mountain air. "All of you are pigs! I wish I'd killed every one of you!"

"I brought you out here to give you some private advice, Clay," Seth said. "I want you to remember I'm the leader here. You know what that means, Clay? It means nobody backs me down. Nobody!"

Clay glanced at his Colt, now stuffed behind his brother's belt, next to his belly. "What are you going to do to me now?" he asked.

"I'm going to tell you about your ma, Clay. Once and for all."

"I don't want to hear it."

Seth held up a finger. "I'm tired of back-talk, brother!"

"My mother was a decent woman, Seth! What if she did have her men? So what? She was only trying to feed us, wasn't she?"

Seth shook his head. "When Sal Bonner was in her prime back in Tennessee, she wasn't no decent woman, Clay. Ask Buck or Mick, if you don't believe me. She didn't care who she bedded with in those days. Two, three at a time, it didn't make any difference to her. She was a no-good slut."

"I don't believe you!"

"Well, believe me, because it's true. The thing was, all of a sudden, she got religion. One day, she took a hard look at that dumbhead Deke and figured she'd better start doing some changing right away. That's when she started making Thomas memorize all them sayings from the Bible. It damned near ruined the bastard."

"Momma wasn't like that, Seth," he muttered weakly. "I know she wasn't!"

"Not for long, no, because all that Bible stuff didn't do any good. She took to making the next one 'civilized.' Sent her pretty little Clayton with his blond hair all slicked down off to school, so he could read and write and turn out better than we did. Only you had to come back and join us, didn't you?"

"I'm doing what you want," Clay defended himself. "I did everything you told me to do in town, didn't I?"

"You're not listening to me, Clay."

"I don't need to listen to you! You're lying!"

"A man don't lie about his own ma, boy, no matter how bad she is. I'm telling you the truth. You got to know how it was, Clay. What kind of woman do you think would put a dress on her own boy, huh?"

"It wasn't like that, Seth. I swear it wasn't!"

"Don't tell me how it was. I know. None of us six boys even knows who his poppa was. Could've been anybody. One of them cowhands or railroad workers that was always dropping by, or some Indian or slave or Chinaman, or a greasy Mexican off the street—"

"She was doing it for us, Seth!"

"She was doing it because she was no good, Clay. She'd drag anything into that room!"

"She had to!"

"She didn't have to. She didn't have to take *me* in

there, did she? Huh, Clay? And she didn't have to take the twins in there, did she?''

He felt something raw and ugly grab at his insides and twist hard. "She wouldn't do that—"

"I'm saying she did, Clay. She took her own kids into that room and closed the door—"

"No!" He shook his head wildly, but the words kept ringing in his ears.

"She was worthless, Clay."

"No! Momma sent me to school—"

"Sure, she sent you to school. And what do you think she was doing while you were there, Clay? Sewing clothes?"

"You bastard, I'll kill you!" In a rage, Clay leaped out of the trough with outstretched hands, pounced on the other man, and crashed to the ground on top of him. Managing to snare his fingers around his brother's throat, he began to gouge his thumbs into flesh as hard as he could.

But he was no match for Seth. He felt the huge body beneath him tighten, twist, then all of a sudden buck up into the air, slinging him back and knocking his head against the water trough. Groggy, Clay tried to steady himself, until he caught sight of his pistol on the ground, two feet away. With a groan, he lunged for the weapon, reaching it at the exact moment his brother's big hand clamped down on it and snatched it away.

Before he could rise from his knees, the black metal barrel was swooping out of the sky like a terrible great bird. In a heartbeat, it was smashing into the top of his head with a bone-shattering thump, sending him flat to the ground.

For a long time, he lay still on his back, heaving drily, his brain spinning and swirling in a maelstrom of spots and lights. Soon he gradually became aware of a wrenching pain throbbing inside his skull, then the rhythmic sound of metal banging against wood. Under a jarring wave of pain, he struggled up to see his brother pounding the Colt revolver over and over against the top of the trough.

After a while, Seth stopped, ran his finger and thumb over the broken hammer, and tossed the pistol into the water. "I don't reckon little sisters ought to be handling guns," he declared. He looked down at Clay and shook his head in disgust. "Sometimes I think you ain't worth saving or killing, Clay," he sneered.

"I'm worth more than you pigs," he countered.

"Look here, if you want to stay with the Bonners, you're going to have to do just what I tell you to do. And that means cooking and cleaning and keeping your mouth shut. You hear me good, Clay Bonner?"

"I hear you. But I'm going to do what I want to do."

Seth instantly dropped to his knees, grabbed Clayton's collar, and jerked his face near his own. Clay could feel his hot, smelly breath puffing against his eyes as he talked. "Listen to me, boy," he said. "We got a deal going here in Central City, you understand? A deal! We got a chance to be something big, Clay. Big as the James boys. I just can't let you screw it up."

"I don't care about your deals."

"Well, you'd better care, because it's your deal, too. We got to stick together, Clay!" Getting no response, he released the collar and stood up. "You see what I'm saying, don't you?"

"Yes."

"Well, then, I reckon you've had enough lessons for one day, school-boy," he said. "Come on to bed."

"I'm not going anywhere with you. Never!"

"Damn it, Clay!"

"I'm staying here, Seth."

"It's getting cold out here!"

"I don't care. I'm staying."

"Well, stay then. Freeze to death, I don't care."

Clay waited until his brother had disappeared into the house before he scrambled over to the trough, thrust his hands into the cold water, and started groping for the pistol. When he finally located it, he brought it up before his eyes. One look at the uselss hammer, and he jumped up and angrily hurled it down the side of the hill.

Shivering from the increasing cold, he paced up and down the yard a few times, lingered near the mouth of the abandoned gold mine for a while, finally coming to light on the warped and splintered steps of the mining shack. But he found no peace there. His skull was pulsating in agony, and his mind was flashing ugly, distorted images—things it sickened him to see. He tried his best to stretch and bend his thoughts to other matters, but it did no good. Momma always came back to haunt him.

Freezing from the icy wind whipping against his damp clothes, Clay leaped up from the steps, started for the door of the cabin, then stopped. The thought of snuggling in with those pigs in the sty for another night was more repulsive than the cold. What he needed to make him forget all this was a woman.

His mind ran quickly over the possibilities. There was Billie Simms at the Mercer Hotel, a rancher's daughter named Donna in Blackhawk, and that special girl—the pretty little cripple he had noticed when he delivered Seth's letter to the Canfield mailbox. The one time he had passed Alice Canfield on the street, she had shot a snooty glance straight through him, like an arrow. That had rankled him.

What right did a rich little girl with a limp have to look down on him—a good-looking, healthy man who could not only read and write, but handle a gun and knife as well?

Whomever he chose, the place to find her would be Central City. For a mining town, it had more than its share of women. He would ride down there, latch on to one of them, and forget every single lie that Seth had ever told him. Yes, he decided, if he were ever going to sleep this night, he would have to do it in the arms of a loving woman.

Later, as he seized the saddle horn and slung his leg over the back of the bay mare, he found himself shaking uncontrollably from the cold. Clay Bonner was confused and disoriented. Never in his life had he felt so many ways at once! He was tired and angry and cold. Something inside his stomach was gnawing like a pack of starving rats; his ribs were aching from the beating Seth had given him; his head was exploding with pain. And worse than anything else, his mind was convulsing in terrible, wicked thoughts about his mother.

All he could be sure of was that he had to *do* something— now, in Central City. If Seth hadn't ruined his gun, he would have burst into the sty and slaughtered the pigs. That would have helped. And if his momma had been alive, he could have crashed into her room and plucked her soft little body out of that wicked bed and cracked her neck between his hands like a chicken bone. But Sal Bonner was already dead. And all he could kill now was time.

Darkness swiftly gathered around him on the way to Central City. By the time his horse shuffled into the northern outskirts of town, Clayton could see the lighted windows of the Opera House and the Teller House on Eureka Street. Guiding the mare slowly down the dusty street, he turned her right on Main and proceeded up the grade until he noticed the big square window of the *Centry City Banner* office, glowing in the darkness of the rows of businesses closed for the night. He would have kept going if he hadn't noticed the buxom figure of a woman pass by the window. But one glimpse of her long dark hair, exactly the shade of his mother's, was enough to make him rein the horse.

He felt nauseated as he leaned over the saddle horn and waited for her to appear again in the window. When she finally showed herself, he was having to gasp for breath. But he still could see how tall and proud she stood in the light, with a stack of papers in her hand, like the nasty teacher he had in school. But as he stretched forward in the saddle, he concluded that she wasn't like Mrs. Stadler at all. In fact, he decided, the woman she resembled the most was his own mother. It was true! Maybe the face wasn't exactly the same, but the hair was identical!

He let out a grunt of pain the instant she turned toward the glass and gazed out into the street. He was almost convinced now that she was the very image of his dead mother. Yes. She had the same hair, precisely. She was like his own loving momma. Pretty little Sal Bonner. Mother of the six fine Bonner boys. Finest little chippie in Tennessee.

Filthy, worthless bitch.

10

Katherine Haynes curled away from the window with a cold, hollow feeling in the pit of her stomach as she watched the ghostly figure on horseback outside slump toward her in his saddle, grip the horse's mane, and seem to leer at her and try to speak—

Yanking the blind down over the window, she quickly stepped back into the *Banner* office. For a long time, she listened intently, hearing nothing but the never-ending clank of picks and shovels and the hum of loaded cars of ore rolling along the tramway north of town. After a while, she decided that she must have seen nothing more than a drunken man passing by the office on the way home from a saloon. Before long, she managed to relax and return her attention to the stack of printed editorials she had found earlier that day in Alex's apartment.

Reading her brother's thoughtful essays was a discouraging task. She had decided long ago that the only reason Alex would have ever ventured into the bowels of the earth would be to research an important story. Under that assumption, she had searched through nearly two hundred of his essays for a piece on mining. The unfortunate result of all her efforts had been that she was now convinced that mining was undoubtedly the only subject on earth that Alexander Haynes had *not* written on!

Certain sentiments in his work she found disturbing, too—particularly his recurring attacks on the mavericks of society, such as outlaws and prostitutes. Once again, her eyes skimmed his editorial on the recent death of Billy the Kid:

A man named William H. Bonney is dead. He met his timely and desperate end in a cold and darkened hallway in a place called Maxwell's Ranch. He was the recipient of two perfectly placed bullets from the waiting gun of a man named Pat Garrett.

May God rest his immortal soul.

But now that Mr. Bonney is under the ground, we must ask ourselves this: Is the infamous Billy the Kid dead, as well? Or will we continue to keep this dauntless folk hero, created by the greedy editors of *The National Police Gazette*, fresh and alive (and murdering innocent lives in tales and novels) in our compassionate hearts and feeble brains? How long must we speak with awe and admiration of such reprobates of society as Billy the Kid? How long must we glorify the cowardly deeds of these vicious, predatory animals we call outlaws? How long can we—

Katherine could read no more. She found Alex's ideas shocking. Her brother had always been so independent himself, it was startling to learn how much he despised the outlaws of society. Another of his favorite targets was the Mercer Hotel in Central City.

To our chagrin, a few days ago we learned that our fair city has taken a far back seat to its sister mining town of Leadville. We are referring to this curious (and sobering) statistic: that Leadville now contains one parlor house for every 150 of its citizens!

But there is yet room for hope, citizens. We happen to know that in order to keep in step with the competition, Central City has decided to change the tune of its own steady little march of progress. Now the old Mercer Hotel, once that fastidious old matron of silver spoons and linen sheets, we are told, is soon to be transformed into a madame of silver coins and silken sheets!

Move aside, Mammy Pleasant and Julie Bulette and Cattle Kate. The town of Central City now has an Andrea Sherbourne. We now must turn our tired eyes to the East again, not to the rising sun, but to those ladies of darkness who will be arriving shortly on the Central City Train.

Weary of reading, Katherine set aside the newspaper articles, picked up Alex's key, and tapped it nervously on the top of the desk. After all these years, she was finally beginning to understand her brother. Though she disagreed with much of what he said in his editorials, she had to admit there was a sense of responsibility in them, combined with a powerful strength of purpose. Unlike her father, Alex lashed only at the enemies of decent society, not merely the enemies of the world he himself had created. Perhaps, after all, there was some meaning to that much-maligned description, "the public servant." Perhaps Alexander Haynes had truly been one.

But if Alex were such a dedicated newsman, then his

death in a mine cave-in was still mysterious. If he wasn't researching a series of editorials on mining disasters or worker abuse, what was he doing there?

Idly flipping the key over in her hands, she gazed around the office for the fiftieth time. She was still convinced that it fit something in this room. But so far, after reading every sheet of paper, cracking open every drawer and door, and searching every cranny in the room, she had turned up nothing.

Deciding to give up for the evening, Katherine walked over to the window, peeled back the corner of the blind, and peeked out into the darkness to see if the way was clear. But there again was the stiff, still figure of the man leaning forward on his horse, lurking outside in the shadows of the street. He must have passed out from liquor, she concluded. She would linger a while, until he moved away.

As she turned back into the room, the old daguerreotype of Gardner Haynes, Jr. caught her eye. Once again, the resemblance to Alex seemed uncanny. On an impulse, she went over to the wall, looked directly at her father's youthful expression for a moment, then laid her hands upon the frame. Removing the picture off the nail, she found on the other side of the photograph exactly what she had been looking for all day—a secret compartment.

She had no trouble turning the little key in the lock of the small black safe recessed in the wall. Her excitement mounted as she clicked the steel door open and pushed it aside. When she saw the handful of manuscript pages in the safe, she whisked them out and took them over to Alex's desk to read.

This is it! she thought. Soon I will know the reason for

my brother's death. Then I can go to Matthew Pilgrim and tell him!

The rough, ink-stained pages were written in tight, thin little letters that looked at first like a code of some kind. But after a bit of practice, she mastered the handwriting and could make out every word. Some of the material seemed irrelevant to her—notes on the Panic of 1873 in North Dakota and Minnesota, facts on "bonanza farming" in the Midwest, and financial figures on the holdings of companies such as the Amenia and Sharon Land Company. Most of the scribbling, though, had to do with the railroad.

Alex had written a long, angry paragraph on "railroad magnates," such as Hall and Gould. He had instructed himself to "develop the Pacific Railroad Act of 1862." And he had started a diatribe against the Congress for its "inverted logic, maintaining that the increased value of public lands justifies the irresponsible allocation of enormous public grants."

But after poring over those four thousand words, all Katherine could do was set the stack of papers on the desk, drop the key on top of them, and bury her head in the palm of her hand. She felt defeated by her own brother. However important the hidden compartment had been to him, it had turned out to be meaningless to her. She could see no connection at all between all this material on the railroad and a cave-in at the Get Lucky Mine.

As she massaged her eyes and tried to assess what she had found, a sudden sharp *clunk*! outside made her jump. A moment later, she heard another noise, like the sound of a boot coming down hard on the wooden plankway. She sat paralyzed as she heard three more steps, then saw the metal knob on the door start to turn.

With the image of the man on horseback flashing in her

mind, Katherine sprang up and lunged for the door, just as it cracked open a couple of inches. Somehow she managed to fling her shoulder against the door and slam the bolt into the lock. Pressed against the door and breathing hard, she could hear a low, guttural sound through the wood. Then someone started banging hard on the door.

"Who's there?" she asked in a wavering voice.

Her answer was a series of pounding knocks on the wood, so hard they rattled the panes in the window.

"Henry?" she called out. "Is that you?"

The doorknob turned again.

"Matt?" A dry lump formed in her throat when she heard a thin, reedy voice murmuring close to the door, inches form her face.

"Open the door," a man was saying.

"Who are you!"

"I said, open the door, damn you!"

With the palm of her hand pressed flat against her heaving bosom, Katherine backed away, unable to do anything but stare helplessly at the door.

"Do you want me to break it in?" the voice cried out.

"I want you to go away!" she countered.

"I can break it," he grunted and began kicking his boot against the bottom of the door. "I can do anything I want to do."

Katherine's eyes eagerly searched the room for a place to escape to when the door crashed open. But there was nowhere to go.

She was completely defenseless.

The instant Matt Pilgrim caught a glimpse of the slouching figure of a man whining and battering away at the door of the *Banner* office, he broke into a run, sprinted across

Main Street, and came to a quick stop on the walkway a few yards away.

When the blond young man looked up, Pilgrim could tell immediately that he had recently been in a fight. His drooping jaw was cut and bloody; his left eye was swollen, and he was standing bent over, with his right hand clutching at his stomach.

"What are you gawking at?" the man mumbled. "Get out of here! Leave me alone!"

"The *Banner* office is closed, friend," Matt informed him.

"So what?" he retorted defiantly.

"What do you want in there?" he asked.

"That's none of your business, is it?"

"I'm afraid it is. I think maybe you'd better be moving along."

"Why should I? I don't have to move anywhere."

Matt stiffened. "You're going to move because I'm telling you to," he said.

"Well, you can just stop telling me!" he snorted. "I'm sick and tired of people always trying to tell me what to do!"

Matt moved toward him cautiously. "All right, why don't we say I'm suggesting it, then? Is that better?"

"Stay right where you are, you bastard," he said. "I'm warning you, if you make me angry, so help me, I'll kill you!"

"You're in no condition to do anything."

The other man ground his teeth angrily. "You think I'm nothing, don't you?" he charged. "Well, let me tell you something: If I had my Colt right now, you'd be the one who was nothing, dude. Nothing but buzzard meat!"

143

Matt eased forward. "It won't do you any good to make threats to me—"

The man quickly pointed an accusing finger at Pilgrim. "Don't you act superior to me, you son-of-a-bitch," he threatened. "I'm worth something! I can read and write!"

"Good for you—"

"Stop it, damn you! I'm a better man than you'll ever be!"

Matt took three steps toward him. "All right, you're a better man. Now can you climb on your horse—"

"Don't come any closer!"

"Let me help you up."

He glared hatefully at the detective for a minute, then looked away. "I can do it myself," he said.

"Well, do it then."

The other man tried to straighten out his back, but couldn't. He stumbled over to the mare and leaned against the saddle, and faced Matt. "One day, I'm going to come back here and blow your eyes out of your head," he said weakly. "I'm going to scatter your brains in the street."

"I'll be waiting," Matt replied.

He remained on the walkway while the blond man struggled, groaning, to pull himself into his saddle. Once there, he reached down for the reins, knotted them together, and jerked the mare's head toward the detective.

Without warning, he rammed the needle points of his spurs deep into her flanks and let out a wild whoop as the horse spurted ahead. Even though Matt sprang instantly to his left, he still caught enough of the shoulder of the oncoming horse to lose his balance and tumble out into the street.

After lying for a minute with his face in the dirt, he heard the thundering sound of the charging horse, only a

144

few feet away. Instinctively, he spun away toward the walkway, rolling out of the animal's path just in time to miss the hooves by inches.

This time the man didn't bother to turn his mount around. Racing straight toward Eureka Street, he flailed his arms in the air and hollered out in a shrill, weak voice: "I'll be back to kill you, you son-of-a-bitch! I'll be back!"

Rising to his feet, Pilgrim followed the rider until his horse dug into the dirt around the corner of Eureka and disappeared. Then, dusting off his trousers and coat, he stepped over to the *Banner* office and rapped softly on the door.

"Katherine?" he called out.

"Matt?" she returned in a scared, tentative voice. "Is that you!"

"It's me, Kate," he assured her. "It's all right; he's gone. Let me in."

Seconds later, the bolt snapped, the knob twisted, and the door flung open. And Katherine Haynes plunged without hesitation into his arms.

"Oh, Matt—" she cried.

"Whoa!" he said as she squeezed him tightly. "Take it easy—it's all over!"

But she wouldn't let go. "Where have you *been* all day?" she sobbed into his shoulder.

"I had no idea I'd be missed," he said.

"Well, you were missed!"

He pulled her back, to look at her face. "You really are scared, aren't you?" he said.

"Yes, I'm scared," she confessed. "I'm terrified!"

He touched the soft, dark curls on her forehead. "The man's gone, Kate," he told her. "He won't be back."

"It's not just that man, Matt."

"Then what is it?"

She eased away from him. "I don't know. It's this town, this place, these people—"

"We'd better go inside," he advised.

Once in the office, he made sure to shut and bolt the door. Katherine, he noticed, was drifting over to the window. A minute later, she was peeling back the edge of the blind and staring apprehensively out into the dark street.

She looked so vulnerable standing there alone, he yearned to rush over to her and take her into his arms again. He knew now the attraction he felt for her was rapidly developing into a consuming passion. The robust urge to take her to bed was extremely strong, to press her smooth, white body against his, to make love to her and comfort her.

"I guess the people back home were right, Matt," she said, turning around. "I really shouldn't have come out here."

"There are men like that back home, too, Kate."

"I don't mean him. I was thinking about poor Alex," she explained. "And Henry Aldrich." After a pointed pause, she added, "And you."

"Kate—"

"Stay where you are, Matt," she warned him. "I'm trying to keep a clear head. I want to think this through."

Subduing his natural impulses, Pilgrim forced himself to take a seat on the edge of Alex Haynes' desk. "Then why don't you try it on me?" he suggested. "I listen well."

She hesitated a minute, nodded, then proceeded to tell him everything she knew, from the ransacked office and apartment, to Aldrich's peculiar conduct at his house, to the hidden compartment behind the portrait of her father in the *Banner* office.

"I'm not sure I want to admit it," she said finally, "but

146

I guess what I need now more than anything else in the world is a Pinkerton detective.''

"Was that so hard to say?"

"You'll never know how hard."

To distract his mind from the sensual lure of Katherine Haynes, Matt picked up the pile of handwritten notes she had mentioned and read through them. "It looks like your brother was building up to a massive campaign against the railroads," he concluded.

"Yes, but why? What was so important about it?"

He shook his head dejectedly. "I have no idea, Kate," he admitted.

"Oh, Matt," she erupted, "why did Alex have to die! Why!"

"Kate—"

"It all seems so useless! Why did they plunder through his things like that? And why are they still trying to break in here? In another minute, that man would have come through that door!"

"Katherine, let's try to take it one step at a time."

She went to check the window again. "I keep expecting to see another one out there," she said.

Unable to sit still any longer, he stepped briskly over to her. "Listen to me, Katherine Haynes," he told her. "Everything is going to be fine. Do you hear me? We'll work at this together."

She turned around. "Will we?"

He shrugged his shoulders resignedly. "Why not? If I can take on one unscheduled partner, I can take on two. Especially one as clever and pretty as you."

She looked directly at him. "Matt, can you ever forgive me for the way I acted on the train?"

"You were beautiful on the train, Kate," he said, moving toward her.

"I was not. I was rude and condescending. It's just that. . . ." Her voice trailed off as she gazed longingly into his eyes.

"Just that what?" he prompted.

"Well, I found myself liking you, and I didn't want to. When you told me you were a Pinkerton detective, I thought you represented everything I couldn't stand—"

"Kate?"

"What?"

"Hush!"

"Matt, don't—" She retreated from him a few inches, then stopped.

Pilgrim framed her bright, lovely face in his hands, lowered his lips to hers, and kissed her gently. Meeting no resistance from her, he circled his arms firmly around her and began kissing her passionately, probing eagerly with his tongue, until it touched against hers and sent a strong yearning ache through his chest and stomach. Then he felt her breasts push hard against his chest as she boldly returned his kisses.

His blood was surging violently through his veins, turning his warm desire into an urgent, burning need. He could feel his passion for her pulsating hotly in his loins now as he stripped off her jacket and laid his hand upon her bosom. The touch of such luscious flesh beneath the sheer silk of her blouse took his breath away. By the time he plucked open three of her buttons, he was struggling to breathe.

Inside the flimsy fabric, he slid his fingers, gliding the tips along the moist softness of her skin, to the firm, round shape of a naked breast. Covering it with his hand, he quivered to feel the hardness of the nipple pressing up against his sweating palm.

"Matt—"

"Kate, I love you," he whispered.

She began to stir uncomfortably in his arms. "Matt, please don't," she begged softly.

But he held her closer than ever. "I loved you the first time I saw you in Union Station—"

"Matt, stop it!" She broke away from him. Backing into the printing press, she quickly started fastening her blouse. "Couldn't we please think about this a minute?" she pleaded.

"I don't have to think about it, Katherine."

"Well, I do! Everything is happening too fast, Matt. How can you believe I could jump from being scared to death one minute to making love with you the next!"

"I didn't mean to rush you."

"Then, for Heaven's sake, give me a little room to breathe!"

Collecting himself somewhat, Matthew reluctantly saw her point. "I'll give you all the room you need, Kate," he agreed resignedly. "But it's not going to be easy."

"Thank you," she said, picking up her jacket. "Now, could we please leave this place?" she asked.

"We can leave, but you're not going back to Aldrich's," he stipulated. "Not after what you told me about him."

"Unfortunately, that's where I happen to be staying."

"Not anymore. Tonight you're staying at the Teller House."

"My father sent me to Henry Aldrich, Matt."

"And I'm sending you to the Teller House. Come on." He grabbed her wrist and tugged her toward the door.

"What about my clothes?"

149

"I'll send somebody for your clothes tomorrow."

"Matt, I can't just walk out. Henry will worry about what happened to me!"

"Let him worry."

Locking up the *Banner* office, Pilgrim led Katherine Haynes by the hand north to Main Street, swung left at Eureka, and stalked into the lobby of the Teller House. As soon as the desk clerk saw them enter the building, he hopped up behind the mahogany counter, straightened his necktie, and ran his palm over his slick bald head.

"Any problem, Mr. Pilgrim?" he asked, eyeing the woman.

"There's no problem, Simmons," he answered. "Miss Haynes needs a room."

"Yes, sir," he replied. "One room, coming up. If you'll sign for the lady, I'll go get her luggage—"

"She doesn't have any luggage, Simmons. Just give her the room. I'll take her up."

A frown clouded his shiny face. "Oh, I see," he said.

"Her luggage will be here tomorrow," Pilgrim explained.

"Yes, sir, any way you want to handle it is fine with me. Now, if you'll just sign the lady's name on the register. . . ."

Katherine stalled at the top of the stairs on the second floor. "I'm not sure the desk clerk cared for this arrangement any more than I do," she informed him.

"It's not an arrangement, Kate," Pilgrim countered. "It's a place to sleep. At least, here, nobody will be breaking into your room."

"I wasn't referring to the hotel, Matt. What I mean is, you're staying here, too, aren't you?"

"Your room's down this way," he announced, and led

her down the hall. Turning the key the clerk had given him, Pilgrim shoved open the door to the room and lit the oil lamp with one of the matches on the dresser. After surveying the place for a while, he yanked down the blind and headed for the door.

"Kate," he said at the threshold, "do you really want to help me on this case?"

"Yes!" she replied emphatically. "I have to know why Alex died."

"We'll know before long," he predicted confidently. "But first, we need to do a bit of spying."

"On what?"

"On the Bonners."

"Oh. Well, I guess I asked for it, didn't I?"

"Yes, you did. Good night, Kate."

As he stepped out into the hall, she reached out and grasped his arm. "Wait," she began, then hesitated.

Looking at her voluptuous body and clear, beautiful face in the glow of the oil lamp, he had to sigh and shake his head in disbelief. "You have to be the most attractive woman in the world," he concluded.

"Matt, I wanted to tell you I was feeling the same way you were, back there in Alex's office," she confessed. "I didn't want to stop either."

Holding down his urges, he forced himself to nod his head slowly. "I guess I was moving too fast," he acknowledged.

"We both were."

"Which means we'll have to watch ourselves from now on."

"Yes, we will."

"Good night, Kate." He started to go.

"Matt?"

The instant he turned to her voice, she flung her arms around his neck, thrust her breasts hard against his chest and kissed him passionately. For one exciting moment, her soft body seemed to sink into his, and her lips seemed to beg hungrily for him. Then she backed away.

"I'm sorry, Matt," she said, flushed.

"Kate—"

"Of all the men in the world, I had to go and choose a Pinkerton detective!"

Before he could react to her words, Katherine had slipped into her room, closed the door softly behind her, and left him standing alone in the hall.

11

Clay Bonner felt as if he were going to burst at any moment. If he didn't have a woman soon, he was going to set the town of Central City ablaze and burn every man, woman, child, horse, dog, and cat in it.

For an hour now he had been stalking the dusty, dark streets on his bay mare, plodding up and down the avenues, allowing his pain, anger, and frustration to mix and blend and simmer, and finally come to a boil inside. At last, at eight o'clock, he guided his horse to the hitching post in front of the Mercer Hotel, slid off the saddle, and crashed through the door.

Although the enormous house was a gaudily decorated palace, with garish red velvet sofas and chairs, burnished brass spitoons, and elaborate crystal chandeliers, Clayton didn't notice. His eyes were peering into the formal-looking parlor, searching through the lounging company of men and women for a certain prostitute.

"Where is Billy Simms!" he demanded of the woman approaching him.

Andrea Sherbourne, the large-boned, fleshy, but still attractive madame of the house, bustled into the foyer, sliding the parlor door closed behind her swishing silk skirts. "Mr. Bonner!" she reprimanded, "you're disturbing my guests!"

"I don't care about your ignorant guests," he countered. "I'm looking for Billie Simms."

Andrea Sherbourne touched the tiny white rose hanging from a gold chain over her bosom. "I think perhaps you'd better go, Mr. Bonner," she advised.

"Sure, I'll go. I'll go upstairs and jerk every whore out of bed till I find her."

"Now you wait a minute, sir—"

"No, you wait a minute. You may be the big sow in this fancy sty of yours, but you're not going to push Clayton Bonner around."

"You impudent, little—"

"Don't call me names! You hear me? My name is Clayton Bonner. And I want Billie Simms!"

"Molly!" Andrea called out. Within seconds, a thin black woman with graying hair burst through the adjoining door, carrying a broom.

"Yes, ma'am?" she said.

"Molly, I want you to go get Sheriff Potts. Go on, hurry!"

"Yes, ma'am."

"And tell him to bring his gun!"

"I'll sure tell him, Miss Sherbourne," she said, moving toward the door.

"Hold it right there, darkie!" Clay stepped into her path. "You're not going anywhere."

"Miss Sherbourne—"

"Do as I told you, Molly," Andrea commanded.

Bonner braced himself and pointed a trembling finger at the frightened woman. "I'm in no mood for you, darkie," he warned her. "If you move one more inch, so help me, I'll wring your ugly black neck!"

"Miss Sherbourne—" she fretted.

Aware of the danger brewing, Andrea hastily changed her expression. "There's no need for us to get so excited," she suggested. "Why don't we keep everything on a business level?"

Bonner moved the finger to Andrea Sherbourne. "You just get me what I asked for, sow," he told her. "That's all."

"I will, Mr. Bonner," she replied, gritting her teeth. "But you're going to have to wait. Billie isn't available right now."

"Don't you send me another man's leavings, woman!"

"No, no. She's not with anyone; she's just getting ready. I promise you'll be the only man with her this evening."

Clayton lowered his hand and clutched his belly with it. "Well, you just let her know that Clayton Bonner is down here waiting for her."

"I'll tell her. In the meantime, Molly will take care of you."

"I don't need taking care of," he retorted. "Not by the likes of her anyway."

Andrea forced a polite smile. "I'm afraid you're not ready for one of my girls yet, Mr. Bonner," she informed him. "Look at yourself. Your clothes are wrinkled and dirty, your hands are grimy, and your face is covered with cakes of dried blood."

"What does a little dirt matter—"

"I'll grant you it doesn't matter up on Casto Hill. But here, it does. My girls are clean."

He rubbed his bloody jawbone. "I'm not going to let this darkie touch me," he told her.

"You can do it however you want to. But let me tell you something, sir. You will not have Billie Simms this night or any other night, until you lower your voice, wash your face, and act like a gentleman! Now, is that clear to you, Mr. Bonner?"

"It's clear, you old sow."

"And you will also watch your language, sir. I do not allow profanity or abuse of any kind in this house!"

"All right, all right. Just go get her. Tell her I'm ready."

"One item of business first, Mr. Bonner. Can you afford the services of this hotel?"

"I've paid before, haven't I?"

"I'm talking about now, sir."

Glaring angrily at Andrea Sherbourne, Clay plunged his fist into his trousers pocket, drew out a wad of damp, crumpled bills, and tossed them on the floor. "There's my money, *madame*. Pick it up."

Andrea hesitated, then took three steps foward, knelt down to the floor, and scooped up the money. "Thank you," she said, stuffing the bills into her cleavage. "Molly will show you where to wash."

"You just get Billie Simms down here in ten minutes," he told her. "Do you hear me? No more than ten minutes. That's as long as I can wait!"

While Clay Bonner was swabbing the dried blood off his face over a wash basin, a small, frail young woman, above him on the second floor, was putting the final touches on her blonde wig in front of her dresser mirror. With meticulous care, she tucked in every strand of her natural dark brown hair and ran through the wig once more with an ivory comb.

This was the last ritual in her nightly transformation. During the day, she walked about dressed in proper, tailored gray, instead of rustling red silk. She tied her hair in a bun and wore the pince-nez spectacles she still had on. Occasionally a visitor to Central City had actually taken her for a schoolteacher or librarian. But those who frequented the parlor houses in mining towns knew better. They had no trouble at all recognizing the youngest and most popular prostitute in the Mercer Hotel, Miss Billie Simms.

Billie hated to look at herself in the mirror. She despised her way of life. At eighteen, she had already climbed out of the ranks of the saloon whores of Leadville and Aspen to become a successful crib girl in Denver. It was there that Andrea Sherbourne had hired her as one of the parlor prostitutes in Central City. This was the final trial for her, she told herself in the mirror. This would be the end of the line. In a few weeks, she would finally be able to make the break to a new life.

With small, delicate fingers, she pried open the ivory and jadestone jewelry box on the dresser, slipped out a thick stack of bills, and clutched them hard against her breast. There was no need to count the money. She knew exactly what the sum had risen to: $368.00. She needed only a few dollars more to pay Miss Sherbourne the $462.00 she owed her for room and board, and then she'd buy herself a ticket to glorious New Orleans on the Union Pacific Railroad.

After carefully putting the money back and tidying up the room for the night's work, Billie sat down very properly on the rosewood chair in the room and waited for her first customer, like a girl about to be courted by the boy down the street. But soon she became uncomfortable and began to squirm in her chair. When a cold, dry harshness seized her throat, she got up to pour herself a glass of water. But, as she expected, the cool liquid sliding down her throat had no effect. She understood it was not a physical ailment. It was always this way when something terrible was about to happen. First came the dryness in her throat, then the queasy feeling in her stomach. . . .

"Billie?" Andrea Sherbourne rapped two times on the door, opened it, and swished into the room with a warm smile. "Don't you look lovely!" she said. "But what have I told you about wearing those glasses, sweetheart?"

"Miss Sherbourne, I don't feel very well," Billie complained.

A serious look crossed Andrea's face as she closed the door behind her. "This wouldn't be another one of your feelings, would it, sweetheart? Another one of these 'impressions' of yours?"

"Yes, ma'am." She hugged herself with her slender, bare arms.

"Now darling, you know those feelings never amount to anything," she said, bringing her to her feet. "You're just nervous for some reason, that's all. But you're going to have to be good, Billie. There's someone downstairs, asking for you."

"Miss Sherbourne, I was wondering if maybe just for tonight—"

"No, Billie," she cut her off. "I've told you before, you can't keep a man waiting. The longer he waits, the rougher he gets."

"I thought maybe I could stay up here and write letters, or something," she said weakly.

Andrea smiled sadly. "Now, who would you write letters to, darling? You have no family, and I'm sure most of your friends back in Denver can't read."

"But I don't feel good, Miss Sherbourne. My stomach feels funny. Can't you tell the man downstairs to pick someone else?"

Andrea stroked her shoulder. "You know it doesn't work that way, honey," she told her. "If a man comes in here asking for Billie Simms, then he's looking for one thing: a precious, fragile little songbird in a gilded cage. Nothing else in the Mercer Hotel will do."

She nodded. "I wish he'd asked for someone else though."

"Well, he didn't, sweetheart, so please be good for me, all right? Anyway, how are you going to pay me back that money, if you don't work?"

"I'm real close to it now, Miss Sherbourne," she announced.

"I know you are, darling. And we're all very proud of you." Andrea reached up and carefully removed Billie's spectacles. "I want you to go downstairs and be what nobody else in this place can be, Billie. Will you do that for me?"

"Yes, ma'am."

"I swear, child. You have such a wonderful innocence about you," Andrea told her. "I've never seen anything like it. After four hard years in this business, you still look like everybody's little sister. I wish you would learn to use that, honey. I keep saying, you could rise to the top in this business, if you only wanted to."

"But I don't want to, Miss Sherbourne! All I want is to get on the train to New Orleans!"

"And you will do that, darling, I promise." Andrea

159

wrapped her thick arm around Billie's bare white shoulders and eased her toward the door. "But in order for it to happen, we have to take care of some business, don't we?"

"Yes, ma'am."

"That's my girl. Now, are you feeling any better?"

"I guess so."

"Good. Then why don't we go meet this gentleman caller of yours? He's very anxious to see you."

Reluctantly, Billie followed Andrea Sherbourne out into the hall and started descending the thickly carpeted stairs to the main floor. A dozen steps later, she stopped abruptly, clutched the railing tightly, and refused to move. Below her, a disheveled young man with wet hair stood glaring up at her with hard, accusing eyes.

"It's about time!" he growled at her.

At the sound of Clayton Bonner's voice, Billie felt the heavy sickness in her stomach again. "Miss Sherbourne," she said shakily, "couldn't I go back?"

"No, Billie."

"But I can't do it, Miss Sherbourne!" she protested in a loud whisper. "Not with him!"

"Billie, sweetheart—"

"Oh, please don't make me!"

"Billie, he's already paid his money."

"I don't care! I won't do it!"

Andrea patted the back of her hand. "Billie," she admonished, "I want you to stop this! The man is waiting!"

"No!" She screamed, jerked her hand away, and wheeled around. Stumbling frantically up the steps, she raced breathlessly down the hall to her room, slammed the door, and locked it.

Minutes later, as her chest heaved up and down excitedly,

she sidled near the window and listened to the terrible sound of a master key clicking loudly in the lock. When the door pushed open, she turned her head to avoid Sherbourne's look.

"Sweetheart—" she said softly.

"Couldn't he take someone else?" she cried.

"I asked him, darling. He won't have anyone but you. I'm sorry."

"Miss Sherbourne, please—"

"Billie," she bargained, "if you do this for me, I will see to it you get an extra ten dollars. I'll leave it under your plate tomorrow morning."

"Miss Sherbourne, he scares me!"

"Ten extra dollars would mean leaving two weeks ahead of your schedule, Billie," she pointed out. "I should think that would appeal to you."

"It does," she said.

"Then will you do it for me?"

At last, she sighed and nodded her head.

"You're a very sweet girl, Billie. Now you know if he gets rough, all you have to do is scream."

"Yes, ma'am."

Andrea walked over to her, took her into her massive arms, and hugged her tightly. Then she stepped back, opened the door, and let Clayton Bonner in.

At the slam of the door behind him, Bonner grabbed his stomach with his left hand and winced. "What happened to your hair?" he grunted painfully. "Why is it that ugly color?"

"It's a wig, Mr. Bonner," she explained.

"Clayton," he corrected. He moved closer, grimly examining her from head to foot. "I don't like it," he declared. "It looks cheap and vulgar. Take it off."

Silently, she peeled off the wig and unconsciously tried to straighten her matted dark brown hair.

"Something's missing though," he reflected. "Where is that string of pearls you usually wear?"

Her heart stuttered when she caught his eyes moving along the surface of the dresser. It nearly stopped when she saw his lean arm shake out and his fingers snap up the lid of the jewelry box.

"Stop it!" She screamed and ran to him and groped behind him for the money. "Leave that alone!"

But he had no trouble keeping the box away. "Well, would you look at this," he taunted, drawing out the stack of bills. "Have you ever seen so much money!"

"Give it to me!"

He shoved her away and thumbed through the bills. "There must be close to four hundred dollars here," he said.

"Give it to me!" she demanded. "I earned that money! I saved it!"

He grinned at her, tossed the money back into the case, and clapped it shut. "I don't want your dirty whoring loot," he sneered.

Billie's heart was still pumping fast. "I need it, Mr. Bonner," she explained weakly. "All of it."

He grimaced as he massaged his stomach with both hands. "I'll let you keep it, Billie," he said, "if you'll promise to do everything I tell you to. If you don't, I'm going to walk out of here with it. Do you understand?"

"Yes, sir."

"I told you to call me Clayton."

"Yes, Clayton. I understand."

"Good. Only next time, say my name sweeter, like you really cared who I was. Now, I want you to go right over there and take off your dress. Then sit down on that chair.''

Under his attentive eye, Billie obeyed. She slowly unhooked the back of her red silk dress and pulled the smooth, cool material over her head. Wearing only her petticoat, she eased down on the rosewood chair. Instantly, Clay Bonner dropped to his knees in front of her.

"Now curse me," he ordered.

"What?" she said, puzzled.

He clenched his teeth. "You heard what I said. Curse me! Say ugly things to me. Say every filthy thing you can think of!"

"No, I won't!"

"Do as I say, girl. Don't forget, I paid for you!"

"But cursing isn't allowed," she protested. "Miss Sherbourne doesn't let us use those words."

"Forget Miss Sherbourne and start thinking about that $400.00 of yours. Do you want to keep it or not?"

"I've got to have it, Mr. Bonner."

"Then speak!"

She swallowed dryly. "What do I say?" she asked softly.

"I want you to call me a bastard," he answered eagerly. "Call me your little bastard."

She braced herself. "Clayton, my little bastard," she mumbled.

"Louder!" he demanded. "And uglier. Make it uglier!"

"I'm sorry. I just don't know what to say! I don't know how to use those words—"

"Come over here." He jumped up, grabbed her arm, and hauled her over to the bed. "Go on, lie down!" He slung her against the bed.

"Do you want me to take the rest off?" she asked.

"I didn't say to, did I?" he growled. "You just do what I say!"

Quivering under his words, Billie pulled down the bedspread, climbed on the mattress, and lowered her head slowly down upon the white satin pillow. "What do you want me to do now?" she asked innocently.

"Tell me to come to bed. Say, 'Come to bed, Clayton, you little bastard.' "

She repeated the invitation in a low voice.

"Say it again—and mean it!"

Once more she uttered the words, and opened her arms enticingly, the way men always liked her to do.

Within a heartbeat, Clayton Bonner had ripped off his trousers and was hopping like a crazed animal on the bed beside her. Groping at the lower part of her body with his shaking hands, he tore away her pantaloons and exposed her naked skin to the cool, dry air of the room. Then he flattened himself on top, split apart her legs, and violently plunged his weight into her.

The rest was automatic for Billie Simms. While the outlaw rose and fell above her, she expertly ground her hips against his bony frame and thrust her pelvis up and down in rhythm to his. Digging her nails into the coarse thick material of his wrinkled cotton shirt, she squealed and moaned and whined in pretended delight, as Bonner pumped madly into her again and again, until at last he erupted into a shrieking howl, and collapsed lifelessly on top of her.

Billie lay quiet under his dying pulsations. Tomorrow, she thought, she would have ten whole dollars extra. Two weeks sooner she would be riding in style to New Orleans. Then never again would she rent her body to the likes of a Clayton Bonner.

After panting a while into the pillow, Clayton whispered into her ear. "That was good," he complimented. "Very, very good."

She knew exactly what to say now. "Yes, it was, Clayton," she told him, hoping desperately it would be enough for this night.

"You're too good for this place, you know it?" he informed her. "You need to get out of this parlor house. You need to be free."

"I will be free," she told him. "Some day."

"You're right, because I'm going to take you out of here myself," he declared. Raising his head up, he looked down at her with puffy, drooping eyes. "What do you think of that, Billie Simms?" he wavered. "What do you think of leaving Miss Sherbourne and taking good care of me for a change?"

"I can't even take good care of myself," she replied.

"You just look after Clayton Bonner and you'll be fine," he assured her. "From now on, you'll be my own sweet little Mom. Won't you?"

She didn't answer him.

"But I need to get another gun first," he said, dropping his head to the pillow again. "My stupid brother broke mine tonight."

"Why don't you go to sleep, Clayton?" she said.

He sighed heavily and dropped his head to the pillow again. "I need to sleep," he agreed drowsily. "I'm very tired. And my bones ache."

"Then close your eyes and relax," she advised.

Billie lay still beneath him until, at some time during the long night, he let out a loud, guttural noise and plopped over on his back. For a time, she gazed up at the shadows playing fancifully on the white ceiling above her and imagined how it was going to be in that magic city on the exotic Mississippi River. She would stroll down Canal Street in fancy tailored wool and black velvet and ostrich feathers and smile coquettishly at all the rogues in waistcoats and derby hats. "Evening, ma'am," they would say—to Miss B. Simms, of Royal Street, in New Orleans.

Drifting from that reverie to peaceful sleep, she barely moved a muscle until just before dawn, when, all of a sudden, she sprang up in the bed. With a terrifying thought gnawing at her brain, she felt with her hand for the man beside her, and found nothing but cool, empty sheets. She knew now that Clayton Bonner had slipped away during the night.

"Oh, no!" she cried as she fumbled with the lamp on the stand next to the bed. Somehow managing to strike the match and light the wick, she nervously replaced the globe. Then, holding her breath in a cold, gripping terror, she moved her eyes across the foot of the bed, over a few feet of braided rug, to the top of the dresser.

She felt her spirit sink like a stone in water when she caught sight of the open ivory jewelry box. Rising from the bed, she told herself it was still possible he hadn't actually taken her money. He had said he didn't want it, after all. And she had done everything he had asked her to do.

Slowly and apprehensively, she moved toward the dresser, holding the lamp above her head until a blanket of light fell straight into the jewelry box.

Then there was no longer any doubt. And for Billie Simms, no longer any hope.

For every single dollar of her precious money was gone.

12

As Matt Pilgrim scraped the last splotch of dried shaving lather off his chin, he gazed into the mirror and noted with pleasure the light of dawn pouring in through the window behind him. After spending much of the night worrying about mines and railroads and Katherine Haynes, he was relieved to see a new day breaking at last. In just a little while, he would go knock on Katherine's door and invite her to go to breakfast with him.

A quick, sharp series of taps on the door quickly broke his thoughts. Tossing the razor on the dresser, he stepped over to the door and swung it open. He was surprised to discover a plump, pretty blond girl standing in the hall, then brushing past him into the room.

Matt reached over to the bed for his shirt. "Miss Canfield, what are you doing here!"

"I've come about Reuben, Mr. Pilgrim," she said excitedly.

"No doubt." He pulled on the shirt and began buttoning it. "What's he up to now?"

"You have to come get him, Mr. Pilgrim," she insisted. "I can't do anything with him!"

"Get him from where?" he asked.

"He's over at the Mercer Hotel, looking for clues."

Matt couldn't help but smile. "What kind of clues is he looking for in a parlor house?"

"I don't know. I told him not to go into that place, but he wouldn't listen. You know how he is."

"Yes, I know." He tucked in his shirt and grabbed his coat. "We'd better go see what he's doing," he said, guiding her out into the hall.

"What happened was," she explained as they headed for the stairs, "ever since Reuben found this clue of his outside my bedroom window this morning, he's been real upset. He's been poking around all over town, trying to find more like it."

"Why didn't he tell me about it?"

Alice Canfield used his arm to steady herself as they started down the steps. "He said he didn't want to wake you up," she answered.

"Very thoughtful," Matt observed.

As they reached the lobby, the bald desk clerk behind the counter perked up his head. "Is everything all right, Mr. Pilgrim?" he called out.

"Everything's fine, Simmons."

"Aren't you and the lady going to have breakfast this morning?"

"No, Simmons."

Alice glanced back at the prying clerk as they passed through the front door. "Why was he looking at me like that?" she asked.

"He was probably thinking you don't look much like Katherine Haynes."

"I don't understand."

"He doesn't either."

"Mr. Pilgrim—"

"It's not important, Alice." He took her arm. "Let's go see what Reuben has gotten himself into."

In front of the Mercer Hotel, Matthew deposited Alice Canfield next to a lamppost and instructed her not to budge an inch until he came out.

"But why can't I go in with you?" she asked.

"Because I said stay here."

"That's no reason," she replied stubbornly.

"Alice, you're as hardheaded as your brother."

"You won't let me in because you think I'm a lady, is that it?" she exacted.

"That's reason enough. But to tell you the truth, I don't think I could handle more than one Canfield in a parlor house at a time."

"Well, it isn't fair!"

"Few things are, Miss Canfield. But at least it's safe. Wait right here, and I'll be back in a few minutes."

"If you're in there very long, I'm coming in after you," she threatened.

"I'm sure you will," he said, and burst through the doors into the hotel. In the foyer, he naturally turned to the noisy confusion of loud voices coming out of the parlor room to his left. Marching through the wide doors, he discovered a neat, red-headed young man in a business suit standing eye-to-eye with a large, fleshy woman in a low-cut white dress.

"Reuben," he said to the man, "don't you ever sleep?"

"Mr. Pilgrim!" He sprang over to Matt and pumped his hand up and down. "I certainly am glad to see you this morning. I've picked up a trail!"

"So I see."

"I'm sure our suspect has been in this house!"

169

"Sir," the woman said to Matt, "if you have any control over this young man, would you please try to remove him from the premises?"

"I apologize if I'm upsetting you, ma'am," Reuben said quickly to her. "I don't mean to."

"Reuben," Matt addressed him, "what suspect are you talking about?"

"The man who stole the black powder from Miller's Store, Mr. Pilgrim," he answered. "The one who killed the fellow we pulled out of the mine. I'm positive he was here last night. I found his heel print in a cake of mud on the front steps. Evidently, he'd gotten wet somehow."

Andrea Sherbourne broke into a laugh. "This boy is crazy," she declared.

"No, I'm not. I found the same heel print outside my sister's bedroom window this morning."

"Ah, well, then maybe you ought to ask your sister about him."

Reuben's face flushed red. "Alice has never even seen this man, Miss Sherbourne. She doesn't know anything about this."

"Well, neither do I, Mr. Canfield. Now, if you gentlemen will excuse me—"

"Miss Sherbourne," Matt broke in. "Wait a minute, please. My name is Pilgrim. I'm with the Pinkerton Detective Agency. Would you answer a few questions for me?"

She toyed with her gold necklace as she looked him over. After a minute, she shook her head. "The Pinkertons are not the law, are they?" she asked.

"No, ma'am."

"Then I don't have to answer any questions," she concluded.

"Miss Sherbourne," Matt said, "you should know the man we're looking for is extremely dangerous."

"Then he hasn't been here, sir. I don't allow that kind of people in my house."

Matt heaved a sigh. "Could you at least tell us how many men came in here after dark last night?"

"Last night was slow," she replied guardedly. "A few miners and cowboys, and a couple of business folk. But no murderers."

"How do yo know!" Reuben exclaimed. "You can't always tell criminals by the way they look!"

"If I ask you something, Mr. Canfield," she said, looking directly at Reuben, "will you answer it?"

"Yes, ma'am," he said confidently.

"Could you identify a prostitute if you saw one?"

"I don't know," he fumbled. "I never thought about it."

"Well, think about it. Could you?"

He shrugged his shoulders. "I'm sure there would be a number of clues," he decided. "I suppose you could."

"And I can identify a criminal, young man. In my business, you have to. So don't preach to me!"

"Miss Sherbourne," Matt said to her, "If you'll give us the names of the men who came in here last night, we'll leave without another word."

"Mr. Pilgrim, there is nothing on earth that will make me give you those names. I know you won't understand this, but I have my own integrity. But it's here, sir. What my clients do outside this hotel is their own business."

"This man may commit murder, Miss Sherbourne," Reuben blurted.

"Don't you raise your voice to me in my own house," she warned. "You just remember, if a man acts like a gentleman here, then that's what I assume he is—until I have proof to the contrary.''

"We're working against time, Miss Sherbourne!" Reuben pleaded. "We need to know who we're after!"

"Why don't you go look in the streets then? Or in the mines—"

"But he was here!" Reuben argued. "I know he was here!"

"Will you gentlemen please leave? Or do I have to call for Sheriff Potts to throw you out?"

Reuben flung up his hands. "Mr. Pilgrim, she knows exactly who it is! She knows his name! We can't just walk off!"

"She's only trying to protect herself, Reuben," Matt pointed out. "We can't force it out of her. Let's go; your sister's waiting."

But Reuben wouldn't move a muscle. "May I ask you something now, Miss Sherbourne?"

"I'm running out of patience, sir."

"Of all the men who came in here last night, is there one who you believe is the man we're after?"

She sighed heavily. "Yes, Mr. Canfield," she admitted. "For all the good it does you."

"You absolutely refuse to tell us who it is?"

"Yes, I do. I can't tell you."

"I can!" said a small, soft voice drifting down from the stairway.

Matt looked up to see a delicate, blonde woman about Reuben's age, standing on the steps, looking down at them with sad, tearful eyes. With a trembling hand, she raised a linen handkerchief to her face, covered her thin red lips with it, and started to cry.

Andrea Sherbourne shot a hard, accusing glance up at

172

her. "Get yourself back upstairs, Billie!" she ordered. "Go on—you've got no business down here."

"But he took my money, Miss Sherbourne!" she wailed.

"You heard what I said, Billie—go to our room!"

"Who took your money, Miss?" Pilgrim asked her.

Before Billie Simms could utter a word, Andrea Sherbourne had turned on him. "I will have to ask you to leave my girls alone, sir!" she commanded. "What happens in this hotel is my concern, not yours. I will take care of it!"

"But it wasn't hotel money, Miss Sherbourne," Billie sobbed. "It was mine!"

Instantly, Andrea lunged toward the stairs. "You'd better come with me, Billie," she ordered as she quickly mounted the steps. "We're going to have to talk about this."

"No!" she said, retreating. "I don't want to talk about it. I want my money back!"

Andrea stopped a few feet below her. "Now, sweetheart," she reminded her, "you know the rules of the house. None of my girls is allowed to talk to anyone about a client."

"But these men can go look for him. They can find it for me."

"Don't you understand, darling, these men are not the law. They have no right to pry into our business."

"But I've got to find it somehow," she cried. "I've got to get to New Orleans, somehow."

Andrea reached up and grasped Billie's thin, white arm in her chunky fist. "I want you to forget about New Orleans, Billie," she ordered her. "Just put it out of your mind."

"I can't! I've been saving for it for so long, I just can't."

"There's nothing we can do about it, sweetheart." She stroked her arm.

"But they can!"

"No, Billie," she insisted quietly. "You are not going to tell them. Do you hear me?"

Matt took a couple of steps forward. "Miss Sherbourne—" he began.

"Stay out of this, Mr. Pilgrim," she warned.

"We're only trying to help—"

Andrea Sherbourne bristled at the offer. "We know better than that, sir," she responded. "Nobody ever helps a whore. No matter how polite you people act with us, you always keep us in our place, don't you? Wives and mothers always sneer at us; miners and cowboys call us by the names of animals, and little boys and girls snicker when we pass them on the street. And when the stares and giggles don't make us shudder enough to suit you, then a newspaperman like Alexander Haynes starts telling everyone that we're nothing but a nest of diseases, descending on this pure and proper town like a deadly plague."

"Miss Sherbourne, we're not here to censure you," Matt assured her. "As long as Central City wants and needs the Mercer Hotel, it will stand on its own, without our interference. But we are trying to preserve the law. And we need cooperation."

Andrea kept her eye on Pilgrim as she wrapped her arm around the sobbing Billie Simms and squeezed her softly. "I'm not going to cooperate with you, Mr. Pilgrim," she declared. "So you might as well save your breath."

Now Reuben came forward. "But we're detectives, Miss Sherbourne," he argued. "Don't you want us to help her get her money back?"

"If I need detective help, I won't be calling on Barton

Canfield's little red-headed boy, sir," she countered. "I'll be calling on Sheriff Potts himself."

"Sheriff Potts!"

"Let it go, Reuben," Matt advised.

"But, Mr. Pilgrim, you know he can't—"

"Let it go, Reuben!"

"But Sheriff Potts couldn't find her money if she sent it to him in the mail!"

"You ignorant little boy," Andrea scolded him. "The sheriff may look like a drunkard to you, but let me tell you something: Underneath all that whiskey odor and dirt and grime is a good man. And mark my words, some day that man will come out. And when he does, everybody in this town will be ashamed of the way they've been laughing at him all these years."

"I wasn't laughing at him, ma'am."

"I don't really care what you were doing, Mr. Canfield. Nobody in this hotel cares about anything the upright citizens of Central City do. We take care of ourselves by sticking together."

"Miss Sherbourne—" Billie squirmed in the other woman's arms. "I'm not feeling so good."

"Now look what you've done," Andrea accused Reuben. "You're making the girl sick."

"I didn't mean to upset her—"

"Get out of my house, sir," she ordered. "Both of you!"

Reuben frowned with concern. "We don't want to hurt anybody, ma'am," he told her. "We just want to know the man's name."

"You won't be getting it in the Mercer Hotel, sir," she stated flatly. Then, clutching Billie Simms close to her side, she started up the steps.

When Reuben lurched after them, Pilgrim instantly snatched the tail of his coat and held him back. "Let them go," he said.

"But we have to know, Mr. Pilgrim! Alice's life is in danger!"

"We'll get it some other way."

"I know she wants to tell us. I could see it in her eyes."

"But she can't tell us. Not as long as Andrea Sherbourne hovers over her like a mother hen."

176

13

On the wooden plankway outside the Mercer Hotel, Alice Canfield sprang forward at the sight of Matt and Reuben coming out the front door.

"What happened?" she asked them anxiously. "Are you all right, Reuben?"

"Nothing happened, Alice," Reuben answered dejectedly. "The trail stopped with Miss Andrea Sherbourne."

"You mean the madame? Oh, what was she like?" Alice asked. "Was she poised and confident? Did she use any bad words? Did she wear a wig and revealing clothes?"

"I didn't notice."

"Oh, Reuben, stop. I want to know!"

Matt smiled at her exuberant expression. "Miss Sherbourne is a very protective woman," he told her. "She wouldn't give us much information."

"She was certainly protective of that pretty blonde girl," Reuben offered.

"What blonde girl?" Alice inquired eagerly.

"Just a girl, Alice."

"How old was she? Did you actually talk to her?"

"Alice, stop asking questions—"

"Because neither one of you is going to bother to answer them, isn't that so? You want me to die an old maid, in total ignorance."

"We'd rather you went home and stayed there, sister," Reuben told her.

She looked directly at him. "Did you know this is why I'm going back East, Reuben? I'm going to learn! I can't find out anything here. This is as close as I've ever been to a place like the Mercer Hotel—"

"And it's as close as you're going to get, too."

She looked at him in innocent bewilderment. "I don't understand why you never want to tell me what's going on," she said.

"Alice, we don't know what's going on," Reuben explained. "That's why we're investigating—"

"I declare, you can be so exasperating, Reuben," she accused. "When will you and Daddy ever realize I'm not a little girl anymore? And when will everybody else stop believing because I walk with a limp, I'm about to fall apart!"

"Nobody believes that, Alice."

"Oh, of course they do. They're always going out of their way to help me! That doesn't bother me so much; I'm used to it. But I do want to know what people think about things, Reuben. I hate for folks to suddenly lose their voices whenever I come near. I may be crippled, but I'm not going to break if I hear something I don't like!"

"I don't know what you're going on about, Alice. We told you about Seth Bonner's note—"

"I know—'If you don't close the Get Lucky Mine, your daughter will never reach New York.' That's not anything. I don't even take that seriously, Reuben."

"Well, you'd better take it seriously!" he said with alarm.

"How could I?" she countered. "I don't even know this Seth Bonner."

"What does that matter, Alice—he knows you!"

After considering that for a while, she looked over at the Pinkerton detective. "Don't you think this is nonsense, Mr. Pilgrim?" she asked. "You don't really believe my life is in danger, do you?"

"I believe your brother's right, Miss Canfield," he answered. "Don't ever forget, the Bonners are outlaws. They're living in a world of their own making, up there on Casto Hill. And in that world, they're not obliged to honor any of the rules of decency any of the rest of us have. They have their own. If an outlaw wants something, you'd better assume he is incapable of recognizing any reason why he shouldn't have it. No matter who gets hurt."

"I realize the Bonners are dangerous, Mr. Pilgrim, but they never even come into town."

"One came into town last night," Reuben jumped in. "He planted his feet under your very window!"

"You don't know that for certain, do you?" she exacted.

"Not for certain, no. But all the evidence points to it."

She shook her blonde locks in fond disapproval. "You and your evidence," she said. "People aren't nearly as bad as you and Daddy make them out to be, Reuben. That silly footprint of yours probably belongs to a man who just happened to be passing by."

"A man who also just happened to amble on down to the Mercer Hotel? No, Alice, I don't believe that. Somebody is after you. We're just not sure if it's the Bonners or not. Someone else may have composed that note. We just don't know. We have a lot of clues, but nothing has come together yet."

"Well, when it does, let me know. Meanwhile, I'm going to be very busy. I've got a thousand things to do before I leave."

"Alice, I'm telling you to be serious about this. You could get hurt!"

She smiled sympathetically at her brother, then reached over and kissed his cheek. "I'll be all right," she assured him. "Really, I promise, if I see a Bonner lurking about, I'll just turn around and hobble away. In the meantime, I'm glad you're out of trouble for the moment and . . . I've got to go."

"What do you think you're doing?"

"If you must know, I'm going to Miller's Mercantile."

"Oh, no, you're not. You're going home."

"I will, Reuben, I swear. Daddy will be wanting his breakfast soon. But first, I've got to step into Miller's Mercantile," she stipulated. "I have to look over the new straw hats coming in from St. Louis today."

Reuben threw up his hands. "How on earth can you think of buying a hat when Mr. Pilgrim and I are working night and day to keep you from getting hurt?"

She sighed and shrugged her shoulders. "You're really so sweet, Reuben," she complimented. "Both of you are. And I do appreciate it, honest. I promise you, I won't give you any more trouble."

"Then you're going home," Reuben assumed.

"Yes—after I look at the hats."

"Alice—"

"Good day, gentlemen." She curtsied, waved at them, and limped away toward Miller's store.

After watching her to the corner of Main Street, Reuben

reared back and kicked the lamppost in frustration. "Have you ever seen anyone so stubborn in your life?" he marveled. "Whenever she gets an idea into her head, she'll wade through hell to follow it through."

Matt laughed. "Runs in the family."

Reuben didn't hear the pointed reference. "I wish Alice were already on that train," he was saying. "I'd feel a lot better if she weren't so easy to get to. She's not nearly as strong as she lets on, Mr. Pilgrim. And she's just too trusting!"

"Why don't you keep an eye on her, Reuben?" Matt suggested. "I'll see if the telegraph office has received the Agency's report on the dead man yet."

Reuben nodded. "I'm willing to go look after my sister, Mr. Pilgrim," he said, "but I'm not through with the Mercer Hotel yet. I know I can learn more here."

"From the girl who was robbed, you mean," he surmised.

"Yes, sir. All the clues lead straight up those steps to her bedroom door. And that's where I'll go, too, if I have to."

"You won't even get to see her, Reuben," he warned. "Andrea Sherbourne will never let you slip past the foyer."

"Well, Miss Sherbourne is pretty formidable all right. But it can be done."

"If anybody can manage it, I'm sure you can," he complimented.

Just as Matt started toward the telegraph office, he happened to see a stocky man in faded overalls trudging down Main Street toward the hotel. Pausing to spray the dusty street with tobacco juice, Ben Watkins, the mine manager, climbed up on the walk and lumbered straight up to them.

"Morning, gents," He greeted the detectives with a

wide grin which amply displayed the gap in his yellowed teeth. "Have yourselves a nice night, did you?"

"Mr. Watkins, we didn't stay in there!" Reuben disclaimed. "We've been working."

"Is that so? Well, I'd say you've been doing some mighty agreeable work then," he declared, gazing up at the facade of the hotel. "I hear they got some real nice pieces of trade up there on the second floor. I wouldn't've expected to see a Pinkerton detective and the supervisor's son hanging around a whorehouse, though."

"We're not hanging around," Reuben protested.

"No? What do you call it, then—"

"What do you want, Mr. Watkins?" Matt cut in.

He grimly swallowed down a slug of his tobacco juice, then cleared his throat noisily. "Everybody on the hill is saying you gents are real heroes, you know that? They're going on about how you saved the lives of that crew of Cousin Jacks you brought back to the surface with you."

"Unfortunately, there was one man we didn't save," Matt regretted.

"Yeah, well, that particular dude didn't have no business in my mine anyway. I wouldn't worry about him. He probably got just what he deserved."

"We can't know that until we know who he is, Mr. Watkins," Matt pointed out. "It's possible he wasn't anywhere around the mine when he was stabbed. It looks like he was thrown down the shaft."

"Close enough for me. I always say that nobody belongs in a mine that ain't a miner."

"I'll remember that," Matt said ironically.

"You do that, Mr. Detective," he replied. "And you might remember this, too: I don't cotton much to seeing Pinkerton badges and bowlers around my men, Mr. Pilgrim.

It ain't good for them. We may have to put up with this boy here, on account of who he is, but we don't have to put up with the likes of you. You understand what I'm hinting at here?''

"I think so."

"Good. Then you're going to keep your butt out of my mine."

"Mr. Watkins, I'm going to do whatever it takes to do the job I was hired for. If that means I will have to poke around in the Get Lucky Mine, or close it down, or blow it up, that's what I will do—with the permission of the mine manager or without it."

"You're a regular blowhard ain't you, bud? Well, chew on this fact, Mr. Pilgrim. Right after Mr. Harrison promotes Barton Canfield as a supervisor, he has to hire a Pinkerton detective to keep the place from caving in and killing more people. Does that tell you something or not?''

"Should it?"

"It tells me this boy's daddy ain't the right man for the job. Apparently, the Get Lucky miners ain't behind him the way they might be with somebody else."

"Meaning you, I suppose," Reuben said accusingly.

"Now I didn't say that, Mr. Canfield," he denied. "You know I didn't. Your daddy's a real good man, I'll tell anybody that. Only the mine ain't been working right ever since he became supervisor. Like it or not, that's the truth of it."

"But it's not truth enough, Mr. Watkins," Reuben contented.

He pursed his lips and ejected a splash of juice that spattered in the dry dust with a dull poof. "All I'm doing is telling you the facts, that's all," he argued. "Ain't that what you Pinkerton detectives are supposed to be after, Mr. Pilgrim?''

''We're getting them, Mr. Watkins,'' Matt said, starting off.

''Wait a minute there,'' he called out. ''I ain't through.''

Matt stopped. ''Mr. Watkins—''

''I'm just saying I've got something for you gents,'' he interrupted. ''Something you're going to be real interested in.''

Matt watched the mine manager very slowly and carefully extract with two fingers from the chest pocket of his overalls a pale yellow envelope. After a quick spit across the walk into the street, he wiped his lips with his sleeve and raised the envelope into the air for the detectives to see.

''I'm told this here's a telegraph for Mr. Matthew Pilgrim,'' he revealed, ''from none other than Mr. William Pinkerton himself, of Denver. I wonder if either of you gents might be interested in it?''

Matt snapped the envelope from him. ''What are you doing with this?'' he asked.

''Doing just what you see, Mr. Pilgrim,'' he replied. ''I'm delivering a message off the telegraph. Thompson said as long as I was going past the whorehouse, I might as well bring it over to you. He acted like it was urgent.''

''It is,'' Matt confirmed.

''Well, you'll notice it's still sealed tight as a drum. I figure you ought to respect a man's privacy, even if you don't necessarily respect the man himself.''

''Well, I appreciate your bringing it over, Mr. Watkins,'' Matt said. ''We've been waiting for this since last night.''

''Who knows, there could be good news in that message.

I reckon there's even a chance Mr. Pinkerton might be sending you back East, huh? That'd certainly make it worth all my trouble, wouldn't it? Well, I'll be saying good morning to you, gents,'' he saluted them and proceeded down the street in the direction of the Harrison mine.

"I'd say Ben Watkins is still high on our list of suspects, Mr. Pilgrim," Reuben reasoned. "He can't forget for a moment my father was promoted over him. He might be willing to do anything to see him fail."

"Yes, he might," Matt allowed. He split open the envelope, popped out the paper, and read the message.

"What is it, Mr. Pilgrim?" Reuben asked anxiously. "Is it about the dead man?"

Matt nodded. "Our photographs made it fairly easy for the Agency to identify him. The man's name was Thomas J. Farrell. He was thirty-one years old, married, and had three children. Mr. Pinkerton wants us to send his body back to Omaha on the next train."

"Is that where he was from?" Reuben asked, surprised.

"It looks like it. He'd been working for the Union Pacific Railroad in Nebraska for five years—as a detective."

"A detective!" Reuben exclaimed. "Then we were right, Mr. Pilgrim! There is a direct connection between the railroad and the Get Lucky Mine!"

"There is," Matt qualified, "if Thomas Farrell was investigating the mine. We don't know for sure whether he was."

"He had to be!"

Pilgrim scratched the bottom of his lip as he read over Pinkerton's communication again. While his brain was working fast to piece together the various fragments of the mystery, he knew that what he was looking at now did little more than stir the muddy water a bit. He had hoped to receive a crucial fact or two that would establish a definite link between the mine and the railroad, but it was obvious he wasn't going to be that lucky on his first case as a Pinkerton detective.

"Mr. Pinkerton says that Thomas Farrell was in Chicago two weeks ago," he reported. "According to the Union Pacific files, he witnessed a secret conference of five financiers, two railroad executives, and the banking firm of Hargrove and Son, on Washington Street."

"Why did he do that?"

"They don't know. Evidently he was pursuing his own case and hadn't told his employers exactly what he was doing yet. He was supposed to meet with them after his trip to Colorado."

"Then Farrell was killed because he knew too much, just as we thought."

"They were all killed for that reason, Reuben—the detectives, Haynes, and Farrell. But they weren't murdered because they knew everything. I have a feeling each one knew a little, but no one of them knew any more about what's going on than you and I do now."

"Which means you and I had better start looking over our shoulders," he concluded.

"I think you're right, partner," he agreed.

"Mr. Pilgrim, what about that secret conference in Chicago?" Reuben asked. "Does Mr. Pinkerton happen to know why they were meeting?"

"All he says is this: 'Agency files indicate banking firm of Hargrove and Son, Washington Street, Chicago, could be involved in massive land deals in Nebraska. Bank previously under surveillance. Currently investigating all possible connections.''

"But what kind of connection could there be between a gold mine, the Union Pacific Railroad, and a land deal in Nebraska, Mr. Pilgrim? I don't see it.''

"Neither do I, Reuben," Matt admitted. "But I know where I'm going to look. One of the last things Alex Haynes wrote about was the Pacific Railroad Act of 1862," he recalled. "The link we're looking for may be in that piece of legislation.''

"What do you mean?''

"There has to be a good reason why Alex Haynes locked these notes in a safe, Reuben," he answered. "I'm going to find out what that reason was.''

"Then I'll follow up on my bootprint lead, Mr. Pilgrim," he said.

"Right now, I want you to follow up on your sister.''

"But, Mr. Pilgrim—''

"Don't let her out of your sight until she's safe at home," he told him.

"Yes, sir.''

"Meanwhile, I'll wire William Pinkerton about that payroll train," he decided. "Whatever else is going on, the Agency must be told that somebody is going to try to rob that train tonight!''

"As soon as Alice is home, I'll execute a plan of my own,''

"Do what you have to do, Reuben. Just keep me informed.''

"Yes, sir, in the best Pinkerton tradition! Where are you going to be?''

Matt started off. "I'll be at the *Central City Register*, plowing through old newspapers.''

"Mr. Pilgrim?" Reuben called out.

He stopped and looked around. "What is it?"

"We are getting close, aren't we?"

Matt nodded. "Yes, we are," he confirmed. "Very close indeed."

14

At one o'clock that afternoon, Matt Pilgrim stepped wearily up to the registration desk at the Teller House and asked the clerk for his key. While Simmons was digging it out of the cubbyhole on the back wall, Matt leaned against the counter and massaged his brow.

"How's your day been, Mr. Pilgrim?" the clerk inquired.

"It's been a very unproductive day, Simmons," he replied. "I've spent all morning poring over records and newspapers."

"That would be pretty rough all right," he acknowledged, handing him the room key. "If that's really what you detectives did."

"What?"

"I've read about you Pinkerton men," he said wryly. "I know about all your ladies in distress, or what-have-you."

Matt smiled. "It's not usually like that, Simmons," he assured him.

"Oh, now, Mr. Pilgrim, I'm here a lot of hours during the day. And I keep my eyes open."

"I hate to disillusion you."

"Don't worry; you won't." He grinned and gestured behind the detective.

Matt automatically turned his head toward the stairs, where the lovely sight of Katherine Haynes descending the steps nearly took his breath away. She was dressed in high black boots and a gray riding skirt with a matching jacket and derby hat. For a moment, all he could do was stare at her. If possible, she looked even more beautiful now than she had the night before in the *Banner* office. He recalled fondly the soft, exciting touch of her lips and the warm arousing feel of her firm luscious breast in his hand.

"Good afternoon," she greeted him at the bottom of the stairs. "Are you ready?"

"Ready?" he puzzled.

Glancing at the desk clerk, she lowered her voice. "You haven't forgotten what we were going to do today?"

Now he remembered he had told her they would be spying on the Bonners today. "I think we'd better cancel our plans, Kate," he suggested.

"Oh, no, you don't," she countered. "You promised me I could help in the investigation!"

He grasped her elbow and led her away from the prying eyes and pricked ears of the desk clerk. "The situation's becoming too dangerous, Kate," he told her. "Why don't you go back upstairs—"

"I will do nothing of the kind."

"Katherine, things are going to start heating up soon. I don't want you to get hurt!"

"Then stand by my side and protect me, Matt," she suggested. "Come with me to the Bonner house."

"Katherine, how can I make you understand—the Bonners are outlaws! We can't just sally up to their front door and solicit information!"

"You underestimate them, Matt. I don't care if they are outlaws; they're still people. Down deep they're decent human beings."

Pilgrim sighed and shook his head in dejection. He wondered how he would ever convince her that outlaws were not decent human beings. How would he ever make her realize that a family like the Bonners could never fit into society? They were immoral misfits—hard, callous people with absolutely no regard for human dignity or life.

"You don't know who you're dealing with, Kate," he stated.

"Yes, I do. I've seen men like the Bonners all my life. They work like pitiful slaves in the factories until people like my father decide they're not needed anymore, and then they're thrown out. With no way of earning a living, they're forced to scavenge and steal—"

"Damn it, Kate, these are not the same kind of people! How can you forget what happened at the *Banner* office last night—"

"That man was drunk, Matthew."

"But he was acting like an outlaw! He was unpredictable. He was capable of doing anything to you!"

"But he didn't! So how can you say what he was capable of?"

Pilgrim blew through his teeth in exasperation. "And I thought we were making a little progress," he regretted.

She looked straight at him with large, pleading eyes. "Matt, you know I have to find out why Alex died. I can't sit around this hotel and wait for something to happen. I have to help you!"

"But not this way. Not now."

"All right, Mr. Pilgrim, if you won't go with me, I'll go alone!" she declared. Stepping briskly over to the desk, she summoned the clerk. "Is there a place in town where I can rent a buggy?"

Simmons nodded his head agreeably. "Couple of places, ma'am. If you want me to, I'll send a boy after one."

"Thank you."

He eyed her curiously. "I'd sure be careful where I was going though, ma'am," he warned her. "You know, these mountain passes are mighty treacherous."

"I'm sure they are," she acknowledged, looking at Matt. "But I imagine I can handle a buggy."

"I hope you can, Miss. I'll see if I can find my boy—"

"Never mind, Simmons." Matt strode over to the desk. "You don't have to send anybody. I'll be taking Miss Haynes myself."

He rubbed his palm over his bald head and grinned. "I figured you'd come to her rescue," he said. "A lady can always count on a Pinkerton man."

Katherine smiled at Matt. "Sometimes the lady wonders—"

"Let's go, Katherine." He placed his hand on the small of her back and pushed her gently toward the door.

Later, after crossing the tramway north of town, Matthew guided the covered buggy through Eureka Gulch, then up along the steep, rocky wagon path gouged years ago into the side of Winnebago Hill by hundreds of miners hauling down their gold into Central City. When he finally reached the cover of a small clump of yellow pines, he jumped down and offered Katherine a hand.

"That's Casto Hill down there." He pointed at the slope below them. On the bald, stony hill, the rickety, old shack occupied by the Bonners was quite conspicuous. The whole structure was leaning toward the town, and away from the mouth of the disused mine.

"Why don't we move closer?" Katherine asked.

Matt yielded enough to lead her forward to a pair of stunted spruce trees set between boulders on the incline. Then he announced that they were close enough.

"Now, Matt—" Katherine regarded him suspiciously— "you know that if you and Reuben Canfield were doing this, you'd be right down there on top of them. Wouldn't you?"

"Maybe," he allowed. "But this is as close as you and I are going to get," he informed her in a calm, steady voice.

"Well, it's not close enough, Matt—"

"Whoa—hold it, Kate!" He grabbed her arm and pulled her behind the trees. "Someone's coming up to the house!" They stood close to the spruce and watched a big, burly man in a wide Western hat jerk back the reins of his bridle, sling his leg over the rump of his spotted horse, and step down to the ground. "That looks like one of the gang that shot at us on the train."

She nodded. "It is. I recognize the horse."

Matt's eye followed the man as he encountered a younger man, in an ankle-length black coat, a few feet from the front porch. For a moment, they stood talking, until the larger man promptly stepped into the other one and rammed his fist between his legs.

Pilgrim couldn't help but cringe at the thought of the shocking pain of such a blow. Then, as the first man followed it with two quick slaps across the face and a punch to the stomach, he felt a strong impulse to spring to the smaller man's defense. But he held himself in check, having been taught in Chicago never to butt into the family feuds of a clan of outlaws.

"Why is he doing that!" Katherine grimaced.

Matt stirred again as a pair of still smaller men stormed out of the shack, eagerly engaged the larger man, then buckled under his command and retreated backwards to the porch. It was an eerie feeling to see, but not hear the words of the violent men on the hill below; it was like a strange, silent drama being acted out for their benefit.

"Take a look at your pitiful slaves. Kate," he said bitterly. "They're even vicious to each other."

"How do you know they are?" she callenged.

He was almost ready to throw up his hands. "Just look at them, Kate!" he told her. "Look at how they live!"

"We can't judge them if we don't even know what they're saying!" she pointed out stubbornly.

"We don't have to know," he insisted.

"Oh, Matt—"

"Wait!" he stopped her. "Look down there, under the roof of the porch, Kate. Can you see him? The man in the business suit!"

"Where?"

"He's in the doorway now, talking to the others. Now he's going inside."

After straining her eyes a while longer, Katherine shook her head. "I couldn't see him," she said. "Who was it?"

Matt stared at the mining shack for a minute. "I don't know who he was," he ruminated. "But I believe I know what he was."

"What?"

"That man must be our mastermind, Katherine. He has to be the one who's behind all of this. He's the one who's manipulating the Bonners!"

194

"If you think he is, shouldn't we go back to Central City and tell the law?"

"The law in Central City is the sheriff, Kate," he reminded. "How much good do you think telling Alvin Potts would do?"

"What do we do, then?" she asked.

"We do this: I'm going down for a closer look; you're going to stay here."

"Oh, no, I'm not."

"Katherine—"

"If you think I'm letting you slip away that easily, Matt Pilgrim, you're crazy. I'm going with you."

"Kate, we don't have time to argue about this!" he admonished.

"Then let's not argue. Let's go!"

"Stop!" a high-pitched voice behind them cried out. "You just make one more step, and I'll swear I'll shoot you dead!"

Matt and Katherine wheeled around to see a ragged young man in a torn and rumpled hat, which he'd pulled low and snug over his forehead, standing next to their buggy with a Springfield rifle pressed tight against his shoulder. The long black barrel of the gun heaved up and down as he breathed.

"Now take it easy," Matt held up a palm to caution him. "We don't mean any harm."

"Nobody's supposed to be up here," he said in a small, childlike voice. "He don't like anybody at all around this place."

"Who doesn't?" Matt asked.

He looked at him quizzically. "My brother Seth," he answered. His brown cow eyes moved over to Katherine.

"You shouldn't be here with him," he told her. "You're real pretty."

Matt took a step toward him. "You don't need that gun," he said. "We're not going to do anything."

"I do need it!" he said. "I need it to shoot the rabbits. Seth sends me out to shoot them. My brothers eat them every day."

Matt advanced a few more feet. It was fairly evident that this man had the mind of a child. Perhaps he could be talked out of holding them.

"Shouldn't you be doing that now?" he suggested. "I saw a rabbit down in Eureka Gulch a while ago. Right down there—"

"Stop!" he commanded, the barrel of the rifle trembling in his hands. "Don't move your hands anymore!" he warned. "Move it again, and I'll shoot you dead. I'll blow your head off!"

Matt drew up. "All right, I'm still. I won't budge."

"I don't want to shoot you, mister, but I will. I don't want to shoot the rabbits neither, but I do. Seth tells me to." He looked at Katherine out of the corner of his eye. "You shouldn't be with him," he said to her. "He's bad. You're real pretty and all, but he should be killed."

Katherine moved next to Matthew and quietly reached for his hand. He could feel it tremble in his fingers. "What's your name?" she asked the outlaw.

"What?" he breathed heavily.

"You do have a name, don't you?"

He pointed the rifle at her. "I have one," he told her. "It's Deke. My brothers send me for things. I get them, too. I went and got the paper for Clayton to read the other day. Seth said it was the right one."

"Deke," Katherine said softly. "Mr. Pilgrim and I

were out for a ride in the buggy. Don't you think that was all right to do? We certainly don't want to hurt you or your brothers.''

"You've got real pretty hair," he muttered behind the wobbly gun barrel.

"Thank you."

"My mother's hair is like yours. It's the same color. My mother's pretty, too."

"Where is your mother, Deke? Could I meet her?"

"My mother's dead. She had a bad disease, Clayton said. Seth wouldn't even let me look at her in the box." He lowered the rifle a few inches. "That's a good hat you're wearing," he said to her. "I like that hat. Only it ain't fit for a woman."

"Is isn't?"

"No. I bet you didn't know that's a man's hat you got on. Women's hats have feathers. I could wear one like that though. Clayton would be proud of me in that hat.

Katherine pulled her hand out of Matt's and reached up to her head to take off the hat. "Why don't I give it to you—''

"Kate!" Pilgrim exclaimed. "You can't bargain with an outlaw!"

But she persisted. "Deke," she said, taking off her hat. "I want to give you this as a present. But you've got to promise to take good care of it."

"You'd better stop!" He raised the rifle to eye-level. "Better not move!"

"I just want to give it to you, Deke," she explained.

"Put it down!"

"Can't I hand it to you?"

"Put it on the ground—right there!" he ordered.

After hesitating, Katherine nodded, stepped up, and set

the derby hat on top of a boulder. "There it is," she said tentatively.

"Now back up!" he yelled.

At the wave of the black barrel, they retreated out of the shelter of the spruce trees into the open. Matt shot a quick glance down at the Bonner cabin, then whispered to Katherine, "When they come out of that shack, they're going to see us. We have to do something to him, fast!"

"But he doesn't want to hurt us!" she whispered.

"You can't trust him."

"Matt, he's like a baby!"

Pilgrim braced himself as Deke circled the buggy, then emerged bareheaded from behind it with a cotton sack soiled with dirt and blood. Propping the Springfield clumsily against his hip, the outlaw moved slowly and suspiciously toward the hat. When he finally reached it, he quickly flicked it off the boulder, picked it up off the ground, and popped it on his head. Although it was too small for him, he grinned his approval. Then he drew a bleeding rabbit carcass out of the sack and spread it carefully on the rock.

"This one here's yours," he said to Katherine. "Take it!"

Repulsed at the sight of the dead animal, Katherine turned away and shook her head. "No," she said, gagging.

"Come get it," he urged her.

"Why don't you save it for your brothers, Deke?" she suggested.

He pulled the derby down lower on his head. " 'Cause that ain't their rabbit," he told her, his face flushing a bright crimson. "It's yours. I traded it to you."

After hesitating, Katherine decided to step tentatively

toward the boulder. "It's a very good trade, Deke," she complimented.

"Be careful, Kate," Matt stirred uncomfortably. "His trigger finger's moving!"

"He's harmless, Matt," she returned, moving closer to the rock.

"No outlaw is harmless!"

A few steps from the boulder, Deke suddenly thrust himself in front of her. Wearing a stupid grin, he reached out with his left hand and touched her hair.

"Feels real good," he commented as he stroked. Staring blankly at the strands of dark hair wrapped around his fingers, he muttered, "Feels soft, too."

"Deke, don't do that, please—" She tried to back away.

But he immediately squeezed a lock of her hair into his fist. "Don't!" he growled and twisted her neck to the side. "I don't want you to go!"

"Deke, you're hurting me!"

"Bonner!" Matt yelled. "Let her go!" He leaped toward him, but stopped dead in his tracks as the barrel of the rifle sprang up at him.

"I'll shoot you!" Bonner threatened.

"If you don't let her go—"

"Shut up!" he cried. "I'll kill her!"

"Deke, please—" Katherine pleaded.

Breathing rapidly, he yanked her head back and stared blankly at her with his large, brown eyes. "I don't want to hurt," he sobbed. "I don't like to hurt."

"Then let go of me, Deke!"

He glared at Matt for a minute, then released her. "There," he mumbled. "I'm sorry."

She rubbed the back of her neck and tried to catch her breath. "Thank you," she said to him.

"I'm sorry," he moaned. "I'm real sorry."

She looked at him with pity. "Why don't you move your gun away from Mr. Pilgrim?" she suggested.

Deke knitted his brow as he thought over the request. "That man ain't my friend," he declared. "I should kill him."

"Matt—" Katherine called to him.

But Pilgrim's attention was on the mining shack on Casto Hill. Below them, at the moment, three of the Bonners were spilling out of the house onto the front stoop. While the man in the dark suit lingered in the shadow of the porch, nearly out of sight, Seth Bonner stepped past his spotted horse, cocked back his wide hat, and pointed a finger up at Winnebago Hill.

"They've seen us, Kate," Matt announced. "And they're mounting up! We've got to get out of here!"

"No!" Deke warned. "I'll have to kill you!"

"Deke," Katherine entreated, "your brothers are coming after us. Please let us go."

"No," he refused. "Can't."

"But you don't understand—they want to hurt us!"

"No," he shook his head. "They want to hurt him."

"They'll do it to me, too, Deke—"

"No, they won't," he stated.

Matt took the opportunity to move a few feet closer. "Do you really believe you can stop your big brother, Deke?" he pressed.

"Seth won't never hurt me."

"But he'll make you hurt this woman." Pilgrim tried to keep his voice calm and steady. Out of the corner of his eye, he could see the Bonners on horseback, thundering up the hill, only a few minutes away.

"Seth is good to me," the outlaw protested.

"Deke, listen to that sound," Matt implored, stepping toward him. "That's your brothers coming up here with guns!"

Deke lowered the rifle of the barrel a foot or so. "Seth won't make me shoot her," he contended in a weak, quivering voice.

"Yes, he will, Deke," Matt argued. "He'll make you shoot her down like a rabbit."

"Uh-uh." He shook his head. "Not a woman!"

Matt's brain was working fast as he drew close to the boulder. He had to think of some way to move this man—quickly. "Just what do you think that is, Deke?" He pointed an accusing finger at the carcass. "That dead rabbit's a woman. Didn't Seth make you kill her?"

Deke's brown eyes shifted back and forth from the body on the rock to Pilgrim. "But I didn't know it was," he whined. "Nobody said so!"

"Come see for yourself, Deke. Look at her! Your brother made you kill a woman rabbit."

The outlaw's chin began to tremble as he stared at the carcass. "I didn't mean to hurt her," he said sadly. "But nobody said!"

"Deke," Matt told him after a moment. "We're out of time. We have to do something!"

"I wish I hadn't done it—"

"Deke!"

He planted the butt of the rifle on the ground. "I don't want Seth to tell me," he decided. "I'll make you get away." He suddenly sprang toward the buggy. "I'll take this," he announced.

"Wait a minute—" Matt called out.

But he was already clambering up to the seat and wrapping the reins around his hands. "One time Seth made the posse chase me in a buggy while my brothers got away," he said. "I did it real good."

"Do you mean you'll let your brothers chase you?" Matt asked.

"Yes," he said to him. "I remember how. All the posse did was laugh at me. It didn't hurt none."

With those words, he popped the reins on the rump of the horse and hastily pulled away.

"Come on, Kate," Pilgrim said, "we've got to get out of sight." Back at the two spruce trees, he nestled down beside her behind a bush. As soon as he heard the mighty rumble of horses nearby, he raised his head to see the band of outlaws bursting up from the slope to the path in a cloud of dust.

The burly man in the wide hat jerked the bit in his horse's teeth. "Where the hell are they?" he growled fiercely.

"Look there, Seth!" one of the others shouted. "There they go, headed down to Eureka Gulch!"

Seth Bonner pricked his pointed spurs in the horse's flanks. "Let's go, Bonners!" he hollered. Only a second later the whole gang was digging out after the single buggy speeding recklessly down the hill.

After the swirling dust had settled to earth, Matt raised up. "We have to move fast now, Kate," he told her. "They'll be catching up to him soon."

"Move where?"

"Down the hill," he answered. "We're going to search the cabin."

But she resisted him. "I don't think we should do that," she stated.

"We can't do it if we don't hurry."

"Matt, that old shack is their place," she argued. "We don't have the right to plunder through it!"

"Those men are outlaws, Kate!"

"I don't care who they are. I don't think we should break into people's houses just because we don't agree with the way they do things."

"Then we'll knock on the door first," he told her. "Come on."

"I don't want to do it!"

He started down the hill. "Then stay here," he advised. "I'll pick you up on my way back." He skidded and slid down the grade through twenty feet of loose rock before he heard her call to him. Grabbing the limb of a pine tree for balance, he turned around and waited while she struggled down the side of the mountain. When she reached him, he offered her a hand.

She politely turned it down. "I still don't approve of this," she told him.

He looked straight at her. "If we can find out who the mastermind is, Katherine," he explained, "we just might be able to save a few lives. Don't you think that matters more than the rights of Seth Bonner and his brothers?"

"I suppose so," she relented.

"It's part of the job, Kate," he said, moving down the slope. "And I'm going to do it."

Matt was pleased at how briskly they descended the hill to the Bonner shack. Katherine Haynes stubbornly managed to climb all the way to Casto Hill without taking his hand once. When they reached the flat path leading up to the old mining shack, though, she came to an abrupt stop.

She stood and waited for him while he proceeded straight to the porch.

With Kate at his back, the detective crept quietly across the boards to the closed glass window of the cabin. When he held his breath and looked in, he saw something that made a hard knot form in his throat. Sitting unnaturally erect and stiff at a cluttered dinner table in a room full of filth, was the slim, blond man he had chased away from the *Banner* office the night before. Matt berated himself for allowing a Bonner to slip so easily from his grasp.

He felt very uneasy about the way this man looked and acted. At the moment, he was stroking the long black barrel of a shiny new Colt .45 with the palm of his hand, caressing the metal as if it were the soft fur of a pet animal. With a smirk on his face, he popped out the cartridge cylinder, rubbed the cases of each of the six bullets with his finger tips then gave the cylinder a spin.

At the instant Katherine called out Matthew's name, Bonner immediately clicked the cylinder back into his revolver, slapped his chair to the floor, and leaped up. With the pistol poised in front of his belly, he lunged for the door, groping with his left hand for the latch.

Pilgrim's only thought at this moment was to prevent the outlaw from shooting Katherine. he pulled his arms in to his chest, lowered his shoulder, and thrust himself with great abandon through the windowpanes. As he struck the pine wood boards of the cabin with a crack, he had to shield his eyes with the crook of his arm as a jagged sheet of glass fell from the window and shattered near his face.

A second later he looked up to see the threatening black barrel of Bonner's big revolver. Then he heard Katherine again.

''Matt!'' she was crying as she raced toward the shack.

"Kate!" Matt hollered, for the outlaw's benefit. "Stay with the others! They have him covered!"

As soon as Bonner heard those words, he whipped open the door, bolted through it, and scampered away.

"Matt!" Katherine shrieked when she burst into the cabin and saw him on the floor.

"I'm all right," he protested, pushing himself up from the glass.

"No, you're not. You're bleeding!" She quickly took his left hand. "Just look at this cut! Did they teach you to do this at the Pinkerton Agency?"

"I don't know. It never came up."

"I don't wonder." She popped the handkerchief out of his coat pocket and started wrapping it carefully around the wound. "You're lucky that glass didn't slice off your hand, Matthew Pilgrim," she stated.

"No, I'm lucky the man I broke in on was a coward," he corrected. "He had me dead in his sights and couldn't pull the trigger."

"I don't call it cowardly to spare a human life," she differed. "I would say it's humane."

He decided not to argue with her. After she finished wrapping his hand, he proceeded to search the place. The simple task of looking into a couple of nail kegs, a torn carpetbag, an old trunk, and a dresser in the bedroom became a tough chore in the dirt, debris, and stench of the house. Strewn about the floor were bits and pieces of uncooked and rotting animal flesh, moulded chunks of bread, and dried pools of eaten, but undigested food. In the corners of the shack, Matt could even smell the strong, rank odor of human waste.

"How could anybody live like this, Matt?" Katherine asked, clinging close to the open window.

He kicked aside a pile of chicken feathers. "I've been telling you they don't live the way we do, Kate," he said.

"I know, but this. . . ." She covered her mouth and nose with the palm of her hand.

"This is the life of an outlaw," he said, searching the fireplace for loose bricks. "At least," he added, "that's how they described it in Chicago."

She lowered her hand and looked at him with curiosity. "You don't mean you've never even seen an outlaw's hideout!"

"Where would I see one, Kate? This is my first case as a detective."

"It's what!"

He gave up on the fireplace. "You won't tell Reuben that, will you?" he asked her. "He'd never forgive me."

"Well, I'm not sure I will either. All this time I thought I was adjusting myself to a man who was a Pinkerton detective to the core—"

"And you were only adjusting yourself to a man—" At the rumbling sound of approaching horses, Matt instantly snatched hold of Katherine's wrist and darted for the bedroom. After struggling with the window a minute, he finally succeeded in throwing it up, then boosting her up through the opening. "Let's head for the mine," he said as he crawled out behind her.

They were safely inside the mouth of the cave when the Bonners stormed up to the cabin, leading the rented buggy. Katherine gripped his hand as Seth Bonner, scowling with anger and frustration, slid off his horse and lumbered back to the buggy. With a loud grunt, the huge man plunged his fist inside the carriage and jerked out the unconscious body of his brother Deke. Displaying incredible strength, he lifted the body over his head and dashed it to the ground with a thump so loud it seemed to echo in the bare hills.

"Oh, Matt—" Katherine gasped.

"Shhh." He held her back out of sight. But he knew what she was feeling. Even though they were a hundred feet away, they could easily see that Deke had been severely beaten. His legs were curled back and twisted under his thighs, his arms were limp, and his face and hair were saturated with blood.

Gripping Katherine's hand tightly, Pilgrim recoiled at the sight of Seth Bonner stalking over to Deke, dropping down on his knees beside him, and yanking him up roughly by the hair. "Who were they?" he demanded. "Tell me!"

"He can't even talk now, Seth," one of the twins asserted. "You beat him good."

Seth rattled Deke's head violently in his big hands. "Moron," he sneered, then slammed him to the ground. As he rose to his feet, he pointed at the others. "Leave this piece of dirt alone," he ordered coldly. "I don't want nobody touching Deke till I say so."

"We won't, Seth," the other twin replied quickly.

After glowering at them for a long time, Seth turned his back and headed for the cabin. He banged around inside for a minute, then came back out. "All right, the momma's boy's gone," he roared. "Go find him."

The twins stole a look at each other. "But we're hungry, Seth—"

"I told you to go find him! And that don't mean tomorrow!"

While the twins hurried to their horses, the Bonner in black lingered over the body on the ground. "What do we do with Deke?" he asked Seth.

"We let the bastard rot, Thomas."

His brother nodded. " 'There is treachery, O Ahaziah,' " he quoted, then mounted his horse and rode away with the others.

Matt and Katherine stood silent in the mouth of the cave, staring at the unconscious body of Deke Bonner. Matt felt numbed by what he had just witnessed. Then his stomach wrenched with a sick, empty feeling as he watched the injured outlaw stretch out his arms and start to drag himself like a wounded snake across the dusty ground to the water trough. At that moment, he decided he had seen enough.

"I'm going out there, Kate," he announced.

"But Seth is still in the house—"

"Maybe he won't look out."

"And the others will be back soon."

"I don't care. After what Deke did for us, I can't just let him lie there!"

Without another word, Matt broke out of the mine and marched straight for the water trough. With Katherine following close behind, he crossed the flat, fully exposed to anyone in the cabin or on the hills around the mine. At any moment he expected Seth Bonner to smash through the door of the shack and pounce on them. After what seemed forever, they reached the water trough undetected.

"Oh, Matt—look at him!" Katherine cried. Instantly, she lifted her skirt, ripped off a piece of her petticoat, formed it into a pad, and dipped it into the water. Dropping to her knees, she raised the outlaw's head, laid it in her lap, and began gently absorbing the blood away from his battered face. "How could anybody do this!" she gasped.

Pilgrim knelt down beside them. "Deke?" he said to him, but got no response.

"Is he going to die, Matt?" Katherine fretted. "He's bleeding so."

"The blood's coming from his face, Kate," he assured her. "I don't think anything is broken." Leaning closer to the outlaw, he said, "Deke? Can you hear me?"

Bonner painfully made a slit between his swollen eyelids and nodded his head slightly. "I didn't tell Seth," he muttered thickly. "Never told him."

"Deke, how badly are you hurt?" Matt exacted.

He paid no attention, as he was smiling with a grimace at Katherine. "I didn't tell him," he said proudly. "I swear."

"I know you didn't," she comforted him. "You did fine, Deke. You did the right thing."

Matt made sure to keep the front door of the cabin in view as he talked to Bonner. "Deke, we have to hurry, because your brothers will be coming back any minute," he told him. "We're going to put you into the buggy."

"No," he groaned and writhed. "Don't do that!"

"Be still, Deke," Katherine told him. "Let us help you!"

"Nobody helps me," he insisted.

"But you can't just lie there! You're in pain!"

"Leave me alone!" He twisted his bloody face in agony. "Want you to go!"

Matt stirred uncomfortably. They had been exposed on the flat for a long time now. "Deke," he said, "we can take you to a doctor in Central City."

"Can't," he declared. "I'm staying home with my brothers."

"Why—"

"Momma told me to!" he whined. "She told me to stay with Seth. I have to stay with Seth!"

Katherine carefully touched a corner of the damp cloth to a swollen bag of flesh under his eye. "But Seth is a bad man, Deke," she said, tears coming to her eyes. "Look at what he did to you!"

"Momma told me to stay with my family," he asserted firmly. "I have to."

"Matt?" She looked pleadingly to the detective. "Can't we do *something* for him?"

Pilgrim stood up. "The best thing we can do for him now is to make sure Seth Bonner doesn't see us out here with him." he replied. "Let's you and I get into that buggy and go, Kate—right now!"

Kathering lingered a moment, wiped a trickle of blood off Bonner's cheek, then eased his head to the ground. On her feet again, she looked down at him and cried.

"He's so defenseless, Matt," she said pitifully.

Matt hesitated while Deke Bonner struggled to prop himself against the trough. When he finally succeeded, the detective quickly checked the cabin again. The closed door at the back of the porch looked like a monstrous keg of black powder, about to explode. Insistently, he hauled Katherine Haynes away from Deke and toward the buggy.

At the vehicle, she stalled. "Do we have to leave him like this?" she asked sadly.

"Yes, Kate." He lifted her into the carriage. "We don't have any choice."

"Seth Bonner's an inhuman monster," she declared as he climbed up.

"Seth Bonner will get what he deserves, Kate," Matt said, popping the reins. After a final glance at the rickety, old shack standing silently near the mouth of the mining cave, he added another vow as they turned toward Central City: "Every one of them will get what he deserves."

15

At dusk, Matt stopped at the lobby desk of the Teller House to leave a message. "I'm writing a note for Sheriff Potts," he explained to Simmons as he scribbled on the paper. "I stopped by his office a few minutes ago, but he was gone. Would you see that he gets the message, please?"

"Of course," the bald clerk responded politely. While Matt wrote, he showed Katherine a toothy, admiring smile, then cast his curious eye on the detective's bloody bandage. "What happened to your hand, Mr. Pilgrim?" he asked.

Ignoring him, Matt finished the note. In it he told Potts that he was convinced the Bonners were going to rob the payroll train tonight. He recommended strongly that the sheriff take a posse out to the tracks to protect it. He ended with a promise to meet later in the evening.

"I'm sorry, what were you saying?" he responded to Simmons.

"I was saying your hand looks hurt," he prompted him.

"It feels worse than it looks." He stuffed the note into an envelope and sealed it.

"I would say that hand of yours is the result of another adventure, Mr. Pilgrim?" he deduced.

"It's the result of putting it where I shouldn't have, Mr. Simmons." he replied, handing him the envelope.

"Yes, sir," the clerk said blandly.

Matt could feel Simmons' interested eyes glued to his back as he escorted Kathering Haynes up the steps. At the door to her room a few minutes later, he took the key from her and clicked open the lock. When she hesitated in the doorway, he looked straight at her.

"May I come in?" he asked.

She searched his eyes for a moment. "There is something I would like to say to you," she said nervously.

Unhesitantly, he stepped into the room. "I have a confession to make, too," he admitted. Making a quick survey of the place, he noted that while this room was identical to his in color and furnishings, it felt very feminine. He was stimulated by a light, powdery fragrance hovering in the air around him.

Katherine moved restlessly through the room to the window, then turned to face him. "I've been thinking about this all the way back," she began. Fidgeting with the collar of her blouse, she collected her thoughts a minute. "I wanted to say you were right about what you said on the train, Matt," she offered after a time. "Western outlaws are not at all like the factory workers back home. And they don't even resemble those romantic vagabonds in dime novels."

Listening with great interest, Matt leaned back against the dresser. "What led you to this conclusion?" he asked.

"Seth Bonner," she answered soberly. "That family's vicious, Matt. Seth almost killed Deke, and the others didn't even lift a finger to stop him!"

Pilgrim looked at her sympathetically. It was clear she was very disturbed by what she had seen at the Bonners' shack. "I wanted to confess that it was you who were right," he said.

"Me?"

"Yes. I realize now that I've been narrow-minded about these outlaws. I guess that believing they were all bad was a convenient way of dealing with them. But after meeting Deke Bonner, I know I was wrong. They are people, Kate, just as you said. Naturally, if they break the law, they ought to be punished, but sometimes the law itself may not be just. Our only hope is to always remember that a law-breaker is a human being."

Katherine was visibly moved by his words. "Do you really feel that way, Matt?" she asked.

"Yes, I do." He stepped toward her. "But that's not all I feel, Kate."

After gazing into his eyes for a moment, she pressed her palm to her chest. "Maybe you'd better go now," she suggested.

But he kept moving. "I don't want to go," he told her. "I don't ever want to go."

"Matt, you promised you'd give me time!"

"I promised that last night. I've spent an eternity since then."

"Do you think I haven't?" she said, turning her back. "But this can't be the right time—"

Pilgrim grabbed her arm and spun her around. "I want you to tell me how you feel, Kate." He pulled her to his chest and held her. The touch of her bosom against his chest sent a shock of desire through him. "I have to know!"

"How can I know? Everything's happening so fast—"

"Why does it matter how fast it happens? My God, if I had known you all my life, I couldn't care for you any more than I do right now, this very minute. I love you, Kate. I will always love you!''

"Matt, let me go, please."

"Oh, Kate," he held her closer. "I will never let you go. Never!"

She raised her hand to his cheek. "What on earth am I going to do with you?" she cried. "I'm not sure I can handle this."

"I want you, Kate," he insisted.

She didn't resist him as he pulled her close and kissed her. The blood in his veins pumped faster the moment he felt her soft, moist lips press hard against his. His breathing quickened as he touched his tongue to hers. Then suddenly, abruptly, she pushed away.

"Matt—"

"Damn, Kate!"

"I'm sorry!" she said loudly and wriggled out of his embrace. Near the window again, she turned and faced him. "I don't know what to say," she muttered softly.

"Do you want me to leave, Kate?" he asked.

"Yes," she answered. But the moment he moved away, she blurted, "No!"

He waited, looking at her with patience. "Exactly what do you want, Kate?" he asked her seriously.

She stared through the windowpanes at the sky darkening around the hills. A flash of lightning that illuminated a bank of gray moving clouds was followed seconds later by a low rumble of thunder crossing in the heavens.

"I think it's going to rain," she observed flatly.

"Kate—"

"Matt, it's so scary out there. Mines are caving in; people are being killed; angry men like the Bonners are running around loose—and nobody seems to be able to do

216

anything about it. I didn't expect anything like this when I came out here. All I wanted to do was find out about Alex.''

"We'll find out about him, I promise you."

"But all of this is so upsetting. I'm still shaking from that horrible business with Deke Bonner."

He came to her and wrapped his arms around her. "It doesn't do any good to think about it now," he told her.

"I can't help it, Matt. I have to say I asked for it. I insisted on going out there. But when I saw what Seth Bonner had done to poor Deke—''

"Stop it, Kate."

"Matt, I keep seeing Alex's wrecked office, and that dead body from the mine, and Deke Bonner's bloody face. I'm afraid.''

"You don't have to be afraid, Kate." He hugged her tightly. "Nothing will happen to you as long as I'm here. I'll stay with you as long as you want me to."

She looked at him with tears in her eyes. "I feel so inept, falling apart like this," she confessed. "I guess it's been building up ever since I got here."

"You don't have to worry about it now, Kate. Everything is going to be fine."

"Is it?"

"Yes. I promise you."

"Oh, Matt—''

"Kate, I love you so much."

He pressed his eager lips to hers and kissed her tenderly. When he felt her bosom begin to rise and fall against him, he showered her lips and cheeks and eyes with harder, hungrier kisses that teased his urgent passions and made his body ache to touch her. Sucking in the hot breaths of air brushing his face, Pilgrim boldly opened the collar of her blouse and started loosening the buttons. In a daze, he thrust his hand between the folds of cloth and clasped one of her soft, warm breasts in his fingers. His breath nearly left his body when he felt the hardness of the erect nipple rubbing against the skin of his palms.

Without a word, he pulled away his hand, lifted Katherine up into his arms, and carried her to the bed. Easing down beside her on the mattress, he seized a handful of dark curls as he made their lips come together again. Anxiously he stroked and caressed every inch of her body he could reach. The firm, luscious curves of her hips, and the tight, easy slope of her legs tantalized and excited him, until he could stand it no longer.

"Kate—" he panted.

"Don't stop, Matt," she pleaded. "Please don't stop!"

Spurred by her words, he pulled open her blouse and began deliriously covering her neck and chest with kisses. Suddenly Katherine unfastened something behind her back, freeing her breasts. Consumed by a fury of desire, Matthew buried his face in her naked bosom.

He couldn't even remember later how they managed to get out of their clothes. In the thrilling madness of the moment, somehow the skirt and blouse and petticoat and trousers seemed to fly away from their bodies on their own. Soon he found himself warmly surrounded by the lovely, naked arms of the most desirable woman he had ever known. But the closeness of her body was torturing him. He had to make love to her, or die.

As hard as it was to control his surging emotions, Pilgrim forced himself to move slowly and gently into her, until he was sure her craving was as overwhelming as his. Then they moved together in a passionate, throbbing rhythm, deliberately at first, then rapidly, rising and falling until they reached a final grand thrust that left them both exhausted and content.

For a long time afterwards, they lay holding hands beneath a thick layer of quilts, staring contentedly at the ceiling. Although his body was warm and content next to hers in bed, Matt could see his breath condensing like puffs of smoke in the cool, darkened room.

"You're being awfully quiet, Kate," he observed, speaking for the first time since they had made love. "Are you still afraid?"

"I'm confused, Matt," she replied.

"Confused about what?" He faced her.

"Don't you realize what I'm doing, lying in bed with you? A week ago I didn't even know you!"

He squeezed her hand lovingly. "My father used to say, if God can make a world in a week, a man ought to be able to make a decision in a couple of days. And I've made mine."

"What is it?"

He touched her cheek softly. "I want to marry you, Kate," he said. "I want us to always be together."

Although he expected an immediate response, he got nothing but silence. Then she pulled away her hand and moved.

Rolling to the edge of the mattress, she quickly slid off and moved behind the dressing screen. A while later, she came out from behind the shield, tying the sash of a bone-colored silk robe, around her waist.

"It's so cold in here," she complained, wrapping her arms around her chest.

Matthew raised himself up against the headboard. "What is it, Kate?" he asked. "What's wrong?"

"I don't know," she replied in a quivering voice. "I'm so cold all of a sudden. It feels so unsafe here!"

"Why don't you come back to bed?" he suggested.

"No" she declined with a nervous laugh. "I don't think we should do that again."

"I had the impression you enjoyed it."

"I did, Matt. It was wonderful. That's what's wrong with it. It's too much too soon. Oh, I thought I was such a big girl, coming out West all by myself, but I find I can't really deal with it. I haven't even let myself consider marriage. And there's so much about it to consider."

"Such as what?"

"Such as my parents, Matt. They don't even know you exist."

"We'll inform them. You and I will team up against them, and we'll win them over."

She paused. "Then there is Henry Aldrich," she added. "Somehow or other he's gotten the idea that I'm going to marry him."

"Well, he's wrong."

"But Father sent me to him, Matt," she argued.

"I don't care. I can talk to Father. You just forget Aldrich!"

As soon as she turned her back to gaze out the window again, Pilgrim got out of bed and put on his clothes in the cool room. After waiting for her to consider the situation, he went to her. Placing both his hands on her shoulders, he gently turned her around.

"Why don't you tell me the real problem, Kate?" he said seriously. "Did I assume too much? Do you care for me less than I thought?"

"Oh, Matt, no! I love you! You know I wouldn't have done this if I hadn't!"

"Then what is it?"

"It's this kind of life," she confessed. "I don't know if I would be able to cope with all this violence and misery—and uncertainty. I don't know if I could be the wife of a detective."

"I see."

"Matt, please understand."

"I do, Katherine," he assured her. "I know you. You're beautiful, intelligent, and courageous. You have fire in you. You don't belong in a stuffy carriage, riding up and down Washington Street. You belong here, with me. I need you, Kate. We need each other!"

"No, don't, please." She backed away.

"I'm sorry if I forced you—"

"You didn't force me!" she cut him off. "I wanted to do it! But now I want you to go."

He gritted his teeth. "All right," he said, "I will."

She looked longingly at him. "Matt, please don't be angry," she pleaded.

"I'm trying very hard not to be, Kate."

"I just need time to think—alone."

"Then take it," he said as he headed for the door. "Take all the time you need."

"Matt—"

He paused at the door to look back. "I mean it this time," he told her. "I want you to be sure about this. Absolutely sure," he added, stepping through the doorway into the hall. Hesitating a moment for a word that never came, Matt swallowed hard, shook his head dejectedly, and proceeded slowly down the corridor to his room.

16

At that moment, Clayton Bonner planted his boots in the dry dust in front of the mining shack, with the heel of his hand resting uneasily on the butt of his new Colt .45 pistol. While he watched his four brothers hauling the kegs of black powder down from the mine, he had to flinch under a bolt of lightning that zigzagged briskly across the sky and brightened the hills around him. In that splash of light, he had a clear shot at the four of them. He could have murdered every one with two bullets left in the cylinder of his Colt. But, as usual, he let the opportunity pass him by.

While Clayton drew closer into the glow of the torch stuck in the ground near the hitching post, Seth dropped his keg to the ground with a grunt. Noticing Clayton coming to a stop twenty feet away, he let out a disdainful laugh. "You planning to use that gun on me, little sister?" he taunted. "Or are you just going to stand there scratching your paw with it?"

"I want to go on the robbery, Seth," he asserted.

"Well, you can want all day long," he countered, "but that's one thing you won't ever do."

"But why do I have to stay? Why do Thomas and the twins get to go?"

"Thomas!" Seth bellowed up to the mine. "Stop gaping at that keg. It won't bite you. Pick it up and come on!"

"Seth!" Clayton pressed. "I've got to go!"

The older brother looked at him. "I reckon the Bonners can rob a train without a momma's boy to show us how," Seth declared. "You just do your job, Clay, and we'll do ours."

"But I don't have a job!" he cried. "You won't let me do anything! I can ride and shoot, too. I can do anything my brothers can do!"

Seth shot a wad of spit in Clay's direction. "All you ever learned was how to parade around the house in Momma's drawers," he said contemptuously.

"I did not! You take that back!" he demanded, his hand trembling over the handle of the .45.

"I'm the head of this family, Clay," he reminded. "I don't have to take nothing back."

"Maybe what I've got in this holster says otherwise, Seth," he asserted boldly.

"Why don't you go play with your new gun somewhere else," he growled impatiently. "I've got work to do."

"You'd better take me seriously this time, Seth," he warned. "I know how to use this pistol!"

"Maybe, but you can't use it, Clay. You see, you got no guts. You're not a man; you're a piece of tripe." He turned toward Thomas Bonner, who was struggling with a keg of black powder toward the pack horse. On the side of the barrel in white letters were the words: "No. 4, Coarse Grain. XXX. Miller's Mercantile, Central City."

"You've got no right to talk to me that way, Seth," Clayton accused. "No body does!"

Seth ignored him. "Come on, Thomas," he told the other brother. "Tie the keg on the horse. We don't have all night. We've got to be there and set this robbery up right. According to instructions."

Thomas hesitated, puffing. "Why don't you make Clayton pick it up, Seth?" he suggested. "He never does any hard work."

"That's because *Clayton* is a little girl, Thomas. You ever see a little girl lift up a heavy keg of black powder?"

"Seth!" Clayton hollered. Slowly and deliberately, he moved forward. He rested the heel of his right hand on the belt of his holster and wiggled his fingers menacingly over the handle of his gun. "That's the last insult I'm going to take!"

Seth kept his eye on Thomas. "What are you waiting for, preacher?" he groused. "I said, load it up!"

"Seth!" Clayton called.

"You heard me, Thomas."

But Thomas declined, choosing instead to back sharply away from the scene, leaving it to the other two men. Irritated and disgusted with the whole lot, Seth Bonner let out a sigh, and turned to face his younger brother.

"You're scaring the chickens away, Clay," he told him. "And you're making me mad."

Clayton came to a stop. "You're wearing your gun, Seth," he said. "Use it!"

Seth turned up his nose and shook his head. "I never shoot females, Clay."

"I told you to draw, Seth!"

"You stupid, little—do you want more of what you had

225

the other night? Do you want some of what Deke had this afternoon?''

"Deke and I are having no more of that, Seth. All that's over. I'm going to kill you."

Seth chuckled at that. "How do you figure you're going to do that, little sister?" he teased. "You going to kill me with flowers?"

"No, with this," he patted the gun. "I'm going to shoot you right between the legs, Seth."

"Is that so? Well, go right ahead," he challenged, spreading his legs apart. "Do it, *Clayton*. Shoot a man and feel good about it, why don't you?"

"I will—"

Seth started walking toward him with his legs apart, and his pelvis thrust forward. "Here it is, big boy. I'm giving you a good clear shot at it. Take out that new gun of yours and give it to me!"

"Stay where you are!"

But Seth kept staggering ahead. "If you touch that gun, Clay, you ain't never leaving that house again. Do you hear me? I'm giving you a choice. Come on, little sister. Do it! Shoot me, or shut up. Or didn't sweet little Ma show you how to do that?"

"You're a bastard!" Clayton shrieked.

"And you're a coward!" His brother laughed.

"Don't call me that, Seth. I'm warning you!"

The other brother inched closer. "Let me tell you something, Clay," he said coldly. "You've already shot at me once. If you do it again, you'd better make it count."

Clayton curled his unsteady fingers around the bone handle of the pistol, snapped the gun out of the holster and pointed the barrel. "Seth," he addressed him in a shaky voice. "I refuse to be pushed around anymore. If you take one more step, I'll cut you down!"

Seth defiantly stretched out his leg and made an exaggerated step. "Here's one more step," he sneered. "Cut away!"

"Seth—"

"Here's another one," he said, advancing. "I don't hear no gun going off."

"Better look out, Seth," Thomas cautioned. "His hand's shaking!"

But the older brother blithely kept moving. "Give me that gun," he demanded. "You're not going to use it."

"This time I am, Seth," he threatened in a fluttery voice.

"You gutless snake in the grass!" he growled fiercely. With a loud grunt, he sprang toward Clayton, whipped the pistol out of his trembling fist, and hurled the weapon as far as he could, up the hill. Then he crooked his arm around Clayton's neck and slammed his head against his hip. "Come inside, little girl," he snarled. "I'm going to take care of you." While he dragged Clayton struggling and groaning toward the shack, he directed Thomas to bring a rope.

Mick and Buck sent up a round of cheers at the command. "Yaay, Seth!" they hollered. "Give it to him, Seth! Give Clayton a necktie. He needs a necktie!"

"Tie his hands and feet, Seth!" Thomas urged. "Hang him by his heels before the Lord!"

Clayton could almost feel his neck crack as the big, burly man hauled him across the porch into the cabin and slung him to the floor. He landed on his shoulder and skidded against the wall, next to where Deke was crouching in the corner, holding his knees against his chest.

"You're never going to leave this house again," Seth huffed as he reached down, yanked him up, and heaved him up on the table. Snatching the rope away from Thomas, he looped it around the wrists, wrapped it around the table three times, then spread his ankles and bound them to the legs of the table.

"Let me up!" Clayton pleaded. He squirmed against the piles of plates and food under his back. "If you let me up, I'll go, Seth. And I won't ever come back!"

He wiped his lips with his sleeve. "The Bonners stick together," he muttered.

"But I don't want to be in this family, Seth. And you don't want me any, either."

"Shut up. I'll deal with you later. All right, Bonners," he urged the others, "Let's go. We got a train to stop."

"Seth, don't leave me like this!"

The elder Bonner paused at the door for one last warning. "If you're not on that table when I get back," he said, "I'll be coming after you, Clay. I don't care where you are; I'll hunt you down and break that yellow back of yours like a stick of firewood." With those words, uttered in a chilling, matter-of-fact voice, Seth Bonner stormed out of the cabin and headed for the horses.

When Clayton heard the sounds of retreating hoofbeats in the dirt, he twisted his wrists and ankles to slither free. But it was no use; the ropes were too tight. Sickened by the damp touch of the morsels of half-eaten rabbit and squirrel against his back and the nauseating smell of human filth all around him, he called out to his last remaining brother.

"What you want, Clayton?" Deke replied from his corner.

"What do you think I want? I swear, that newspaper was right, Deke; you are moronic."

"I still don't know what that means."

"It means you should get me loose from here!"

"Can't. Seth did it."

"Listen to me, Deke. I've got to get away. Do you understand? I can't be here when Seth gets back!"

He could hear the other Bonner rise up and stumble over to the table. Then he saw his battered, homely face peering down at him. Deke looked utterly idiotic to Clayton. Why, he wondered, hadn't his mother drowned him when she realized what he was going to be?

"Where you going, Clayton?" Deke asked in a forlorn voice.

"I'm going off with a woman, Deke. I've got a lot of money—over \$250.00. If you'll cut me loose, I'll give you some."

He shook his head. "Don't want it," he replied.

"Come on. Don't be stupid, Deke!"

"You ain't supposed to go," he said sadly. "Momma said to stay together."

Clayton tugged uselessly at the ropes. "Those fools left me lying in their garbage! Somebody will pay for this!"

"You want some water, Clayton?"

"No, I don't want any water! I want to get off this filthy table. Can't you understand simple words? I'm willing to pay you money!"

He shook his head. "I do what Seth says."

"That's a lie, Deke," he challenged. "He beat you up because you didn't do what he told you."

"Uh-uh. Because of that woman."

"What woman?"

"The woman with the brown hair, Clayton. Seth was going to make me shoot her. But I didn't. I showed him. I saved her."

Clayton's mind was stimulated by that confession. Within seconds he had conceived a plan. It was pathetic, he reflected, how easily an educated man could outwit a defective mass of human flesh like Deke Bonner.

"Deke, that's what I want to do now," he solicited. "I want to save that woman from Seth. Just like you did."

Deke's big brown eyes widened at that. "Which woman, Clayton?"

"The woman with the brown hair, stupid. That's why Seth tied me up. They're going to hurt her."

"Uh-uh," he shook his head. "My brothers are going to rob the train."

"Didn't they tell you they're going to blow it up, Deke?" he asked.

He looked puzzled. "Yes."

"That's because *she's* on it," he lied.

"No!"

"I've got to get loose and find my gun. It's the only way to keep them from hurting that woman!"

Deke looked down at him very seriously, with his thin lips pressed tightly together over his trembling chin. "I liked her," he said weakly. "She was real good to me." After a minute, he nodded. "You should help her, Clayton," he said.

"Yes, I will, Deke. Now hurry up!"

Obediently, he rummaged through the debris on the table until he discerned a knife sticking out of a piece of bread. After he sawed a section of the rope in two, he stepped back up. "Did I do right?" he asked.

"Go find my gun," Clayton loosened the rope from his wrist. "Seth threw it toward Winnebago Hill."

"I can't shoot anything else, Clayton. I killed a woman rabbit."

230

"Who asked you to? Just go find my Colt!"

While Deke was limping out of the cabin into the darkness, Clayton brushed off the particles of the greasy food from his arms and back. With a sneer of disgust, he planted his feet against the edge of the table and shoved it over, scattering food, plates, knives, and forks across the floor. Toppling the table felt so good, he decided to do more. He lifted a chair above his head and smashed it into a dozen splintered pieces against the wall.

Then he had an idea. He knew how he could get back at Seth for tearing up his mother's picture. He dashed briskly into the bedroom, snatched up the quilts and bedrolls, lugged them into the main room, and tossed them on the floor. Then, panting with excitement, he grabbed a stick of firewood and raked every single coal out of the fireplace to the floor. Minutes later, he was dumping anything that would burn on the smoldering fire.

Clayton had to grin as a flame popped up and caught the pile on fire. Before long, the flames were spreading rapidly across the cabin floor. The sight of the dismal old shack starting to burn pleased him enormously. He regretted only that his brothers wouldn't be burning with it.

Outside, in front of the porch, he lingered to watch the crackling flames whoosh up the walls and snap across the shingles of the cabin. He had never seen such a satisfying sight as that mining shack of the Bonners being gutted and consumed by those bright orange flames that popped and spit into the cloudy sky.

Deke came running, holding the Colt .45 awkwardly by the barrel. "What happened to it, Clayton!" he huffed, marveling at the fire. "Why's our house burning like that?"

"Because I'm leaving it, that's why," he replied, taking

231

the pistol from him. He slammed the weapon into the scabbard and strode toward the bay mare at the hitching post.

"Where you headed now, Clayton?" Deke asked.

He untied the reins, pointed the toe of his boot into the stirrup, and mounted the horse. "I'm going to take my woman south," he stated.

He nodded. "She was real good to me."

"Not that woman, Deke. I don't even know that one."

Deke grabbed the reins excitedly. "Wait! You said you'd help her."

"Get away!" He kicked at him.

"You said, Clayton!" He reached up for the saddle horn.

"Let go of that, stupid!"

"But you—"

Abruptly, Clayton dug his spurs into the mare's flanks. The horse lunged forward and broke into a fast gallop, with Deke hanging on to the saddle horn, dragging his feet in the dirt.

"Let go!" Clayton yelled as he pounded on his clasping fingers.

"No! He's going to hurt her!"

"Damn you!" While Clayton hammered furiously at the fingers on the horn, he accidentally reined the mare sharply to the left, in the direction of a jagged boulder, a yard off the path. The horse stumbled, then lunged ahead and skimmed the rock, just as Deke's fingers slipped away from the saddle. Staggering helplessly forward, he rammed straight into the boulder with his head. Clayton could hear the loud crack of the skull and Deke's muffled groan, but he couldn't see the splattering of his blood against the stone.

It didn't matter. Once quick glance back at his idiot brother lying dead on the ground, in front of the burning shack, was enough for him. Soon he would be leaving this place and this family forever. So be it.

There was still some unfinished business he needed to attend to, however, before he could take Billie Simms away. He was still seething with the thought of the Canfield girl. That feeble little cripple had looked down on him, as if he were weak and cowardly. Well, before he left this town, he would show her exactly what kind of man Clayton Bonner was. Before this night was over, that snooty little Alice Canfield would be licking the dust off his boots.

Lightning flashed and great peals of thunder rumbled across the dark sky as Clayton tied his horse to the hitching rail on Pine Street and stole to the side of the Canfield house. He peeked in the window and saw the father pacing back and forth in front of the fireplace, checking his watch. A moment later, the Canfield girl and her red-headed brother came past the father to the porch. Clayton sidled along the wall to hear what they were saying.

"Maybe I shouldn't go, after all, Alice," he said dubiously.

"Oh, don't be silly, Reuben. I'll be all right. Daddy's here."

"But he'll be going to that miner's meeting at eight."

"He'll only be gone for a half-hour or so," she pointed out. "What could happen in a half-hour?"

Reuben gazed up at the threatening sky. "I have a feeling this is going to be a bad night," he predicted.

"I tell you, I'll be fine, Reuben. Why don't you just carry out your plan?"

"I'm not sure it's a very good plan, Alice," he confided. "I should've cleared it with Mr. Pilgrim."

"I think it's exciting, Reuben. But remember, you promised to tell me everything."

"I know."

"Remember all the details, now. I want you to notice everything. Especially the clothes and the furniture. And don't forget what they say, Reuben."

"All right, Alice," He said impatiently. "And you watch yourself; I'll be back soon," he finally told her as he stepped off the porch and headed into the night.

When Clayton was certain that the brother was gone, he crept quietly around the side of the porch, keeping his eyes on Alice Canfield standing near the doorway. How easy it was going to be to leap up on the porch, snatch her by that blonde hair, and carry her away! Then, how easy it would be to hurl her to the ground and show her just how much of a man he was. But the moment the tips of his boots touched the porch steps, he saw Alice Canfield suddenly spin around to respond to her father's voice. Only seconds later she vanished inside the house.

Clayton managed to slink back to his place at the window in time to see the plump, blonde girl hug Canfield and kiss him on the cheek, then limp out of the room to the stairway. Now he could do nothing but wait. And each minute was passing by more urgently than the last. He glanced around for a sign of his brothers. If they had seen the fire in the sky, they would be coming for him soon. And they would be coming to kill him.

Five long and desperate minutes later, Clayton watched through the window as Barton Canfield suddenly snapped the cover of his timepiece, slid the gold watch into the pocket of his vest, and marched out into the hall. A little while later, he stepped out on the porch, locked the front door with a key, then stuffed his hands into his pockets and left.

"Hey, you, boy!" Clayton called out to a dirty-faced ten-year-old in a miner's cap.

The boy hurrying down the street came to an abrupt stop at the command, hitched up his trousers, and waited for Bonner to appear out of the shadows. "Yes, sir?" he said nervously.

"How would you like to make a dollar?" he asked.

"I sure wouldn't mind that, sir!" he replied eagerly.

"Good. All you have to do is go over to the Mercer Hotel and tell Miss Billie Simms that I'm coming for her soon. Just tell her that personally, and it's yours."

He clicked his tongue. "The Mercer Hotel's a parlor house, sir," he said.

"I know what it is—"

"What I mean is, I can't deliver that message, sir," he broke in. "They wouldn't even let me in there."

"What if you gave them a quarter?" he suggested.

"Not for nothing," he declared firmly. "They wouldn't let the likes of me in the kitchen, even. But I could deliver a note," he offered an alternative. "For the same price."

"I don't know—"

"I've got the paper and pencil here with me," he said, digging into his pockets. "See, I write up the delivery items for Miller's Mercantile."

After thinking a minute, Clayton agreed. He grabbed the pencil and paper, turned the boy around, then, using his back for a desk, quickly scratched out a note.

"Make sure this gets to Miss Billie Simms," he said, folding it.

"I'll sure do it, sir." He smiled as he took it. The

moment he saw the dollar bill being pressed into his palm, he let out a loud whistle and sprinted down the street.

Clayton watched him scamper away with the note clutched in one fist and the money in the other. Then he stalked slowly back to the house. After carefully knocking in a pane of glass with the butt of his revolver, he fumbled through the open rectangle to unlock the window and raise it up. When he finally reached the hallway, he paused to listen for evidence of servants, but the only sound he could hear was the humming of Alice Canfield upstairs.

Pushing his gun back into his scabbard, Clayton proceeded slowly up the steps toward the soft, easy voice. Outside her room, he lingered a moment to ease his breathing, but it was useless. The rapid pounding of his heart made that impossible. He was aroused and excited to think that he was standing inside one of the finest homes in Central City, with one of the town's most precious little treasures only a few feet away—completely in his power.

When Clayton suddenly smashed open the door, Alice Canfield leaped up from her chair, letting a shirt, needle, and spool of thread drop to the floor. "Who are you!" she gasped. "What are you doing here!"

"You know me—"

"No, I don't! What are you doing in my room!"

"Lower your voice!" he told her as he shut the door behind him.

Alice stumbled against the upholstered chair as she backed up. "Daddy!" she cried frantically. "Daddy—there's someone in my room!"

"Daddy's gone," he told her, advancing. "There is nobody in the house but you and me."

"Oh, no—Reuben, where are you!"

"Be quiet!" he demanded. "I'm going to show you

something, Miss Canfield. I'm going to teach you a lesson about Clayton Bonner.''

"Daddy! Reuben!"

"Damn you!" He lunged for her, grabbed a handful of her blonde hair, and slung her to the bed. "Now," he grunted as he pounced on top of her. "Keep your mouth shut!"

"Stop it!" she wailed. "Get off of me!"

"Not till I show you who's better than who, you little snipe!"

"Oh, please, don't!" she shrieked. "Get off! Please get off!"

"Be still!" He grabbed the collar of her blue dress and yanked it away from her heaving bosom with a loud rip.

"Daddy! Oh, God—"

"Shut up, you bitch!" He fumbled in the folds of cloth, trying to grab her small, pointed breasts. But all he felt was rough cotton. This little vixen he had captured was squirming too much for him to get a good hold on her. "Stop moving!" he growled.

"Daddy! Help me!"

"I said, shut up!"

"Daddy!"

"Be quiet!" He clamped his fingers around her throat. When she struggled to scream, he dug his nails into the soft flesh of her neck.

"Da—"

"Bitch!" He gouged his thumbs into her windpipe and cut off her voice. "Are you going to be quiet?"

She heaved and gasped for air, but said nothing.

"Are you?" He shook her by the throat. "Are you going to shut that mouth of yours and *listen* to me?"

When she still said nothing, he jammed his fingers

deeper into her unresisting neck. Finally, satisfied that Alice Canfield was at last ready to cooperate, he removed his hands from the sticky, bruised flesh of her throat and began groping eagerly through the starchy layers of petticoats for the touch of warm flesh.

It was the moment he touched her that he realized with a cold, sickening shudder that something had suddenly changed. Now he was aware that the still and quiet form he had been so desperately fondling was no longer the body of a frightened female who was relinquishing herself to the superior power of a man. Nor was it that of an uppity little town girl being primed for someone better than she could ever be. No. With a revolting, nauseating horror, he realized that what he was touching had become, in the space of a heartbeat, a body, and nothing more.

For Alice Canfield was dead.

17

"No, Mr. Canfield!" Andrea Sherbourne admonished Reuben in the foyer of the Mercer Hotel. "I told you this morning: I will not allow it!"

"Miss Sherbourne, I must see Billie Simms," he insisted. "It's vital!"

"I'm sorry," she declined. "I can't run a business with detectives running around my house."

"You don't understand," he told her. "I came here to *see* her—you know, the way others do."

His words gave her pause. She knitted her brow with curiosity. "Are you telling me, Reuben Canfield, that you've come to the Mercer Hotel to purchase the services of a woman?"

"Yes, ma'am," he lied without hesitation. "That's what I've come for. And I'm not a detective. I'm a private citizen with money to spend!"

She erupted into a coarse laughter that shook her ample bosom. "What do you think? A Canfield—in a Central City parlor house! Isn't this something! I wish that *Banner* editor could've seen this!"

Reuben colored. "There's no need to shout, Miss

239

Sherbourne,'' he said, glancing uncomfortably around the house.

Her expression became serious as she looked closely at him. ''Are you sure you want Billie Simms?'' she said to him.

''I'm positive.''

''Well, Reuben, I hope you realize you're asking for a very special girl. Billie Simms is a real innocent. And in this business, innocence is expensive.''

''I'll pay whatever it costs!''

''Well, sir, what it costs is fifty dollars.''

Reuben swallowed hard. ''Fine!'' he replied in a quivering voice. Sliding his wallet out of the inside pocket of his coat, he handed her five ten dollar bills and cleared his throat. ''Here,'' he said shakily.

She frowned. ''Do you mean you'll pay that?''

''Yes.''

Andrea shrugged her shoulders, took the money, and stuffed it into her cleavage. ''You'll have to wait until she's ready,'' she said.

''Now wait a minute, Miss Sherbourne—''

''When she's ready, sir,'' she repeated firmly.

''But I just gave you fifty dollars! I don't have time to wait!''

''Miss Simms is with somebody,'' she revealed. ''What do you want to do, sir—run up there and pull them apart?''

Reuben blushed again. ''What am I supposed to do in the meantime?'' he said. ''I don't have much time.''

''Molly!'' she called out. ''Come here a minute, please!'' She looked at Reuben. ''What you do is wait,'' she answered him.

''But I must see her now!''

''I'm sorry.''

"Sorry, ma'am," the thin black woman answered from the stairs. "I was up here delivering a note."

"Never mind that. I want you to come take care of Mr. Canfield here until Billie is through entertaining."

"Oh, she's through now," she informed her. "Must be. I just talked to her."

Reuben brightened. Then I can go up now!" he exclaimed.

Andrea pursed her lips. "I suppose you can," she relented. "Molly," she said to the black woman, "you'd better show him where, before the poor boy explodes."

Molly nodded obediently and led Reuben up the steps to Billie's room. He felt very presumptuous, walking into a woman's room, unannounced. Once inside, he paused to allow his eye to wander along the blue-papered walls to the white cotton curtains, past the dressing screen, to the big, high bed in the center of the floor. His attention caught on a blonde wig resting on the mattress next to a full carpetbag and an open piece of paper with penciled writing on it.

"Miss Simms?" he called out.

Instantly a small, feminine voice spoke from behind the dressing screen.

"Go away. I'm not seeing anyone!" it said.

"I'm not here for that," Reuben said quickly. "I mean, I'm not here as a customer. All I want to do is talk to you."

"I can't stay that long," she told him as she emerged from the screen.

Reuben was amazed to see a pretty and dainty, dark-haired girl, in a neat, tailored gray suit and pince-nez glasses, stepping past him to the bed. He stood numbly by while she snapped the carpetbag off the mattress and headed quickly for the door. Just before she reached it, he came to his senses and sprang ahead of her in time to thrust his body in the way.

"I didn't . . . recognize you, Miss Simms," he fumbled. "I'm sorry. It's just that you look so different."

"If you don't mind, I have to go—"

"No, wait! I'm Reuben Canfield. I was one of the detectives downstairs this morning. Remember? You spoke to us."

"I don't have time to speak now," she told him. "So if you'll please let me pass—"

"Your hair is really pretty like that," he said, distracted. "You don't even look like the same person."

She sighed impatiently. "What is it you want?" she asked him.

He looked at her steadily as he cleared his throat. "I want the name of the man who robbed you," he replied. "This morning you said you would tell us who it was."

She lowered her eyes. "I've changed my mind," she said. "I don't want to tell anybody anything. I just want to go."

"Miss Simms," he persisted, "I know I can help you, if you'll just let me!"

"Nobody can help me," she countered.

"At least let me try!" he begged her.

Billie studied him closely, then nervously adjusted her glasses. "Why would you want to help me?" she asked.

"Because you're desperate! Look at you. That carpetbag and those clothes tell me you're leaving. And since you now have no money, you must be running away."

She frowned. "You're real smart," she noted.

"Just observant," he replied.

She continued to look at him closely. "Well, it's true,"

she admitted. "I am running away. But I've got to. He's coming after me."

"Who's coming after you, Billie?" he exacted.

"The man who stole my money."

"But who is he?" he asked. Unconsciously, he grasped the balls of her shoulders in his hands and looked straight into her eyes. "Give me his name, and I'll protect you," he bargained.

She pushed a strand of her dark brown hair away from her forehead. "Nobody protects a prostitute," she said. "People think because of what we do, we can't be hurt."

"Well, I certainly don't think that!"

She looked at him skeptically. "What makes you so different?" she asked suspiciously. "Why do you want to help me?"

"Because I . . . like you."

"Like me! How? You've never even been in my room before."

"That has nothing to do with it. I'm talking about *you*, Billie. I like *you*."

She looked seriously at him, then let out a nervous laugh. "That's silly," she said.

"What's silly about it?"

"I don't know; it just is. After all. I'm not a lady you happened to meet at the mayor's house. I'm a parlor girl."

"What does that matter?"

"Oh, Lord, Reuben, don't you think I know what I am? I'm a whore! Taking off that wig and putting on these clothes doesn't change anything. I may not look the same, but I am."

He let go of her shoulders. "But you can't just run away, Billie," he told her. "Wherever you go, if this man wants to find you, he will."

After a moment, Billie lowered the carpetbag slowly to the floor. "What else can I do?" she lamented. "I still owe Miss Sherbourne $462.00, so I don't want to go. But if I stay, he's going to hurt me. I know he will!"

"How do you know that, Billie?"

"He said in that note he was coming for me," she answered, gesturing toward the mattress.

Reuben marched straight to the bed, scooped up the paper, and read it:

> *Billie: Don't you move. I will be there tonight—after I take care of a little other business. Soon you will be my own little Mom.*
>
> *"C"*

"What does 'C' stand for, Billie?" he asked her.

"It stands for Clayton," she answered. "His name is Clayton Bonner."

"I knew it!" He flung down the note.

"He's an outlaw," she offered. "And he's real crazy. I'm afraid of him. He makes me shudder all over."

"You've got reason to be afraid, Billie. According to the evidence, Clayton Bonner is not just an outlaw; he's also a murderer."

"Oh, no—"

"He killed a man named Farrell, acting on his brother's orders. And he stole four kegs of black powder from Miller's Mercantile so that the Bonners could blow up the payroll train tonight."

She drifted back into the room. "I don't know what to do," she fretted. "I'm scared."

"Stay with me until Clayton Bonner is caught and thrown into jail," he answered.

244

"But I couldn't," she declined. "It wouldn't be right."

"Why wouldn't it?"

"Because you're a gentleman in this town," she replied. "I know. I've seen you on the street before. You're the mine supervisor's son."

"What does that have to do with anything?"

"It just means I couldn't ever be seen with you," she told him. "I don't mean . . . together or anything, Mr. Canfield. I mean with you. People would say things."

"Let them."

She shook her head. "No, I'd better stay here," she decided. "Maybe that would be best."

"You can't, Billie," he told her calmly. "This room of yours isn't safe. If Clayton Bonner wants you, all he has to do is climb the stairs. Who do you think will stop him? Andrea Sherbourne? Molly?"

"No—"

"How about Sheriff Potts, Billie? Will he protect you?"

She shook her head sadly.

"Then let me do it!" he pleaded.

"But how? You don't even have a gun!"

"We'll go see Mr. Pilgrim," he informed her. "That's what I should have done to begin with. He can tell us exactly what we should do."

Billie backed up against the bed. "I don't want to go now," she told him. "I'm beginning to get this feeling in my stomach—"

"Billie—"

"It's a feeling that means bad things," she cried. "I know when something awful is going to happen."

"All right, then. Why don't we go tell Mr. Pilgrim about it?"

She hesitated. "He wouldn't care—"

"Billie, stop it! Listen to me. We'll go to him together. Mr. Pilgrim's a good man and a good detective. And he's in touch with the Pinkerton Agency all over the country. They can help us!"

Billie took a deep, halting breath. "But Miss Sherbourne—"

"Let me handle Miss Sherbourne," he replied. "Now come on," he told her. "Let's go!"

She took two steps toward him. "I don't want to be difficult," she said apologetically. "I just don't know how to act with you—"

"Then don't act, Billie. Just be. Now, please," he said, holding out his hand, "come on!"

"All right," she decided finally, "I will." She walked up to him and let him take her hand.

It felt tiny and warm in his fist. Only now did he realize just how small and frail this woman really was. She aroused every protective instinct he possessed.

The sky crackled with thunder as Reuben led Billie Simms up Eureka Street to the Teller House. There could be no doubt about it now. A heavy rainstorm was on its way. Why, he wondered, did everything seem to happen at once?

As they approached the stairs, the bald-headed clerk suddenly slid his stout form in front of them. "Excuse me," he said.

"What do you want, Simmons?" Reuben asked impatiently.

"I would like to make a request of you, Mr. Canfield," he answered, glancing over at Billie Simms.

"Then make it. We're in a hurry."

He pulled at his starched white collar. "It would be better if I spoke to you alone," he suggested.

"Why don't you go ahead and say it, Simmons?"

246

"Yes, sir. It's, well, I was wondering if you would consider escorting this lady outside."

"What?"

Simmons held up a defensive palm. "Now, I don't mean any offense by that, Mr. Canfield," he declared. "I just happen to know this young lady works at the Mercer Hotel. And you know I would lose my job if I let Andrea Sherbourne's girls frequent the Teller House."

"She is not frequenting anywhere right now, Simmons," he countered. "Right now she's with me!"

"I know that, sir—"

"Reuben," Billie said softly, "I'll be happy to wait outside."

"You don't have to."

The clerk coughed into his hand. "Mr. Canfield," he said, "I don't want to embarrass you—"

"You're not. Now, if you'll excuse me—" He pushed at the clerk's elbow.

But Simmons held firm. "I've been patient with you detectives up until now," he declared. "But this is going too far."

Reuben gritted his teeth. "Mr. Simmons," he said, "If you don't move out of my way, I'm going to do it for you!"

Before he could make a move toward the clerk, Reuben heard a woman call his name from above. A moment later, Katherine Haynes came hurrying down the steps. "What's wrong?" she wanted to know.

"We were going up to see Mr. Pilgrim," he replied. "Until Simmons decided to stop us."

"I'm only doing my job, Miss Haynes," the clerk defended.

"You wouldn't have seen him anyway, Reuben," Katherine offered, looking at Billie. "He's not in his room."

"Then were is he?" Reuben asked. "We have to see him!"

"I'm sure Mr. Simmons knows," Katherine suggested.

Reuben turned toward the clerk. "Do you?" he asked. "Did Mr. Pilgrim tell you where he was going?"

Simmons straightened his necktie. "Why didn't you tell me you were going to see him? I would have been glad to tell you—he went over to the sheriff's office."

"Then so will we," Reuben declared.

"Reuben," Katherine held him up. "Will you wait a minute? I want to go with you."

"Well, hurry, Miss Haynes."

"I just have to get my coat," she said. "It looks like the rain will be here before long."

18

Matt Pilgrim receded from the drafty window of the sheriff's office and paced anxiously back and forth across the floor. Stopping a moment to spread his palms over the pot-bellied stove, he still had to shiver. The cold, damp mountain air seeping into the office through the cracks in the walls was beginning to sink into his bones. He knew it would take more than Alvin Potts's rusty old heater to bring him comfort tonight.

A hundred times he had considered renting a horse and racing through the night to meet the train himself. But he couldn't have done that without violating a basic principle of his training. Although a Pinkerton detective might sometimes be a member of an official posse, he was never authorized to take the law into his own hands. Besides, he reminded himself, how much good could a single man do against half a dozen of the Bonners?

Pilgrim wheeled quickly around at the abrupt, crashing noise of the door banging open. He stepped aside as the big, lumbering figure of Alvin Potts marched straight for the stove, slamming the door sharply behind him. He watched the sheriff pick up the coffee pot, shake it next to

249

his ear, and, without a word, walk gruffly out the back door into the alley. Minutes later he returned with the pot full of water.

"Why didn't you make me some coffee, boy?" he groused at Matt. "It's starting to get cold out there. Looks like it might rain, too, finally."

"What happened, Sheriff?" Matthew asked impatiently. "Did you reach the train in time?"

"All I reached was a dead end, Pilgrim. I seen nothing but iron, all the way to Blackhawk."

"But you did leave the posse there?" he assumed.

Silently Potts flipped back the lid of the blue metal container on the stove, grabbed a sack of coffee from the shelf, and dumped a handful of it into the pot.

"Sheriff?" Matt prompted. "The posse is still there, isn't it?"

Potts shook his head. "There ain't any posse, boy," he confessed. "I went out there by myself."

"What!"

"Well, what did you expect me to do? I can't go around swearing in citizens on the basis of your Pinkerton 'scientific evidence,' I ain't that big a fool."

"Do you mean you didn't even try!"

Potts clanked open the door of the iron stove. "I didn't have to," he replied. "There wasn't a shred of real evidence of any crime in progress or of one about to be committed. I say we ought to let that fact be the end of it."

"I wish we could," Matt said grimly.

The sheriff tossed a couple of sticks of firewood into the stove and clanged the door shut. "I tell you, boy, there's nothing out there!" he growled. "I covered those tracks like a damn worm, all the way to Blackhawk!"

"The outlaws wouldn't be on the tracks, Sheriff," he

pointed out. "They're going to blow the tracks apart! They were probably lying back in the shadows, watching you—"

"And laughing at me," he broke in. "Is that what you're saying?"

Matt squeezed his fists together in frustration. "Maybe they were," he allowed. "And maybe they should have!"

Potts glared at him. "Why don't you run home to the Pinkertons, Pilgrim?" he muttered. "I'll handle the law in the gulch."

"Is that what you're doing now, Sheriff? Is letting the Bonners run wild handling the law?"

Potts bristled at his words. "All a man can do with the Bonners is kill them or let them be. He can't predict them."

"But he can, Sheriff!" he insisted. "That's what scientific evidence is all about. If you know enough about the criminal and his mode of behavior, you can determine what he will do next."

The lawman scratched his bushy gray eyebrow thoughtfully, then tilted the lid of the coffee pot and peered inside. "Nobody's robbing any train tonight," he stated confidently. "And except for the usual drunks at the Shoo-fly, there ain't anybody getting hurt, either. So why don't you use some of your daddy's good sense and move on, son? Go perch your butt on another roost and leave Central City be."

Matt was simmering with anger as he turned away and headed for the door. But just as he reached for the doorknob, he stopped. He couldn't leave Alvin Potts without pressing one more point—an idea that had been fermenting in his mind since the first time he talked to the big sheriff.

Facing him again, he took a minute to bring back what

251

he had been told about the lawman, then braced himself. "What about this town?" he queried.

Potts was reaching into the desk drawer for a bottle of rye whiskey. "What about it?" he retorted.

He advanced a few steps. "There are good and decent people living in your town, Sheriff," he reminded. "Don't you want to protect them?"

The huge, gray-headed man scrunched up his wrinkled face as he swigged some of the strong rye. "I don't care if I do or not, son," he said. "Those people pay me to do just what I'm doing. And that's the way I like it."

"I don't believe that."

He wiped his wet lips with his sleeve. "People ain't worth very much, when you get right down to it, Pilgrim," he contended. "Let me sum it up for you. Let me give you a keyhole you can peep through, to see the whole mess."

"Go ahead," he invited.

"It's simple. Men are like that skinny-necked miner that run off with my wife. All they want to do is take what belongs to somebody else. Women are like my wife. All they want is to be given something they ain't got. And kids are like my son. They don't have brains enough to know what they want, so they go along with the others."

"That's pretty cynical," Matt observed.

"I don't know about that, but it's true."

"I still don't believe it. I think you do care about what happens to the people you're paid to protect."

"Now, just what in lower Hades would you know about it?" he charged. "If you're thinking you're smart because your old man was some kind of wandering philosopher, I've got something to tell you, boy. You don't have the sense the good Lord gave a braying donkey."

"I have enough sense to recognize responsibility when I

252

see it, Sheriff Potts,'' he countered. ''And I saw it right here in this office yesterday morning. You're not hard and mean, Sheriff. You're compassionate and responsible.''

''Get out of here, boy.''

''You're fighting yourself, Sheriff. You're letting what happened to you form a shell around you—''

''All right, Pilgrim,'' he fumed. ''That's enough!''

''Why don't you forget your wife and son? Why don't you live your own life for a change?''

''Because I don't care about a damn thing in it, that's why!''

After he watched Potts swallow down more of the rye whiskey, Matt turned away from him in disgust. A minute later, the door flew open and Reuben Canfield burst in.

''Mr. Pilgrim!'' he exclaimed.

Matt stood amazed as Reuben, Katherine, and, of all people, the prostitute from the Mercer Hotel, filed quickly into the office. He reached out and took Katherine's hand and demanded to know what on earth they were doing there.

''We're looking for you, Matt,'' she answered.

''All of you?''

''This is Miss Billie Simms, Matt,'' Reuben introduced.

''I know who she is, Reuben.''

''Billie gave me the name of our man, Mr. Pilgrim,'' he beamed.

Matt resisted the temptation of asking him how he managed to extract that bit of information from her. That story would have to wait until another time.

''Who is it, Reuben?'' he asked.

''It was Clayton Bonner.''

''There, you see,'' the sheriff offered, looking into the

253

coffee pot. "I told you, you should've gone up there and burned those Bonners out!"

"Somebody tried that tonight," Reuben informed them. "We just saw a prospector bringing down the body of one of the Bonners in his wagon. He said the shack on Casto Hill has been burned to the ground."

"But this dead Bonner wasn't Clayton," Matt guessed.

Katherine squeezed his hand. "It was Deke, Matt," she told him sadly. "His brothers must have killed him."

"Damn!"

"He looked so sad and pitiful all curled up in the back of that wagon," she said softly.

"Why couldn't it have been Clayton!" Matt exclaimed. Then he looked at Reuben. "Did this prospector happen to see any of the other Bonners?"

"No, sir," he replied. "He said he didn't find a trace of another person on the hill. Even the horses were gone."

"Which means they're on their way to rob the payroll train, Reuben."

"Now hold on there," Potts broke in. "It don't necessarily mean that. It could be they've decided to leave. We might not ever hear from that bunch again."

"I wouldn't count on it," Matt offered.

"Mr. Pilgrim," Reuben entreated, "we have to go after them!"

Matt let go of Katherine's hand and faced the lawmen. "What about that, Sheriff?" he challenged. "Is this enough evidence for you? Now will you get a posse and stop that train robbery?"

Potts poured steaming coffee into a tin cup. "I ain't seen a shred of any real evidence," he stated stubbornly.

Reuben winced at that. "We showed you everything we had!" he erupted.

"Reuben—" Matt cautioned.

"Mr. Pilgrim, if he's not going to do anything, we have to!"

At that moment, the detective became aware of the low rumble of a distant crowd of people outside. Stepping over to the window, he looked out and saw a few boys scurrying excitedly up the street.

"What is it, Matt?" Katherine asked.

"Is it the Bonners?" Reuben asked, joining him at the glass.

"I don't know. The noise is coming from Pine Street."

With Katherine and Reuben on either side of him, Matt waited for the mass of people to proceed slowly in the direction of the sheriff's office. The first individuals he recognized were the Cornishmen he and Reuben had pulled up from the mine.

"What in Hades are those Cousin Jacks up to?" Potts muttered over their shoulders. "It's bad enough, the way they hang around the Shoo-fly. Now they're marching on the sheriff."

Next came more miners, then little boys, and a clutch of women gathered around the slender figure of an older man.

"That's my father!" Reuben exclaimed. "What is he doing!"

"Matt!" Katherine grabbed his arm. "It looks like he's carrying someone!"

"Yes, it does. But I can't make out who it is."

"It's a girl!"

"Are you sure? I can't see for the women around him—"

Matt strained to see into the darkness of the night. In the dim mist, all he could make out was a mob of a hundred people enclosed around one person, a man who was holding a limp, dead body in his arms.

Then a streak of lightning cut across the sky and washed the town in a splash of brilliant white light, illuminating every face in the street, for less than a second.

"Oh, God," Reuben said, swallowing.

"What is it, Reuben?"

"Oh, God, no!" he cried. "It's Alice!" He pushed past the detective and crashed through the door, screaming, "Alice! Alice!" as he rushed toward the crowd.

Katherine leaned against the detective. "Oh, Matt," she cried mournfully. "She's dead."

Pilgrim felt his eyes moisten and his throat go dry as he witnessed the terrible scene of his friend Reuben Canfield wailing and fighting his way through the mass of people to get to his sister. When he finally managed to reach her, he held out his hand and touched her hanging blonde hair and burst into tears. But his father never paused. He held his eyes fixed straight ahead as he moved toward the sheriff's office.

For the first time since she had been there, Billie Simms spoke. "Is that his wife?" she asked sadly.

"His sister," Matt answered.

"She died tonight," she stated in a quivering little voice. "His sister died when he was with me."

Matt and Katherine went outside and waited for the others to arrive. The early arrivals veered away when they reached the wooden walkway, making room for the Canfields. With cold, unblinking eyes, Barton stalked up to the office, bearing the crumpled body of his daughter in his arms, and walked through the door.

For a long, tense moment, he stared at the hulking gray-haired man in the baggy wool trousers and gray shirt.

Then, as his arms began to tremble, he spoke with teary eyes.

"My daughter's dead, Potts," he said accusingly. "Do you see her? There's not a breath left in her body."

"I know—"

"A slimy little villain slipped into my house and strangled her, Potts. Do you hear me!"

The sheriff stiffened. "I'm sorry, Canfield. What do you want me to do about it? I can't very well bring her back to life, can I?"

"You're to blame for this, Potts," he sobbed. "You've laid around this office swilling your liquor and licking your wounds for so long, you've become useless to everybody!"

"Now hold on here, Canfield—"

"Look at what you've done to me, Potts! Look at what you let happen. You son-of-a-bitch—you let them murder my precious daughter!"

"How do you think I could save her? I was off investigating—"

"She never hurt anybody. She was the sweetest girl who ever lived. And she was so smart. I've never seen anyone so smart. She was going East to school—"

"Damn you! I said I couldn't have saved her!"

"Didn't I show you the note, Potts!" he cried. "Didn't it say they were going to kill her! Oh, merciful God, why Alice? Why take away such a sweet and loving soul?"

"I tell you, it wasn't my doing, Canfield!"

With tears streaming down his cheeks, the mine supervisor eased the limp body of his daughter down on top of the sheriff's desk. "I want you to look at her, Potts," he said harshly. He swept back a lock of the girl's hair, revealing the severely bruised neck. "Look at how they handled my

girl. Put your hand on her skin, Potts. Feel it. It's cold!
Her skin is cold!''

Get her off my desk!'' Potts demanded.

''The Bonners put those filthy blue marks on her throat.
They do anything to us they want to, and you never raise a
finger to stop them!''

While Potts turned away to lace his coffee with rye,
Billie Simms began to sob loudly. ''It was Clayton Bonner
killed her,'' she cried in a halting voice. ''It's because of
me she's dead!''

''Billie—'' Reuben stepped toward her.

But she shrank away, shaking her head. ''You should've
been with her, not me!'' she moaned. ''Then she wouldn't
be dead!''

''It isn't your fault.''

''It *is* my fault. I knew something horrible was going to
happen. I knew it!'' With her hand pressed to her mouth,
Billie Simms broke through the cluster of people in the
room and ran into the street outside.

After staring down at his sister's body for a time, Reuben suddenly plucked a revolver out of a holster nearby
and headed out.

Before he had gone a yard, Matt Pilgrim caught up with
him. ''Reuben, wait!'' he cautioned him.

''Let me pass, Mr. Pilgrim.''

''Just what do you think you're going to do with that!''

''I'm going to get Clayton Bonner,'' he answered coldly.

A man in the crowd cheered. ''That's right, Reuben!''
he urged. ''Go shoot the cold-blooded bastards!''

''We're behind you, Reuben,'' another goaded. ''Kill
them all!''

Matt seized Reuben's right arm and twisted it. ''Put it
down!'' he told him.

"Why don't you let him be, Pilgrim?" the first voice grumbled. "They killed his sister, for God's sake!"

"Yeah, Pilgrim," the other shouted. "The man has a right!"

The detective hated to see his friend, usually so neat and confident, now so dishevelled and shaky. He looked angry and defeated. In his watery eyes there seemed to be all the pain in the world.

"Reuben," he pleaded, "you know this is wrong."

"I know it is, Mr. Pilgrim, but he killed Alice! He deserves to die too!"

"Maybe he does, but you can't just go out there and shoot him down! What if he isn't even guilty?"

"We know he is, Mr. Pilgrim."

"How can you be sure? Where's your evidence, Reuben? Do you have any evidence!"

Reuben hesitated, then sadly lowered the pistol to his side. "No, I don't," he admitted. "I just feel I ought to do something, Mr. Pilgrim," he said pitifully. "I just can't stand around here and *look* at her!"

"Sheriff Potts is still the law, Reuben," he reminded. "Until he acts, that's all we can do."

"Excuse me, please." A buxom woman in red shoved her way through the crowd from outside the office. "I have to see the sheriff."

A minute later, the voluptuous, silk-draped figure of Andrea Sherbourne squeezed through the tangle of arms and legs into the open space around the desk. A hush fell over the crowd as she directly confronted the grizzled man gulping coffee at the stove.

Behind Pilgrim a woman whispered, "What's *she* doing here?" Another hissed a scathing reply. But there was nothing but reverent silence when Andrea Sherbourne opened her mouth to speak.

"Well?" she rebuked the sheriff. "Aren't you going to say something to me?"

"Why doesn't somebody get her out of here?" Potts mumbled vaguely.

Andrea stood like a statue in the middle of the room. "I'm not going 'til I've had my say, Alvin Potts," she stated flatly.

"Nobody wants to hear your say, Hilda Jane," he told her.

"I'm going to say it anyway. I'm going to address you in public—for the first time in eleven years. All this time, I've done exactly as you wanted. I haven't breathed a word about the two of us since the day your wife ran off with that miner. But I was wrong, Alvin. I should've said something! I should've stood by you!"

"This ain't the time for this, Hilda Jane."

"Oh, yes, it is. These people believe you're responsible for this poor girl's death, Alvin! Look at them. They believe you've let them down. They believe you're no good!"

"Well, they're right," he mumbled and swallowed some coffee and rye.

"No, they're wrong! You are good, and you're strong! And I want you to show them!"

He shook his head slowly. "Can't," he said simply.

"Alvin!"

"I can't, Hilda Jane!"

"Now you listen to me," she said, her heavily shaded eyes full of tears. "I've been waiting all these years for you to pull yourself together. I've defended you to practically every man in this town! I've blackmailed and threatened and lied—I have done everything I could think of, to keep you sheriff. And look at what you're doing with it! How can anyone ever respect you, if you do nothing!''

"I don't care, Hilda Jane!" he countered. "Don't you understand? Don't any of you understand—I don't care!''

"Alvin Potts," she said severely, "I've never asked you for anything in my life. You know I haven't. But I'm asking you now; I want you to show these people what you're made of. Will you do that for me?''

He looked straight at her. "They already know what I'm made of," he replied. "Nothing but a lot of bluster and rye whiskey.''

"Lead them, Alvin!" she begged. "Lead them after the Bonners!''

Potts rubbed the wrinkles of his cheek as he gazed around the room. He scanned the afflicted expressions of Barton and his son, then stared for a long time at the convulsive look of anguish frozen in the innocent face of Alice Canfield. Finally, he quaffed the rest of his coffee and set the cup down on the desk beside her.

"Get out of my way," he muttered to the crowd as he started for the door.

"Alvin!" Andrea called out to him.

He stopped and turned around to face her. "Haven't you said enough, woman" he growled angrily.

Andrea seized the tiny white rose of her necklace, ripped it away from her bosom, and held it up by the chain. "You gave this to me a dozen years ago," she reminded him. "Do you remember? You called me your White Rose then.''

"That was a long time ago," he returned. "Two lifetimes ago.''

261

"You told me to give it back to you if I ever stopped loving you. Do you remember that?"

"Woman—"

"I will ask you one more time, Alvin. Will you lead a posse after the Bonners? Will you, once and for all, show these people you're still a man?"

He clenched his teeth as he looked at her. "Why don't you just leave me alone?" he said.

"Alvin, please!"

"Go back to the hotel and take care of your whores, *Andrea*," he said.

"Damn you!" she cried, and hurled the necklace at him.

The little white rose plunked against his wide, solid chest and dropped almost without sound to the office floor. For a second, he glared at Andrea Sherbourne, gritting his teeth. Then he reached down, picked up the necklace, and squeezed it into his big fist. With every eye in the office following him, Sheriff Potts marched through the door and started pushing his way through the crowd.

19

In the gathering mist outside the sheriff's office, Matt could see Ben Watkins perched on the bed of a wagon, spitting tobacco juice and rousing the crowd.

"There he goes, gents!" Watkins was clamoring. "There goes your law! Scurrying off like a wounded rabbit! Look at the coward go!"

A chorus of men nodded and grumbled their agreement.

"Well, I say we forget Alvin Potts," Watkins charged them." Why don't we do it ourselves! Whatta you say, gents!"

"I say them Bonners are murderers!" a miner yelled.

"I agree! And what do you do with murderers?"

"You hang 'em high, Ben," the miner replied. "Hang 'em high!"

"Now ye best hold the lid on here, lads!" said the big Cornishman from the Get Lucky Mine. "There's surely no need to start a row—"

"Keep your big nose out of this, Hawley," Watkins commanded. "Go back to the mine and get to work!"

"But this is not the way to handle it!" he contended.

"What's a Cousin Jack know about anything American, Hawley?"

"I know even Americans need to have some order, Mr. Watkins!" he countered.

The mine manager angrily spit out some juice, then ordered a few of the miners to lug away the Cornishman. "Chuck him back in the hole," he instructed. "That's the only place they're good for!"

When Matt saw the Cornishman being carted off, he knifed his way through the crowd. "Watkins," he yelled at the leader, "why don't you come down from there before somebody gets hurt!"

"Well, look at this, gents!" Watkins exclaimed in a mocking voice. "Looks like its our hero, the detective. Butting in, as usual."

"I'm not butting in, Watkins." He came forward. "I'm just suggesting that you break this up. Right now!"

"And why should we do that, Pinkerton?" he said defiantly.

"Because if you go after the Bonners yourselves, you'll be breaking the law."

"What law, Pilgrim?" Watkins sneered. "There ain't no law. The law's headed home with his tail tucked between his legs."

Matt looked anxiously around him. The teeming crowd was made up of men now, two hundred or more frightened and angry faces, glaring at him. He felt as if he were cutting through a current of tension as he moved past them and closer to the wagon.

"Before you go after the Bonners, let me say something." He turned around and addressed the crowd.

"You're in our way, Pilgrim!" a miner called to him. "We've got things to do tonight."

"You men listen to me!" he exclaimed.

"Go talk to Potts, detective!"

"I said listen, damn it!" When he finally got silence, Matt cleared his throat. "If you're that determined to go, I can't stop you."

"Now that's more like it!"

"But some of you stay here. The Bonners aren't the only ones involved in this. Our evidence indicates that someone else is manipulating the Bonners."

"What evidence?" Watkins asked. "Who is he?"

"I don't know who he is," Matt admitted. "But I do know if you ride out after these outlaws, you may be leaving the town in his hands!"

"This dude don't know what the hell he's talking about, gents!" Watkins boomed. "We're going after the Bonners now! We ain't letting this happen again."

"Let's go, Ben!" a miner shouted. "You lead the way!"

Watkins sprayed the ground with tobacco juice. "The old prospector said their tracks led off in the direction of Blackhawk. So that's where we're headed, gents!" He leaped down to the ground and grinned at Pilgrim. "We'll chase those killers all the way to Denver if we have to!" he said.

"Mr. Watkins—" Matt began.

"Now I'll tell you what to do, Mr. Detective," he cut him off. "You sit down on your fat 'evidence,' and let us take care of the law."

"Let's go, Ben!" The others were already spreading out to their horses.

"I'm coming, gents!"

It looked to Pilgrim as if every man in Central City was whooping and hollering through the streets, on the way to his horse to ride after the outlaws. Within minutes they were up on their mounts and thundering across the street toward the road to Blackhawk. Then, all of a sudden, directly in their path at the edge of town, the loud explosion of a gunpowder blast startled them to a halt.

Poised in the middle of the road was a tall, well-dressed man with the butt of a shotgun pressed loosely against his shoulder. "All right, Watkins," William Henry Aldrich said to the leader. "This is as far as you go tonight."

"What the hell do you mean, Aldrich!" Watkins griped.

"I mean to stop your men from being slaughtered," he replied. "I have no desire to live in a town devoid of men."

Watkins curled his lip. "What are you talking about?"

"I'm talking about the darkness, Mr. Watkins. And the coming rain. If you go out there now, the Bonners will pick you off like flies."

"Then we'll get us some torches, right, men?" Watkins urged.

"Yeah—right!"

Aldrich eased the shotgun down. "Just how much good do you think torches will do in a rainstorm! If the outlaws are out there at all, they're probably waiting for you. You'll be massacred before you get out of the gulch!"

"Then what do we do, Mr. Aldrich?" someone asked.

"You wait until dawn," he answered coolly. "You give yourselves a chance!"

A robust-looking miner on a two-horse wagon seat called over to Watkins. "What the man says makes sense, Ben," he decided. "It's plenty dark in the hills this time of night."

"What do you want to do, Eli," Watkins returned, "let them go?"

"Don't reckon I do, Ben, but I don't want to be gunned down in the rain, either."

Ben inspected the dark, threatening sky. "The rain don't scare me any," he contended. "I figure we got enough time to find them, if we stop all this yapping and go!"

Aldrich dropped the butt of his shotgun to the ground. "Men," he said to them, "if you will wait until dawn, I'll ride with you! Maybe the law won't be behind you, but the railroad will!"

"That's good enough for me," the miner declared and pulled away. "Let's do it at daybreak."

"Now hold on there, gents!"

"At dawn, Ben," they replied. "We do it at dawn!"

"The Bonners may be in another state by then!" he hollered at them.

Paying no attention to him, the men slowly separated and began to drift into the alleys, saloons, and dance halls of the town, to wait for the light.

When Katherine reached Matthew in the street, he was watching closely the angry, unsettled men as they moved deliberately about Central City, wielding their shotguns, rifles, and pistols. Then he turned his attention to the tall, thin man in a new suit and derby hat, walking toward him, with his weapon propped on his shoulder.

"Henry did you a favor, Matt," Katherine observed, "stopping them like that."

"I wonder," he said skeptically.

He stiffened as the other man came to a stop only a few feet away.

"It would seem," he offered, as he lowered his gun, "that even the natives can act on reason occasionally."

"They're acting more out of fear than reason, Mr. Aldrich," Matt reasoned.

The other man smiled and nodded his head. "Yes, they probably are," he acknowledged, then looked at Katherine. "It looks as if that's what you're doing too, my dear," he said to her. "I'm surprised to find a lady of your breeding clinging to a man in the streets."

"I'm not clinging to him," she retorted.

"No, of course you're not. I'm being unforgivably crude. Shall we say you're being seen in the streets in his company?"

"Maybe she prefers my company, Mr. Aldrich," Matt contended.

"That could be," he allowed. "But, then, that's only temporary, isn't it?"

"Is it?"

"Oh, yes. You see, given its chance, quality will always assert itself. And one day soon, I will be giving Miss Haynes such a chance. She will respond, Mr. Pilgrim, because I know exactly what she needs."

"I don't think you have any idea what she needs, Aldrich."

"Oh, but I do, Mr. Pilgrim," he grinned. "Just wait and see. Katherine," he said, taking her hand, "I'll be waiting for you."

His words brought a flush to her cheeks. "Henry," she protested, "I meant what I said. I'm not going to marry you."

"Yes, I'm sure you meant that when you said it. But when you see what I have to offer, you'll change your mind. Well, I won't keep you." He kissed the back of her hand. "I'll say good night to you both."

"Now wait a minute, Aldrich—"

"Matt," Katherine interrupted, "let him go."

"Yes, let me go, Mr. Pilgrim," he said and jerked the

shotgun to his shoulder. "While you strut about the streets with your woman, I will be home making some important plans."

Although Matt was greatly irritated by this parting shot, he stood firm and allowed the other man to leave quietly. While he considered Aldrich very annoying, he also found him just as puzzling. While the man never openly threatened or challenged, he still somehow managed to convey anger and resentment in every word he spoke.

Before Aldrich was out of sight, Matt and Katherine started walking slowly back to the sheriff's office. But they unconsciously stepped up their pace as the sky exploded with light and peals of thunder rolled through the dark, ominous-looking clouds hovering low above the town.

Matt found the sheriff's office cold, sombre, and full of sadness. Next to the desk, Barton Canfield sat in a straight-back chair, staring blankly at the floor, holding in his palm the hand of his daughter, who now lay discreetly covered by a woolen blanket. The other man in the room was pacing slowly up and down, with a .45 calibre pistol tucked behind his belt, next to his belly.

Reuben looked up as Matt and Katherine came in. "I can't wait for Sheriff Potts to come around, Mr. Pilgrim," he announced. "When the posse leaves tomorrow, I'm going too."

"No, you're not," Barton Canfield said in a calm, measured voice.

Reuben faced his father. "What do you want me to do?" he asked. "Just sit—the way you're doing?"

"You've done all you can, Reuben," he stated. "Now, please, for God's sake, let it be!"

"I'll never let it be," he vowed.

"Reuben," Matt broke in, "you can't throw aside your

knowledge and intelligence and join up with that mob outside!''

"Yes, I can, Mr. Pilgrim," he disagreed. "All I have to do is look at the tortured body of my sister and think of Clayton Bonner.''

"All right, suppose you do catch up with the Bonners. What happens then? Are you going to personally string every one of them from a tree?''

"No, sir. Just the one that murdered Alice.''

"You know I can't let you do that, Reuben.''

"Neither can I," Barton Canfield said, rising to his feet. "We've had too much lawlessness in this town. We can't have any more!''

"No matter what's happened, Reuben," Matt agreed, "we have to do things according to the law. We have to use the evidence. If you want to convict and punish Clayton Bonner, you need proof.''

"Then I'll get it," he declared. "I'll put together so much scientific evidence, the courts will have to hang him. I'll produce the bootprint in the black powder, the fingerprints on the knife that killed Farrell, and I'll tie them all to Alice." He gazed forlornly at the corpse on the desk. "Somewhere on my sister's body, or in her room, are Clayton Bonner's latent prints," he said. "They will match the ones I take from his fingers.''

"The courts may not accept the idea of fingerprints, Reuben," Matt warned. "The procedure is too new.''

"I'll make them accept it," he said. "And somehow, I will connect Clayton Bonner with the man who composed this note." He drew a slip of paper out of his coat pocket and held it out. "I know the fingerprint I took from this letter signed by Seth Bonner belongs to the man who's behind all of this.''

Katherine raised her eyebrows at the sight of the note. "May I see that, Reuben?" she asked. After he took it to her, she stared at it with curiosity.

"What is it, Kate?" Matt asked.

"I'm not sure. There just seems to be something familiar about this."

Reuben perked up. "Could you be recognizing the handwriting, Miss Haynes?" he asked.

"I've seen it before, Matt," she explained. "Or some like it. But I can't remember where."

"Was it in Chicago?"

She shook her head. "I don't think so. I believe I saw it here."

"Does it help to know that the paper is made from cloth instead of ground wood, Miss Haynes?"

"No, I'm afraid not."

"What I mean is, that's a high grade of paper," he told her. "It's a better quality than the paper they make from wood—the kind used in dime novels and newspapers."

"Newspapers!" she exclaimed. "That's it, Reuben! That's where I saw it—at Alex's newspaper office. It was in the files I was looking through yesterday."

Matt felt a surge of excitement go through him. "Could you find it again, Kate?" he wondered.

"I don't know. I must have seen a couple of thousand letters in Alex's files. He kept everything."

"But you could try?" Reuben encouraged.

"Yes—"

"Then what are we waiting for?" He bounded for the door. "Let's go!"

With the others outside, Matt took a look back at Barton Canfield, who was staring under the blanket at the face of his daughter. "Sir—" he began.

"Never mind me, son," the older man anticipated. "I'm all right, I'll just stay here with Alice."

"This could be the connection we've been waiting for, Mr. Canfield," he said.

"Then go track it down, Matt," he urged. "But I would like you to do one thing for me."

"Yes, sir."

"Watch Reuben," he said in a shaky voice. "Keep him safe, I don't think I could live through another loss like this one."

"I'll watch him," he promised, and closed the door to the sheriff's office as he left.

272

20

The vague figures drifting in and out of the town streets looked like phantoms through the foggy window of the *Banner* office. While Matt and Reuben rifled noisily through the files, Katherine rubbed a clear spot on the glass with her palm and peered out into the dark. Nearby, two men in dirty clothes were arguing beneath a street lamp. One was waving his arms and grumbling loudly; the other was silently shaking his head. Farther away, at the mouth of a dark alley, a woman was herding her three little boys home. The whole town was anxiously waiting for the dawn to come.

She flinched at the loud crack of thunder and shivered as it rolled across the heavens. She could feel all around her a cold, hostile air charged with danger.

"I've never seen so many letters in my life!" Reuben observed to Matt behind her back. "And none of them matches this one!"

"One of them does. We just haven't seen it yet."

"I think we've already been through this batch, Mr. Pilgrim."

"Then we'll go through it again."

"Yes, sir."

Katherine felt her nerves tighten and ache as she watched a scattering of raindrops in the dirt outside. If she were still in Chicago now, she thought, she wouldn't even notice the coming of a storm. She would be in her parents' house, protected and insulated from harm. She could curl up on a thick warm rug in front of a crackling fire and comfortably read her novels about outlaws and lawmen and never have to touch the lives of such destitute people as Billie Simms or Deke Bonner.

But then, looking at the serious, dedicated expression on the handsome face of Matt Pilgrim as he searched through Alex's papers, she wondered if the comfort and security of her home in Chicago hadn't lost its appeal in the last few days. Even though she was nervous with the dread of what might happen next, she still felt more excited and more alive than she had ever felt before. All she wanted at this moment was to be with the man she loved. After that, she believed, everything else would fall into place.

"I've been through this stack twice," Matt complained. Rising to his feet, he glanced over at Reuben, who was flipping through the files of another cabinet. "Anything in that batch?" he asked hopefully.

"Not yet," he answered.

"If you don't come up with anything, we'll go through them all again."

"Yes, sir."

"Matt," Katherine said in a worried voice, "it's becoming so tense out there. Everybody is restless. The men are walking around with their guns loaded, just waiting for something to happpen."

Matt nodded knowingly. "After the cave-ins and the

274

murders, Alice's death was too much. They want to get it over, one way or another.''

"So do I,'' she said.

He smiled at her and touched her cheek. "This has to be pretty hard for a Chicago girl,'' he noted. "Standing in the middle of a little mining town, waiting for it to explode.''

"I don't care where I am,'' she replied, "as long as I'm with you.''

He lowered his hand to her waist and looked at her curiously. "Do you really mean that?'' he asked her.

She backed up a step. "I guess it just slipped out,'' she said.

"Kate—'' He stepped toward her.

All of a sudden, Reuben erupted. "Mr. Pilgrim!'' he cried. "I've got it!''

After a long moment's glance at her, Pilgrim turned around and marched over to Reuben. Taking the two sheets of paper next to the lamp, he compared them closely. One was the threat signed by Seth Bonner; the other was a note dated September 2, 1879, requesting a one-year, $5.00 subscription to the *Central City Banner*.

"Katherine was right,'' Matt concluded. "It is the same paper.''

"The handwriting is different, but I'm sure these notes were written with the same pen,'' Reuben offered. "Look at how the blunt point smears the capital letters.''

Matt nodded. "These two pages definitely came from the same desk,'' he agreed.

"Then we've done it, Mr. Pilgrim!'' Reuben exclaimed. "We've found the man we've been looking for—the mastermind!''

"Who is it, Matt?'' Katherine asked. "Or are you going to keep it from me?''

Pilgrim hesitated. "We can't be certain the papers are identical yet, Kate," he said.

"I understand that, Matt. Just tell me who wrote it."

"Maybe Reuben can lift a fingerprint off the second letter and compare it to the one he took off the first one."

"Matt, tell me!"

He pulled in a long breath and let it out slowly. "The man who wrote this letter to your brother," he said, bringing it to her, "was William Henry Aldrich."

His cold, leaden words made her feel sick inside. Unsteadily, she took the note and read it. Her heart sank when her eyes fell on the name, written with a practiced flourish, at the bottom of the page.

"I can't believe it," she said, deflated. "It must be a coincidence."

"It fits, Kate," he claimed.

She felt the blood rush hotly to her face. "What do you mean, 'It fits?' " she challenged. "You're talking about a respected businessman. A friend of my father's. A civilized man! There is no way on earth William Henry Aldrich could ever commit a murder!"

"He didn't do it himself, Kate," he pointed out. "He's too clever for that. He used the Bonners. Aldrich is the man in the business suit I saw at the cabin on Casto Hill today. He was out there making deals with the Bonners. He's been using everybody in this town for his own benefit."

"I'm sorry, Matt," she declared and turned away. "I just can't accept that! How can you connect a gentleman like Henry Aldrich with mass murder! It doesn't make sense!"

"It is a shock to think of Mr. Aldrich that way, Mr. Pilgrim," Reuben chimed in. "After all, he does work for the railroad. If he were sabotaging the mines in Central

City, he would be causing the railroad to lose business. What would he have to gain by that?''

''Whatever he had to gain, Reuben, it has something to do with that group of railroad men and financiers back in Chicago, and with land in Nebraska.''

''But what?'' he sighed, frustrated.

''We don't have enough information to know that yet, Reuben. All we have now is our own evidence.''

''Matt?'' Katherine had to hear the words from Pilgrim's lips. ''Are you saying that a friend of my family actually had Alex murdered?''

''Yes, Kate. Remember, the notes Alex valued the most, the ones he kept in that secret compartment, had to do with the railroad. It was the connection of the railroad to the mines that drew him down into the Get Lucky. And he died there because he was getting too close to exposing that connection—and William Henry Aldrich.''

Although Katherine's emotions strongly resisted that idea, her clear, sound mind quickly embraced the logic in it. ''Henry has been trying to keep me away from Alex's office and apartment ever since I arrived in Central City,'' she admitted.

''Because Henry was the one who wrecked them,'' Matt offered, ''trying to find any incriminating evidence Alex might have left behind.''

''And the key!'' she recalled.

''What key?''

''The key to Alex's hidden safe. All the time Henry must have been trying to get it away from me. I had no idea! That's why he went through my luggage. And that's why he sneaked into my room. He was searching for that key!''

''He must have made plans for you, Kate,'' Matt deduced. ''After he had devised a scheme that would make him rich, you came out of the East and straight into his house. He instantly decided you'd make a perfect wife for a wealthy man. He didn't even care that he had killed your brother.''

Katherine uselessly tried to shake the idea out of her head. It made too much sense now for her to abandon it. "All that matters to Henry is money and power, Matt," she revealed. "He told me that once. He believes that a man can have no real dignity or worth until he possesses those two things."

"I don't see much of either in manipulating people like the Bonners into murder and robbery and sabotage."

"But he's so well-mannered, Matt. That's what makes it so hard to believe. He's so much like the people I've always known. Like the people back home!"

"Aldrich is a new kind of criminal in this country, Kate. He's an educated, sophisticated man who uses other people to do his dirty work for him, while he maintains the perfect face of respectability for himself. He understands enough of the complexity of a changing world to be able to use it for his own gain."

Reuben took the letter from Kate. "That kind of criminal is too much for a small-town sheriff like Potts," he said.

"Yes, he is," Matt agreed. "And crime of this sort is too much for one or two detectives. That's why America needs the Agency. Only through a cooperative network of information can we hope to deal with it—" Matt stopped at the sight of his partner lunging for the door. "Reuben!" he called out to him. "Where are you going?"

"I'm leaving the Agency business to you, Mr. Pilgrim," he said. "You take care of Mr. Aldrich. I'll take care of Clayton Bonner."

"Reuben!"

"You said I needed evidence, Mr. Pilgrim," He whipped open the door. "I think these two letters are evidence enough, don't you?"

"Reuben!"

Just as Katherine and Matthew burst out of the office after Reuben, the streets all of a sudden began to fill with people from every lighted corner and shadowed alley of Central City. Katherine recoiled at the crack of a gunshot, then another, as a man stormed into town on a sorrel mare, waving his pistol over his head and shouting, "Robbery! Robbery!"

Ben Watkins was the man who grabbed the reins and hauled down the rider. "What's happened, Ellis?" he asked. "What robbery!"

The elderly man hung on to the saddle horn while he struggled for breath. "Train robbery," he gasped. "Payroll!"

"Where did it happen!"

"Outside of Blackhawk."

The mine manager swallowed a load of tobacco juice with a grimace. "Did you hear that, gents!" he shouted to the crowd gathering around him. "The whole damn world's falling apart, and we're standing around here, letting it happen!"

"Who did it, Ellis?" someone asked. "Who hit the train?"

"It was the Bonners," he puffed hard. "They blew up the tracks and stopped the train!"

"All right, let's go get them," Watkins enjoined. "Which way did they go, Ellis?"

"Looks like they're heading down to Denver, Ben," he answered. "And so are we!"

"Count us in on it, Ben!" the men shouted. "We're with you!"

"Then mount your horses, gents. Let's go!"

Before Watkins could move, Katherine felt Matt's thigh touch hers as he broke away from her into the swarm of people in the street. In an instant, he was leaping up on the back of a wagon and calling for quiet.

"Men!" he yelled as a white bolt of lightning zigzagged wildly across the black sky. "Stop! Listen to me!"

Watkins paused as the thunder rolled. "We've already listened to you, Mr. Detective," he returned. "Now we've got work to do!"

"No, wait!"

"We've waited long enough, Pilgrim."

"If you go out there now, you're going to be killed! Do it according to the law, men! We now know who's behind the cave-ins and the murders in Central City. Let's get him first!"

"Who are you talking about, Pilgrim?" a miner asked.

"Yeah, tell us who it is," the others demanded. "If there really is such a person."

"Well, how about it, Mr. Detective?" Watkins pressed. "Is there? If there is, say it. These men want to know."

"I'll tell the sheriff who it is," Matt replied. "He's still the law in Central City."

"Damn the law!" Watkins growled. "I say let's take these outlaws ourselves! Let's make them pay for what they did to Alice Canfield!"

Matt singled out the mine manager. "Watkins, you're trying to turn this into your own personal revenge!" he charged.

"Why shouldn't I?" he contended. "The man that killed

Alice Canfield ain't any better than the bastard that raped and killed my little girl in Leadville, is he?''

"You killed that man years ago, Watkins," Matt charged. "He's paid for his crime."

"But this one hasn't. Right, gents?"

"Right, Ben!"

"But you can't twist the law to suit your own personal feelings! Ben, don't herd all these people into an ambush in the dark just because you're still hurting over the death of your daughter!"

"Shut up, Pilgrim."

"Men!" he appealed to the troubled faces in the crowd of men bearing rifles and pistols in the streets. "Go to Sheriff Potts. Make him arrest the one man responsible for all that's been happening in Central City. Then we can form a legal posse and go after the Bonners."

"Who is this man, Pilgrim?" someone cried. "Tell us!"

Matt hesitated until the men began to move. Then he spoke up. "All right!" he cried. "I'll tell you. The man is Aldrich. William Henry Aldrich."

Ben Watkins broke a long pause of silence with a loud guffaw. "You're touched in the head, Mr. Detective," he accused.

"No, I'm not."

"It couldn't be him. He stopped us from going out a while ago, just like you're trying to do!"

"He stopped you in order to give the Bonners enough time to rob the train, Ben."

"You're talking crazy, Pilgrim. Ain't he, gents!"

The men offered a loud "Yeah!" in response.

"You know you can't believe a Pinkerton!" Watkins

bellowed. "Come on, mount your horses! We've got outlaws to kill!"

"Wait!" Matt pleaded.

"No! No more waiting!"

Pilgrim leaped to the ground as the crowd began to disperse in varioud directions toward the waiting horses and wagons. "Think about what you're doing! You're abandoning the law!"

"Sometimes that's just what a man has to do." Watkins slung his leg over his horse's rump and settled into the saddle.

"Don't you realize, if you break the law, you're outlaws, too!"

"Give it up, detective. We're on our way. We're going to go get these sons-of-bitches, ain't we, men!"

"Yes!"

"Then let's ride, gents!" Watkins let out a croak, dug his spurs into his mount, and lunged ahead.

In a loud, clashing rush of clumping horses' hooves and spinning wheels in the dirt of Central City, hundreds of men suddenly began to pour out of the town and squeeze together in rows of a dozen on the road to Blackhawk. In no more than a few fleeting seconds, the rutted streets were completely vacant, except for Matthew Pilgrim.

Katherine could see the imprint of discouragement and frustration in his face as he walked back to her. But she saw no sign of defeat. She knew Matt Pilgrim well enough now to understand that he was a man who would never give in to anything.

Joining her, he kept his eyes on the noisy receding mob. "For their sake," he said, "I hope the Bonners are on their way to Kansas by now."

"But you don't think they are," she guessed.

"No. They'll hang around long enough for the pay-off from Aldrich." He quickly surveyed the street. "Was Reuben with them?" he asked.

She shrugged her shoulders. "I don't know, Matt," she answered. "I lost him in the crowd."

"He was headed for trouble when he left the *Banner* office a while ago."

"He's taking the loss of Alice very hard," she noted.

Matt nodded hopefully. "Maybe he went back to the sheriff's office to be with her."

"I hope so. I hate to think of him out there in the dark. And the rain," she added as the clouds opened up and at last began to drop water from the sky.

Matt instantly grabbed her hand and hurried her out of the street to the covered walkway. Then, without a pause, they headed through the noise of the pounding rain for the office of Alvin Potts.

21

The only occupants of the sheriff's office were Barton Canfield and the corpse of his daughter. Looking pale and sickly now, the mine supervisor was squeezing Alice's cold, limp fingers in his clasped hands and staring down at the covered body with puffy, tearful eyes.

"Matt?" He looked up the instant they entered the office. "Will you help me?"

"Anything, Mr. Canfield."

"I don't want her here," he stated flatly. "I wanted to take her to the undertaker's. But I guess all this has been too much for me. I couldn't even pick her up—"

"I'll take her, Mr. Canfield," he volunteered.

"Thank you." He smiled grimly and carefully tucked her arm out of sight beneath the blanket. "Even though she was plump, she never did weigh much. I should've been able to carry her again."

"Kate," he said to her as he raised the body up and nestled it in his arms, "Reuben may be coming back."

"I'll stay here," she said.

"Good. Mr. Canfield?" he addressed the older man.

The mine supervisor was making sure Alice's head was

285

covered properly. "She was always very particular about her hair," he said weakly. "Just like her mother."

"Are you ready to go, sir?" Matt asked him.

"Yes," he answered with a sigh. "I am."

After holding the door open for them to go out, Katherine stood on the walkway and watched the two figures glide slowly under cover for a hundred feet or so, then dash briskly across the street through the driving rain. Soon they were turning a corner and disappearing into the night.

She lingered on the walkway to watch the ruts in the empty streets swiftly fill up with water. It was a cold, unpleasant rain riding the gusts of a raw northern wind down from the hills. She couldn't help but think of the men of Central City strung out helplessly along a mountain pass, pushing slowly into a blinding rainstorm, offering their bodies as easy targets for the bloodthirsty outlaws, Seth Bonner and his brothers.

Where, she wondered, was Reuben Canfield? Was he with them on that mountain pass? Was he, like Alice and Deke and her own brother, destined to become another of the Bonners' victims? She shuddered at the thought of watching Matthew Pilgrim stiffly but tearfully lowering the body of his friend beside Alice's in the undertaker's parlor.

Feeling tense and uneasy, Katherine stepped back inside the office and closed out the rain by shutting the door. Alone in the icy room, she felt cold and clanked open the stove to stoke the fire. But it was no use. By now the fire had turned to ashes. Looking around the place, she discovered that the only firewood was stacked outside, soaking up the rain in the alley. Although she tried to warm herself by pacing up and down for a while, she knew it wouldn't help. The cold numbness that was creeping into her flesh and bones wasn't the result of the rain or the drop in the temperature. In the past few days, she had learned to recognize all the morbid effects of fear upon the soul.

A sudden thump on the walkway outside brought her pacing to a halt. She started for the door, then stopped.

"Matt?" she called out.

Immediately she realized it was a useless word to utter. It was clear to her that the hard, heavy footsteps she was hearing on the walk could not be his. The man stalking the office was much larger and heavier than Matt—a man the size of Seth Bonner! When she heard the sound of leather against the wood of the step, she clutched her throat and pressed her eyelids tight and prayed that he would turn around and go away.

But the man kept bumping up the walk, increasing his pace as he headed straight for the office. He was close now—too near for her to have time enough to reach for the lock. All she could do was brace herself and wait for the intruder.

The door flew open and banged against the wall as a mammoth older man in rumpled gray clothes lumbered in.

"Sheriff Potts!" she gasped in relief.

"What are you doing here, lady?" he rebuked and slammed the door shut.

"I'm . . . waiting for someone," she fumbled. "Matt Pilgrim."

"Who went off with the Canfield girl?" he asked.

"Matt and Mr. Canfield took her to the undertaker's office," she replied.

"Good," he grumbled. "That's where they should've taken her in the first place."

Intimidated by the massive bulk of Alvin Potts, Katherine withdrew a few steps as he ambled over to the rifle rack and stuck a key into the padlock on the bar. "What are you going to do?" she asked him.

"I reckon I'm going to do my job for once," he replied.

"I don't understand."

He sprang open the lock and slapped back the steel bar. "Maybe I don't either. Maybe it's the rain."

"The rain?" she puzzled.

"Yeah. Rain always has made me get up and do things. And I'm sure people are saying it's high time old Potts got up and did something, ain't they?"

She let his question pass. "You're not going after the Bonners, too?" she said.

"Not hardly." He snapped down a Springfield rifle, pressed the butt of the stock tight against his shoulder, and aimed down the barrel. "I was out there listening to what that detective was telling the mob a while ago. I heard who's behind all this crime in the gulch. I figure I'll just go and arrest William Henry Aldrich and be done with it."

She waited until he had dropped a handful of cartridges into his trousers before she spoke. "Shouldn't you wait for Matt?" she asked. "He'll be back any minute."

"No need to; Aldrich ain't dangerous," he responded. "This is one job even worthless drunk like Alvin Potts can do." He propped the gun on the desk and looked at her. "But there's one thing you've got to remember, young lady. I don't want you to tell a living soul who threw him in the cell, do you hear me?"

"Why not?"

"Because I don't want to give them the satisfaction of knowing, that's why. I ain't doing this for anybody but me. Understand?"

"No, I don't, Sheriff."

"Well, since you're a woman, you don't have to. All

288

you have to do is make sure you keep that pretty mouth of yours shut tight as a handshake on the subject of Sheriff Potts. Do you follow me, ma'am?''

''Yes.''

''Good.''

Suddenly the door swung open again and the voluptuous figure of Andrea Sherbourne appeared in the doorway. Peeling the dripping red silk shawl off her hair, she stared at Potts, speechless and dumbfounded.

''What's the matter with you, Hilda Jane?'' he muttered. ''Never seen a man with a gun before?''

''I . . . didn't think you'd be here,'' she faltered. ''After what I said.''

''As a matter of fact, I ain't here,'' he returned. ''I just come back to pick up a gun.''

She stepped into the room, keeping her eyes fixed on him. ''Alvin,'' she said anxiously, ''since you are, I want you to—''

''Don't go asking me for help, woman,'' he broke in. ''I can't give it.''

''It's not for me, Alvin,'' she told him. ''It's for one of my girls.''

''I don't care a yap in Hades about your girls, Hilda Jane,'' he stated defiantly.

''It's Billie Simms, Alvin. She's gone!''

''You think I'm going to cry over that? Hell, a girl like that one ought to be home suckling babies anyway, instead of laying on her back in a parlor house.''

''I don't mean she left, Alvin. She was taken! It was that Clayton Bonner. He took her; I know he did. Oh, after the way he acted that first time, I never should have let him see her! But I was greedy—''

"Hold on, there. How do you know Clayton Bonner took her away? Did you see him?"

"No, but who else could it have been?"

"Damn, how should I know? Maybe she left on her own."

"No," she stated emphatically. "She didn't do that."

"Now how can you be so sure of that?" he challenged.

"I'm sure because of these." She opened her clenched fist to reveal a pair of pince-nez spectacles, with the frames bent double and both lenses smashed. "She never would have left without her glasses. She used to say these spectacles was the only thing that made her different from the other girls. She never would have left them behind!"

After staring steadily at the glasses for a long time, Potts finally shook his head. "This ain't enough evidence to act on," he concluded.

"Of course it is!" she erupted. "I swear to you, Clayton Bonner has taken one of my girls!"

The sheriff stirred uncomfortably. "Maybe he has, and maybe he hasn't," he said, fidgeting with the breech of the rifle.

"Alvin, you already have a gun in your hands. Can't you just walk out that door now and find him?"

He ground his teeth. "I didn't count on going after a Bonner," he mumbled. After a moment's hesitation, he eased the rifle quietly down on the top of the desk. "I should've let well enough alone." With a grunt, he yanked open a drawer and drew out a bottle of rye whiskey.

"You're not going to find any courage in that," Andrea reprimanded.

Blithely he pinched out the cork, raised the bottle to his lips, and sucked in the liquor. "I know I won't," he said.

Taking a deep breath, he quickly forced down another big swallow.

"Then why do it!" she admonished.

"Maybe because people won't let me alone!" he retorted.

She glowered at him. "If you really want to be left alone, Alvin Potts, why don't you run off to the hills and crawl under a rock? Why don't you stop pretending you're a man and let everyone who cares about you forget you once and for all?"

He lowered the bottle next to the shiny stock of the Springfield rifle. "I was lying to myself, lady," he muttered to Katherine. "I couldn't have arrested Henry Aldrich. I would've messed it up, somehow. I ain't done anything right in ten years."

"Eleven," Andrea corrected.

"All right, eleven. So there's not much use in acting like I could start now, is there?"

"You could try! All anybody can ever do is try, Alvin!"

"Damn it!" he growled and hurled the whiskey bottle against the wall, shattering the glass and splashing the liquor everywhere. "I can't! Don't you understand, woman? I can't face anything. I've lost my nerve!"

"Then get it back, Sheriff," she persisted. "Help me. Help Billie Simms!"

"Why are you so damned concerned over one little girl—"

"Because I brought her here," she cried. "I'm responsible for her. I can't stand by and let this happen to her!"

A look of pain flashed across the sheriff's wrinkled face as he considered her words. "Well, maybe you can't. But I can," he said resignedly.

"Alvin, don't give up—please!"

The big lawman reached down into his pockets, drew

out a handful of brass-cased cartridges, and dropped them on the desk. "I don't reckon I'll be needing these," he said.

"Alvin—"

"I won't be using this, either." He lifted his .45 calibre revolver out of his holster and held the gun in the palm of his wide hand. "Not ever again." But before he could lay the pistol down, he reacted to the low and pitiful wail of a woman outside in the rain. "What in lower Hades is that!" he said.

"It's Billie!" Andrea exclaimed.

"Uh-uh," he disagreed. "That sounds like an animal, Hilda Jane."

"No, it's Billie!" She whipped open the door and sprang out to the walkway. "It's coming from down there," she noted to Katherine.

"All I can see is rain," Katherine complained, straining to see where the other woman was pointing.

"But I know she's there. That was her voice!"

Still holding his pistol, Potts took Andrea's arm. "There ain't anybody here, Hilda Jane," he told her. "This whole town's deserted."

Annoyed, Andrea jerked her arm free. "She's down the street," she insisted. "I heard her!"

"Well, if that was her, she's gone now. We might as well go back in."

"Not yet," she replied sternly, then inched closer to the street. Gaping into a sheet of steady, light rain, she called out to her—in vain.

"You see?" Potts said nervously. "I told you it wasn't a woman."

"Billie!" she beckoned again. "Billie—answer me!"

Seconds later, a small, feeble voice groaned helplessly through the falling rain. "Miss Sherbourne—help me!"

At the same insant Katherine detected the plaintive cry of Billie Simms, she could see a frail little girl being dragged up the street by the lean blond outlaw, Clayton Bonner. Drawing to within ten yards of the sheriff's office, he abruptly pulled Billie's back against his chest and crooked his arm around her throat.

"Alvin," Andrea fretted, "he's going to hurt her."

"Hush, woman."

"But look at him! He's choking her! She can't breathe!"

"You!" Clayton yelled and pointed his finger at Potts. "I want you to bring me a wagon—right here, right now!"

"Don't give him anything, Alvin," Andrea said.

"He'll murder that girl of yours if I don't," he returned.

"That's right, Sheriff," Clayton warned. "I'll snap her bony little neck if I have to."

"You don't need to do that, Bonner—"

"Then do what I say!" he demanded. "Bring me a wagon. Hurry up!"

"Everybody's gone, Clayton," Potts fumbled. "I don't know if there are any left."

"Well, there had better be, Sheriff. If you want my little lady here to leave this filthy place alive."

"There should be a rental carriage at the livery stable—"

"Then get it, old man!" he commanded. "Now!"

Andrea reached out and snatched his wrist. "Don't do it, Alvin," she pleaded in a low voice. "He'll take her away—God knows where!"

"I don't have any other choice, woman."

"Yes, you do," she argued. "You're holding a gun in your hand. Use it! Stop him!"

He shook his head thoughtfully. "He's holding the aces,

293

Hilda Jane,'' he said. ''I've got to back out and do what he says.''

''People are right about you, Alvin Potts,'' she accused. ''You're nothing but a coward!''

''Damn it, woman!''

''Sheriff!'' Clayton barked. ''I'm waiting. And I don't like to be kept waiting.''

All of a sudden, the startling detonation of a pistol sent a quick convulsion of fear through Katherine's raw and excited nerves. At first, she thought it had exploded in her own brain. Then she realized the sound had come from the direction of the Mercer Hotel, for close to that place, standing in the street with a gun barrel pointed at the sky, was Reuben Canfield.

Katherine felt frozen to the walk as she witnessed the outlaw spinning toward the other man in the street. Her throat grew tight and began to throb with her pulse as the outlaw slapped his hand down to his leather holster and flicked out a shiny, new Colt .45. Without a pause, he brought up the gun and aimed it directly at Reuben's chest. It was then that Billie Simms began to push and kick and wiggle to get free.

''Reuben!'' she screeched. ''Run! Run!''

''Shut up, girl,'' Bonner grunted.

''Oh, don't shoot him, Clayton,'' she begged. ''Please, don't!''

''Be still!'' He tightened his grip on her throat.

In the middle of the street, thirty yards away, Reuben was leveling his gun. Looking down the barrel, he challenged the outlaw. ''You killed my sister, Bonner!'' he charged.

''Reuben, go away!'' Billie pleaded.

''Shut *up!*'' Bonner snapped her hard against his chest.

Reuben cocked his pistol. "Stop hiding behind her and face me, Clayton," he ordered. "Man to man!"

"You stupid miner—"

"Let her go and face me, damn you!"

Bonner was beginning to squirm now. "I didn't want to kill anybody," he whined. "I didn't mean to kill that girl. She made me! She kept hollering and screaming—"

"You're an animal, Bonner—"

"I told you, I didn't want to do it!" He wailed. "I just wanted to leave! But she kept screaming at me. I had to stop her!"

"You—" Reuben threatened, but the sound of his voice vanished in the loud crack of Clayton Bonner's pistol.

Katherine was jolted and bewildered by the devastating shock of what happened before her eyes. As she stood helpless on the walkway, Clayton in one continuous motion pulled back the hammer of his Colt with his thumb and squeezed the trigger with his index finger. In the moment the smoke was bursting out of the barrel of the new gun, Reuben Canfield was buckling and crumbling to the ground. Katherine saw no blood and heard no other sound but the awful, jarring shot of Bonner's gun. And yet, there the man lay—the vibrant, energetic Reuben Canfield, as still as death on the cold, wet ground.

"Reuben!" Billie Simms shrieked. "Oh, no—"

"Come on, girl." Clayton yanked at her.

"Stop it! Let me go! Oh, Lord—Reuben!"

"Come on!"

"He's the only man who ever treated me proper, Clayton. And look what you've done to him!"

"He made me, Billie," he defended himself.

She squealed and wriggled wildly in his clutches. "Let me go to him! Let me go!"

"No, damn you! You're coming with me!"

"I won't! Not ever!"

"I'm ordering you, Billie!"

"I want to go to Reuben!" She whimpered and twisted in his arm.

On the walkway, Andrea Sherbourne turned away in disgust. "Alvin!" she cried. "For once in your life—be a man! Stop him!"

With pain and irritation in his deeply etched face, Potts clenched his teeth and nodded. "I reckon I've got to try it," he declared. "Once." Without another word, he stepped off the wood into the soft mud and deliberately, shakily stalked out to the middle of the street.

With his pistol at his side, the sheriff stopped and faced the outlaw, who was struggling to keep his hold on Billie Simms. "All right now, Bonner," he said in a wavering voice, "I'm ordering you . . . to give yourself up!"

"You're crazy!"

"I'm still the sheriff here, Bonner," he declared fearfully.

"You're nothing but a joke, Potts," Clayton defied.

"You should never have shot that boy, Bonner," he said. "Not in front of me," He slowly lifted his pistol, which trembled uncontrollably in his big fist.

"You people are all crazy!" Bonner exclaimed, "You're making me kill you!"

"You went too far, Clayton. You rubbed my face in it."

Bonner laughed. "Look at you, old man. You're shaking like a leaf! You're pathetic!"

"Even I can still squeeze a trigger, outlaw. And I might even hit you."

"Not a chance—"

"Release that girl and give up, Clayton," he demanded in a quavering voice. "I mean it!"

"Let me tell you something, Potts. It'll take more than you to take my little Mom away from me!"

"How about me, too, Bonner?" A voice from behind the sheriff spoke up.

The absolute worst fear of Katherine Haynes was realized suddenly and without warning, for walking slowly into the range of Bonner's gun was the man she loved. He came to a halt parallel to Alvin Potts, only twenty paces from the deadly weapon.

She leaned against a post and gripped it with all her might. She felt completely helpless. This terrible scene was playing before her and she could do nothing about it. Matthew Pilgrim was standing unarmed against an outlaw with nothing but Alvin Potts' courage and aim to protect him. She cringed at how terribly vulnerable he looked. In the space of a single breath, he could be lying dead in the streets! And she would never hear his voice again.

"Miss Sherbourne!" Katherine cried. "Can't we do something?"

The other woman shook her head sadly. "There's nothing a woman can do," she answered.

"But we can't just *watch!*"

"It's all they allow us to do," she said. "Watch and pray."

Bonner aimed his weapon directly at Matthew Pilgrim. "I'm tired of you butting in, sir," he said coldly.

"Bonner, listen to me," Matt said. "There are other people in this town. You can't see them, but they're here, watching you. It won't do you any good to leave; they'll come after you."

"Don't tell me what to do! I'm smarter than you are!"

"If you're smart, you'll give up while you're still breathing!"

"I said don't tell me what to do!" he yelled. Then, abruptly he cocked his pistol and fired.

The shot went awry when the squirming Billie Simms knocked her shoulder against his wrist. Angrily, the outlaw swung her around by the neck and hurled her to the ground. After watching her scramble down the street toward Reuben Canfield, he pivoted quickly to face Matt and the sheriff.

"Now, sir," he said to Pilgrim, "you've got no one to protect you."

At that instant, Alvin Potts let out a growl and bolted toward Pilgrim, lunging directly in front of the detective, into Bonner's line of fire. A shot rang out in the rain, and a .45 calibre slug of lead thumped into his side, tearing bloody flesh into the air as he doubled over and dropped to his knees .

While Andrea Sherbourne shrieked madly at him, Alvin Potts pushed himself up and struggled to his feet to face the outlaw. Before he could raise his gun an inch, Bonner had squeezed off another shot. This time the bullet struck straight and true and tore apart the sheriff's chest. Under the tremendous impact of the hit, he stumbled backwards, plopped to earth, and stuck like a heavy stone in the mud. Close to death now, he still managed to reach out his arm and grope blindly through the mire for his pistol.

"Alvin!" Andrea Sherbourne clutched at her throat and screamed. "Oh, Lord, what have I done to him?"

Shaking violently, Bonner turned to Pilgrim again. "Now it's your turn," he wavered.

Hearing that terrible threat, Katherine could take no

more. Abandoning all caution, she leaped out into the rain and headed straight for the detective.

"Kate—go back!" Matt warned.

"Matt—"

"Kate, stop!"

Katherine's right foot sank into a watery hole in the street, and she stumbled forward. But she regained her balance quickly enough to see Clayton Bonner fire his pistol again. With horror, she heard the ghastly eruption of gunpowder and saw Pilgrim's head kick backwards as a screaming bullet grazed his skull and shot a spray of blood into the mud.

When she reached him, he was on his back and groaning in pain, too groggy to raise himself up. "Oh, Matt!" she cried, sinking to her knees. She looked at the wound. Although it was slight, it was bleeding profusely. Blood was pouring down his temple and chin.

The moment she pressed her hands against the bloody gash, she became aware of a man standing a yard away, aiming his pistol straight at Pilgrim's face.

"You've seen what Clayton Bonner is made of," Bonner breathed heavily. "Now let's see what's inside this dude of yours."

"No!" Katherine lay her chest over Matthew's head, shielding him from Bonner's gun.

"Move, lady, or I'll shoot you, instead," he threatened.

"Then shoot me!" she cried.

"Kate—" Matt protested beneath her.

"Matt, don't move—please!"

"It's your choice, ma'am," Bonner offered. "You're forcing me to do it!"

"Then do it!" she shouted. "Shoot!"

Katherine recoiled at the faint metallic *click* of the hammer of the outlaw's pistol. Shivering with her fear and the cold from the rain soaking her back, she braced herself for the shot. In one instant, she thought, there would be no more of any of this. No more Matt Pilgrim. All would be lost.

Her whole body vibrated at the sound of the blast of the sheriff's gun. She raised her head and saw Clayton Bonner sprawled in the mud, in the driving rain. He lay on his back, silent and cold, gripping tightly his Colt .45 pistol in his fist. Not a muscle of his body stirred. There was only blood trickling down from the bullet hole in the center of his forehead to the ground below.

"Kate—" Matt groaned.

"Hush, now," she said, her eyes full of tears. Slowly and carefully, she lifted his head and laid it gently into her lap. "It's all over now," she told him. "There's nothing else to worry about. Clayton Bonner's gone."

"Kate, I've got to go look after Reuben," he grunted.

When she peered down the street into the rain, she saw the other detective struggling to raise himself up. "Reuben's alive, Matt," she reported. "Billie's with him."

"What about Potts?"

She shook her head pensively as she moved her eyes to the big sheriff, moaning and spitting blood against the bosom of Andrea Sherbourne.

"You crazy old man," she was crying. "I didn't mean for you to do that! After all these years, you just had to be a hero."

"I . . . did get him, didn't I?" Potts gasped for air.

"Yes, you got him," she replied. "He's dead."

"That boy stood there and rubbed my nose in it, Hilda Jane," he explained. "I couldn't back away!"

"I know."

"I want you to tell that detective for me, Hilda Jane. Tell him we can . . . still do the job. He'll know what that means."

"I'll tell him, Alvin," she sobbed.

He smiled painfully. "I'm sure glad it finally rained," he mumbled. "Feels better now."

"Alvin, do you know how much time we've wasted—"

"It's good it finally rained. I was getting mighty dry."

"Alvin?" She tried to shake him into consciousness. "Alvin—don't die, please! Oh, God!" she shrieked and pulled his lifeless, bleeding body closer to her chest. "Oh, dear, sweet God. . . ."

Katherine turned away from them with tears pouring down her cheeks. When she touched her fingers to the blood on Matthew's temple, he flinched. "I've got to get you to a doctor," she decided. "I can't let you lie there another minute!"

"Kate—" He resisted.

"Matt, if I don't do something soon, you're going to bleed to death!"

"No, listen!"

"I've got to get you out of the rain!"

"Kate, listen!" he moaned painfully. "I hear horses!"

Katherine hesitated at a low, rumbling sound in the distance. "It can't be," she asserted. "Everybody's out with the posse."

"It must be the Bonners," he concluded.

"Oh, Matt, no!"

He pressed his eyelids tight, tried to raise his head, but fell back helplessly. "I can't move, Kate. You're going to have to leave me here."

"I will do no such thing!"

"I want you to get out of the street, Katherine!"

"Well, I'm not going to. Not without you."

"They must be coming for Clayton—"

"Matt, stop it! I'm not leaving you here. So save your breath!"

She could hear the sound clearly and distinctly now, even in the rain. It was close enough for her to recognize it as the pounding of horses' hooves against hard mountain rock. A band of horsemen was headed at full gallop into Central City. Quickly she looked down the street at Reuben and Billie. Although the other detective had made it to his knees, he obviously was in no shape to stand against Seth Bonner and his brothers. And her only other protector, Sheriff Alvin Potts, had taken in his last breath. It was up to her.

"Katherine . . ." Matt said groggily, then drifted out of consciousness.

"I'm sorry, Matt," she said to him. "I'm not going to run away!" She eased his head to the ground and crawled through the mud to the body of the sheriff. "Miss Sherbourne!" she called to the other women over the sound of the falling rain. "Where is the gun?"

"What?" she answered absently.

"Where is his gun?"

"I don't know," she answered, shaking her head. "What does it matter where it is?"

Katherine plunged her hands anxiously into the slimy mud and dug wildly for the pistol, while the noise of the approaching horses grew louder and louder. The mire was cold and oozy as she gouged her fingers close to the still body of Sheriff Potts. At last, she felt the slick, hard finish of metal and the grainy firmness of wood. With her pulse racing, she snapped the big weapon out of the street.

Andrea Sherbourne cuddled the sheriff's body against

her bosom. "You'll never be able to stop them," she warned.

"Deke told me they don't shoot women," she returned. "If that's true, we have a chance."

She shook her head. When they see what we've done to their brother, they won't care if we're women. They'll kill us all!"

Katherine shuddered at the clattering noise of the horses drawing near. Despite what she had told Miss Sherbourne, she had no idea what to expect from these outlaws. How could she have been so stupid about these violent and unpredictable men? They were not romantic Robin Hoods, as she had believed. And they weren't people cut from the herd and struggling to stay alive. They were criminals with a radically different morality and code of conduct from the rest of society. And for that reason, they were terrifying.

She burst into tears to find Matthew lying curled on his side—unconscious, helpless, and alone in the pouring rain. Planting her boots into the soggy ground next to his legs, she wiped the big gun on the folds of her skirt and waited breathlessly as the horses thundered closer and closer to the outskirts of town.

The massive weapon felt incredibly heavy as she raised it to the level of her chest. It felt so unwieldy in her small hands that she knew she couldn't possibly manage much more than a single shot before they leaped off their horses and pounced on her. She suspected it was utterly useless to stand in the street this way and defend her wounded man. But there was no way not to do it. She had to try.

She could distinguish the men on horses now, storming up the road to Blackhawk in the driving rain. Unable to make out the shapes and faces of the men, she was able to

303

pick out something that made the pistol in her hands feel a thousand times heavier—the spotted horse of Seth Bonner!

With every ounce of her strength, she pulled back the heavy hammer of the .45 and clicked it into a cocked position. Spreading her legs slightly, Katherine braced herself for the outlaws. After a final glance at the man she loved, she was ready.

Just as the rain began to slacken, over a dozen horses rushed into town, tramping into the quagmire of the city streets and splashing water and mud into the air. Holding her breath, she pointed the barrel at the man in the lead, tightened a finger around the trigger—then abruptly stopped. A powerful sense of relief nearly overwhelmed her as she determined that the man on the first horse was not Seth Bonner! He was a firm and stout gentleman in a long, black raincoat and a derby hat—a man she had met once in her father's office in Chicago, five years ago: William A. Pinkerton.

Katherine let down the gun, then dropped it into the mud as Pinkerton reined up close and climbed down from his horse. A pleasant, square-faced man with a thick, neatly trimmed moustache, he cordially tipped his hat to her.

"Are you all right, ma'am?" he asked her.

"Yes," she answered, feeling suddenly very tired.

"Benson!" he called to one of the twelve similarly dressed men in the group. "Take care of these people."

A young man with a fresh face and an eager look hopped off his mount. "Be glad to, sir!" he responded.

After checking the dead sheriff, Pinkerton knelt down with Katherine beside Matt. "I think he'll make it without too much trouble," he told her after he examined the wound.

She took a deep breath. "At least he's stopped bleeding," she said.

"It's hard to keep a Pinkerton man down," he smiled.

She steadied herself with a hand on Pinkerton's arm, as two of the detectives hauled Seth Bonner down from his spotted horse and pulled him and his brothers past her. She grasped it tightly as she watched them head toward the sheriff's office, then come to a stop a few feet away from Clayton's body.

As they gazed down on it, Thomas Bonner spoke. " 'The wicked are estranged from the womb,' " he quoted. " 'They go astray as soon as they're born.' "

"Why don't you shut up, Thomas," Seth snarled.

"I was just saying he was bad, Seth," he mumbled defensively. "Clayton was always bad."

"You think you're any better, going around spouting that tripe all the time?"

"I'm sorry, Seth."

"Just keep that filth to yourself, that's all."

One of the twins peeked over the body. "Looks like our brother's sure enough dead, don't it, Seth?" he said.

"That's right, Mick, he's dead," Seth replied. "I told him clear and simple to stay in the house where he belonged. But, like always, he was too stupid to listen. Clayton was damn near as stupid as Deke."

The other twin nodded. "It appears you was right about Clayton, Seth," Buck declared. "He was always itching to die."

Seth took a long last look at Clayton, then spit on the ground. "I swear to God," he muttered and started off with the detectives, "the son-of-a-bitch looks like a damn little girl, laying there."

Relaxing a little after the outlaws stepped into the sheriff's office, Katherine let go of Pinkerton to help the detectives pick up Matt. "Please be careful," she told them.

"We will be, ma'am," Benson assured her. "He's one of us."

She watched apprehensively as two stalwart men in dark beards lifted him up. "Watch it—he's starting to bleed again—"

"We're taking him to the doctor, ma'am," Benson interrupted. "I promise you, he'll be just fine."

Katherine nodded and forced a smile. "I guess by now I should be able to trust a Pinkerton man," she sighed.

"Believe me, you can, ma'am."

"Sir!" the detective attending Reuben Canfield called from down the street.

Pinkerton faced him. "What is it, Rawlings?" he responded.

"This one's all right, sir. All he's got is a broken shoulder!"

"Good. Take him to the doctor's office, Rice!"

Katherine looked at Pinkerton with curiosity. "I don't understand what you're doing here," she said to him. "What prompted you to come?"

"We were following the recommendation of our agent, Matt Pilgrim, ma'am," he answered promptly. "He telegraphed me in Denver that the train was going to be robbed this evening by these men."

"But he didn't know that."

"He knew enough to infer it. And, of course, he was right. We came as quickly as we could and camped out on both sides of Blackhawk. The rain kept us from preventing the Bonners from blowing the tracks. But, as you see, we did catch up to them."

"I'm certainly glad you did."

"Now you'll have to tell me the story of what happened here, ma'am," he said. "That is, after you've had a chance to get into some dry clothes."

"Yes," she said vaguely, watching the Pinkertons lug the huge body of Alvin Potts out of the street.

"In the meantime," Pinkerton said, "we'll need a place to gather, so to speak. Since you're a native of this place, you must know which building would best suit our purposes?"

She didn't bother to correct him. "The Teller House would be best," she said simply.

"Oh, yes, I've heard of the Teller House. All right, men," he called to the others. "Clear the streets! Let's get in out of the rain!"

22

Katherine felt fresh and invigorated as she came down the steps of the Teller House two hours later. At the foot of the stairway, she saw Matt Pilgrim in the lobby, tugging absently at the bandage on his head while he talked to William Pinkerton. Across the room was Reuben Canfield, wearing a wrap and a splint on his left arm and shoulder, but still managing to give a display of his scientific evidence to an interested circle of detectives. And coming up to her now was Simmons, the desk clerk, with a worried look on his face.

"Miss Haynes," he fretted, "this Pinkerton . . . 'convention' is getting out of hand. I wonder if you might persuade these gentlemen to conclude their business soon?"

"Mr. Simmons, I don't have any influence with William Pinkerton."

"No, but I have noticed that you do have some with Mr. Pilgrim—"

"Kate!" Matt hurried over as soon as he spotted her. "You look beautiful," he said as he escorted her into the lobby.

"Matt," she said hesitantly, "a while ago, I sent a telegraph—"

"Ah, Miss Haynes!" William Pinkerton stepped up to her, took her hand, and gallantly kissed the back of it. "May I apologize for not recognizing you out in the street? It's just that I never would have expected to see Gardner Haynes's daughter in Central City, Colorado."

"I can understand that."

"I was just describing to Matt the courageous way you handled yourself out there."

"All I was doing was what any other woman would have done," she said, looking at Matt. "I was trying to protect something I care about."

"Mr. Pinkerton!" Benson's voice rang through the lobby from the open front door. "We have him!"

"Good. Bring him in."

Katherine felt a hollow sensation in her chest when she saw the neat, well-dressed William Henry Aldrich being led into the lobby of the Teller House with his hands cuffed behind his back. She clutched Pilgrim's forearm as the detectives brought him forward.

"There's a rabble outside, hollering for this one's blood, sir," Benson reported.

"No doubt."

"The leader is a man named Watkins. Shall I bring him in, sir?"

Pinkerton shook his head. "Never mind, Benson," he said. "They can't get to him. We're taking Mr. Aldrich back to Denver with us."

"Yes, sir."

The tall, thin man in the brown business suit clenched his teeth stoically. "You've made a dreadful mistake here,

Pinkerton," Aldrich charged. "It's my guess that you have no proof that I am guilty of anything improper."

"You're wrong, Mr. Aldrich," he corrected. "Thanks to some very fine detective work, we have a great deal of proof."

"You overestimate your competence, sir."

"Do I? We happen to have two pieces of your stationery, both covered with your fingerprints, that link you to the murder of Alice Canfield. We also have copies of three letters you sent to financiers in Omaha and Chicago, describing in detail a scheme of sabotage and fraud. We possess five incriminating affidavits from influential men in Illinois and Nebraska who are also involved in that scheme, with corroborating statements from the banking firm of Hargrove & Son of Chicago. Within a few weeks, other such affidavits will be coming in, as we discover the other members of this enterprise of yours. When you combine all this with the evidence the Bonner family is giving us now, I think you'll agree we have enough proof to send you to the penitentiary for life!"

Aldrich glowered at him with cold, penetrating eyes. "You may have me now, Mr. Pinkerton," he allowed, "but some day I will have you."

"I don't think so."

"And you, my darling Katherine," he said to her, "will be mine."

"No, I won't, Henry."

"Some day I will come back to claim you, Katherine," he vowed. "You belong to me. Your father gave you to me!"

"People can't control other people that way, Henry. Not even my father."

"A man as powerful as Gardner Haynes can do anything he wants, Katherine. And so will I. You will see."

"Take him away, Benson," Pinkerton ordered.

"Yes, sir. Come on, Mr. Aldrich—"

"Take your hands off me, sir. I will walk alone!"

Only when he was out of sight, did Katherine heave a sigh of relief. "He always sounds so confident about things," she said.

"He's a clever man, Kate," Matt offered. "He was part of a group of Western railroad men and financiers who devised a plan to bankrupt the Union Pacific Railroad, then buy its farm land in Nebraska for practically nothing."

"I don't understand."

"They got the idea from what happened in the Northwest eight years ago. When the Northern Pacific Railroad went bankrupt in '73, financiers quickly bought into the fifty million acre tract of land, which was granted to the railroad by the Pacific Railroad Act of 1862, at a depreciated cost of about fifty cents an acre. By turning those prime wheat acres of North Dakota and Minnesota into huge farms, they earned incredible profits."

"They called it 'bonanza farming,'" Pinkerton explained.

"Which is what Farrell was trying to tell me in the mine," Matt said. "I didn't know enough to make the connection."

"But Alex did," she assumed. "And that's why he was killed."

"Yes."

"So Henry's part in the scheme was to sabotage the gold mines in Colorado, in order to bankrupt the Union Pacific here, as the railroad greatly depends on mining for its income."

"Of course," Pinkerton added, "stopping that source of

income wouldn't have been enough. But with other devi-
ous railroad men in the West diverting income from the
railroad, it wouldn't take long to bankrupt the great Union
Pacific. When that happened, millions of acres of clear
and very rich Nebraska farm land would be thrown open
for these men and their financiers. With today's new ma-
chinery and milling processes, they would have a fortune
in two years.''

"Where did the Bonners fit in, Matt?" she asked.

"Aldrich used them, Kate. He promised them fame as
outlaws and a lot of money if they would do his dirty work
for him.''

She swallowed drily. "So all these people are dead
because of one man's lust for power" she said.

"One of many, Miss Haynes," Pinkerton corrected.
"But thanks to Matthew's work, we'll now be able to
locate and apprehend the others. This case will very likely
enable us to save the Union Pacific Railroad.''

Katherine was about to say something to Matt when the
front door of the Teller House swung open, and the stout,
authoritative, but still very pale figure of Barton Canfield
walked in. Without a single glance at anyone else, he
marched straight across the lobby floor to his son.

Reuben looked at him from his chair. "I'm sorry, Dad,''
he apologized. "I couldn't stay with her the way you're
doing—''

"I know, Reuben," he said. "I understand. I came
about that girl you were with.''

Reuben popped up from his seat, grimacing under the
pain of his shoulder. "Billie?" he said. "What's the
matter with her?''

"She's gone, Reuben.''

He frowned. "She can't be! I haven't returned what's

313

left of her money to her! Clayton was carrying it in his coat—"

"I don't know anything about that, Reuben," he said. "She told me she was going to use a few extra dollars she had made recently to leave town."

Reuben rubbed his bandaged shoulder. "But why would she tell you? And when did you see her?"

"She came by the undertaker's office while you were with the doctor, Reuben. She was very proper and attentive to Alice, crying the whole time. I felt sorry for her."

"I don't know why she would do that—she didn't even know Alice."

"She felt guilty. She said if you hadn't been with her, Alice would still be alive."

"But it wasn't her fault! I've got to find her and tell her that!"

"I don't know where you would go, Reuben," he said. "She didn't tell me where she was going."

"Well, I'll just have to look until I find her," he declared. He patted his father on the shoulder and strode across the room to Matt. "Mr. Pilgrim," he said, "I'm going to find Billie Simms. You'll probably be gone by the time I get back."

Pilgrim looked at him steadily. "What about the job Mr. Pinkerton offered you, Reuben?" he asked.

Pinkerton stepped up to offer his encouragement. "We'd be happy to have you," he assured him. "From what I've seen, you'd make a brilliant detective."

"I appreciate that, sir," he replied, "but I think I belong here."

Matt smiled sadly. "Maybe you do, Reuben," he agreed.

"We were good as partners, though, weren't we, Mr. Pilgrim?"

"Yes, we were. Very good."

"Maybe we'll have occasion to do it again."

"I hope so. I wonder—have you ever considered running for sheriff, Reuben?"

"Me? No, sir."

"Why not?"

"Well, for one thing, I'd be too young, Mr. Pilgrim."

"You were never young, Reuben."

"I don't know—to be sheriff. . . ."

"Give it some thought. The West needs men like you in responsible positions."

Reuben paused a minute, then shrugged his shoulders. "Well, anyway, I've got to be going," he declared. "Sir!" He shook Pinkerton's hand. "I'm honored to have met you. I admire very much the work you're doing." Then, with a flush of red in his face, he boldly kissed Katherine on the cheek. "Miss Haynes," he muttered, "I want to say I think you're a very great lady."

"Coming from you, Reuben, that means a great deal to me," she said with tears in her eyes.

"Sir," he said to Matt, extending his hand, "thank you for taking me on."

Matt shook it. "Thank you for helping me."

"Well, good-bye, Mr. Pilgrim," he said with difficulty, then turned to go.

"Reuben?"

"Sir?"

"Do you think you could drop the 'Mr. Pilgrim' for once?"

"I'm sorry," he answered. "I meant to do that. I just kept forgetting." Without further word or comment, he walked out of the lobby and out of the hotel.

As soon as Reuben was gone, Pinkerton gathered his

detectives. "Well, men," he told them. "The rain has stopped, and the case is over. Why don't we all get some sleep? Tomorrow we'll be heading back to Denver."

While the others filed noisily out of the room, Pinkerton looked back at Pilgrim. "Take care of that wound, Matt," he instructed. "I've got another assignement for you. I want you to look into the disappearance of a shipment of gold off a Santa Fe railroad car in Kansas City."

"How soon should I be there?"

Pinkerton paused, glanced at Katherine, then smiled. "Why don't we say three or four days," he replied.

"Yes, sir."

"Katherine waited until the lobby had finally cleared. "Well," she sighed, "I guess I'd better go pack."

He looked at her with curiosity. "Pack for where?" he asked.

"For Chicago, Matt."

"Oh."

"I have to explain to my parents in person the telegraph I just sent them."

"You mean about Alex."

"Yes. And this other, too. They might not understand it right away."

"What other are you talking about, Katherine?"

"Oh, you know, this terrible business of their daughter traipsing all about the country, to places like Kansas City, for instance."

His face brightened at her words. "Katherine Haynes, are you saying—"

"What I'm saying, Matt, is that I refuse to be one of those Pinkerton wives who never know what's going on in their husbands' lives. I want to be there."

"You did say 'wives' and 'husbands,' didn't you?"

She pretended not to hear. "Of course, I wouldn't want to go with you every time. Maybe just until I'm sure you can do it alone—"

"What! Now you listen to me, Kate—"

She stopped his words with the touch of her fingers to his lips. "Do you know that before I met you, no one ever called me Kate?"

He took her into his arms. "I'll bet before me, no one ever called you Mrs. Pilgrim either."

She laughed. "Not a single soul. But I guess they'd better start learning to, hadn't they?"

"Kate, I love you," he said, holding her closely.

"I love you, too, Matt."

Their lips met lightly, but their tentative little kiss was interrupted by the clearing of a throat nearby.

"Excuse me, Mr. Pilgrim," said Simmons, the desk clerk. "I hate to ask you this. But I wonder if you and the lady. . . ."

"Oh, it's all right, Simmons," Matt assured him. "We love each other."

"Uh, yes, sir, I'm sure you do. I'm just thinking of the reputation of the hotel."

Matt eased away from her "Exactly what would you have us do to protect its reputation, Simmons?" he asked.

The desk clerk colored. "What I mean to say is, two unmarried people—"

"You're telling us to get married, is that it?"

"Sir, I would never presume—"

"I think you have a very good idea there, Simmons. Would you mind going to get us a preacher?"

"Are you serious, Mr. Pilgrim?"

"Very."

"Ma'am?" He looked at Katherine for confirmation.

"I'm more serious than he is, Mr. Simmons."

"Yes, ma'am," he said. "Well, I guess I should do that, then. I'll be back as soon as I can."

After the desk clerk had gone away, they laughed together, until Matthew cuddled Katherine close to his body. "While we're waiting—" he began.

"Oh, no, you don't." She broke away.

"You don't mean you've already forgotten what happened last night?"

"I'm not likely to forget it, Matt. Which is why we're waiting for Mr. Simmons and the preacher."

He nodded reluctantly, "I see your point," he conceded. After a minute, he sighed loudly. "I wonder how long they'll be."

"It already seems like a long time, doesn't it?"

"Yes, it does." He nodded again, then began to fidget nervously with his bandage.

Finally, she held out her hand. "Will you come with me, Matt?" she invited.

Looking puzzled, he grasped her hand in his and started off.

Silently Katherine led him out of the lobby, past the empty registration desk, and stopped with him in front of the closed door of the Teller House. There, together, they waited for the desk clerk and the minister.